"With its gripping account ~~probes into deep questions a~~ C.S. Lewis' Screwtape Letters, Kevin Albright surfaces dark questions about spiritual battles we all may face with Satan. It's a needed focus on the neglected area of where the battleground for our well being really lies."

- Lorna Dueck, TV Host and Media Commentator,
Context with Lorna Dueck, Faith Commentary Writer;
The Globe and Mail

"I don't know why some people have more pain in their lives than others. Kevin Albright has certainly had his share. But as I read this powerful, engaging journey of his life, the word that kept coming to me was . . . 'redemption'. Pain has a way of bringing that about in our lives. If you're looking for an authentic, frank story of God's redemption in the midst of turmoil, this book is for you".

- Roger Cross, President Emeritus Youth for Christ/USA

" . . . I am struck by the way God has lead and enabled [Kevin] to overcome one obstacle after another in his life journey. You will be too as you read his story as he tells it with inspired imagination and a transformed perspective. Finding My Father is a powerful portrayal of the journey we all need to be on to personally discover the father heart of God and his power to make you an overcomer."

- Shane Gould, Lead Pastor Burlington Alliance, Ontario /Canada

"This fantastic true story is a classic. It represents a young man re-building his life and soaring above his past with insight and vision."

- Bonnie L. Parker, Executive World Missions Director ABEA,
Founder of Living Springs Ministries

"Kevin's story was engrossing, and his spiritual pilgrimage endearing. I rejoice in what he has found in our Heavenly Father a parent who will never fail him, unlike his earthly father . . ."

- Bill Bjork, Senior Pastor Grace Bible Church, Phoenix, Arizona

FINDING
MY FATHER

A journey from the father who caused the scars
to the Father who healed them

KEVIN ALBRIGHT

WESTBOW
P R E S S
A DIVISION OF THOMAS NELSON

WestBow Press books may be ordered through booksellers or by contacting:

WestBow Press
A Division of Thomas Nelson
1663 Liberty Drive
Bloomington, IN 47403
www.westbowpress.com
1-(866) 928-1240

ISBN: 978-1-4497-6403-6 (hc)
ISBN: 978-1-4497-6401-2 (sc)
ISBN: 978-1-4497-6402-9 (e)

Library of Congress Control Number: 2012915936

Printed in the United States of America

WestBow Press rev. date: 08/31/2012

Contents

Dedicated to my wonderful kids,
Amy and Spencer
May you never lose sight of your heavenly Father

Preface

The journey you are about to embark on through the pages of this book will lead you through the scars of a child struggling to make sense of life. The story is told from three views: current, past, and supernatural. The revelations of a man lost in the abyss of a horrifying nightmare are in the current timeline while the reflections of a child haunting his every thought come from the past. An overshadowing glimpse of the struggles of darkness sits between the two in a never-ending quest for a soul. Although dark, the story is overpowered with the passion of a presence that intertwines everything with love while shining light into a dark place. The presence is strong, personal, and never far away.

The book is based on a true life story mixed with the warring struggles of darkness that roam this world. The story started as a journal of notes and a desire to pass on a family legacy. The legacy surrounds the passion of a Father who loves us beyond our understanding and never lets us go. After sharing the story with friends, the author was repeatedly encouraged to write it down. The pages of that journal are what evolved into this book.

Fasten your seat belt and prepare for revelations from a real life story surrounded by the power of a heavenly presence. The revelations are dark and painful, as is the world we live in. However, the power of the presence of light may be revealed to you in a new and real way. If you surrender to your heavenly Father, he might just change your life forever as you take the journey from the father who caused the scars to the one who heals them.

Acknowledgments

When it comes to the subject matter of this book, I know it well, as I have lived its contents for nearly fifty years. When it comes to the transition from life experiences to the pages of a book, I am now aware of how much I owe to so many. My heavenly Father has crossed my path with wonderful people who answered a call, took action, and helped shape my life into what it is today. *Finding My Father* is the culmination of a story that needed to be told but never would have become a book without the help of numerous others.

My wife, Holly, stuck by me when others would have abandoned all hope and walked away. She spent countless hours helping with the editing and reliving the journey with me through the tears and laughter of every page.

The circle of praying men at Burlington Alliance Church walked with me and became my band of brothers. When they meet and pray, the presence of God walks among them. When I first met them and said my situation was going to take a miracle, my good friend Gil replied, "We know the One who does those."

Don Foster, who encouraged me to write the book, but most of all who displayed the model of a man walking passionately with God, kept me going throughout this process.

June Wharton stood by me and even couriered me through the desert and over the border in a midnight relay to get me to court on time in Colorado. She helped with the editing of this book and offered much encouragement. No one could ask for a better mother-in-law.

Teresa and Elgin, Sherrolyn and Steve, Arnie and Phyllis, and Austin all came alongside me when life seemed unbearable, and they gave of their time, opened their homes, and gave me encouragement without even being asked. Each of them played a significant role in the threads of this tapestry that God wove through the story. They don't all know each other or realize how God orchestrated each of them in what became a symphony of beautiful music. They simply answered his call and acted when he asked.

How can I say enough about the many noteworthy people who answered God's call and played a role in this tapestry? I hope this book helps reveal some of the big picture, which now includes each one of them. Most will never fully know the impact they have had on my life. I can't wait until we get to heaven and the finished work of art that connects all of us is fully revealed.

No thanks would be complete without acknowledging the one who continually directed me on the right path. From the very first day of my life, she pointed me toward my heavenly Father and never stopped praying for me. I don't know where I would be today without her. Thanks, Mom.

1

Concealed Betrayal

The devil has a plan for your life—to destroy everything good and to destroy you.

The thief comes only to steal and kill and destroy.
—John 10:10 (NIV)

Be alert and of sober mind. Your enemy the devil prowls around like a lion looking for someone to devour.
—1 Peter 5:8 (NIV)

Quietly from the dead of night, in a suburb on the outskirts of a Southern California city, something sinister slowly crossed the threshold of a once secure residence. The tumblers of the lock clicked into place by the prideful choices of a deceived leader. An evil presence cautiously stepped into the family room, leading a human accomplice in tow. Darkness filled every crevice of the room as evil spilled in. Unaware of the ominous creature or the human accomplice edging quietly closer, an innocent mother slumbered quietly, seemingly safe in her room. A long shadow grew down the hallway as the evil force closed in to clinch its victory.

Darkness continued to claim so many families from this community that once again drama would play out in the morning news. Most people would merely glance at the event. The pain of the beating that this sleeping mother would deal with would be far greater than the steel pipe and shotgun rounds that would become the focus of media personalities.

This mom was not just meant to be left for dead; the plan was to bring destructive blows to a family once sheltered from this type of violence, a family steeped in an unseen battle and a pillar for many.

Many people would ask, "Why? Why here? Why to a family like this?" Some would conjure up a reasonable explanation that would allow them to sleep at night. Others would fall on their knees and pray. A few would recognize the signs and see the unseen battle that was being waged around all of those born of this earth.

The never-ending shadow engulfed everything in its path as it drew the human intruder down the hall to the bedroom where the sleeping body rested peacefully and unaware. Standing silently in the darkness of the doorway, the accomplice allowed the evil presence escorting her to take control.

The sinister presence took power over the accomplice by invitation, not by force. The accomplice reached for the weapons that accompanied her and executed the maliciously prepared plan of evil. Armed with a pipe and shotgun, the accomplice viciously attacked the unsuspecting mother.

The events were unforeseen by humans, but the moment wasn't spontaneous. That moment was the culmination of small seeds that had grown into weeds over months, even years, before this deed took place. Although a sinister force of darkness walked the accomplice through the dark of that night, the deception involved the fall of an even more profoundly deceived leader in the war against darkness of the paranormal variety.

In the seemingly safe place I called home, my mom was beaten and left for dead in an unthinkable act of evil. The act would have devastated any family, but the actions cut deeper than just the act. The actions sliced through many residents in our community and ravaged some for a lifetime because of who the act came from. The one who opened the lock and gave away the key to our lives invited the accomplice and sinister force into our home. The one I idolized and wanted to be like took my life at age nine and crushed my soul. But most of all, this person took away my father and my hopes and my dreams. Or so I thought.

///

Staring at a cold reinforced wall from a concrete bunk, I had nothing but time to contemplate my life. Time became senseless in that overcrowded cell. Flooded with flickering, stale orange light, the bare chamber was filled with motionless bodies. The overwhelming forces of my life raced through my mind over and over again, questioning everything that had ever happened and everything I'd ever done over the past four and a half decades. It was easy to question my decisions, every single one of them, and blame myself a million times an hour when my family was at stake and a piece of me was missing. The question that was never far from the corner of my mind was, "Why, God, why?" Emotions rushed in as self-blame and the what-if game began to play. I had done so many wrong things in my life. My stubbornness and fears that drove me against God's will echoed endlessly in my head. I felt that everything was my fault. Could I have done something better? And if I had, would I still be in that cell? I would have done anything to get my life back and to break free of that dungeon.

Simple desires, like sunlight and a pillow to lay my head on, became luxuries. A toothbrush and a change of clothes became fantasies. Things that once seemed so simple, and which I had taken for granted, became faint memories. I wondered if I would ever again see the sky or feel the warmth of a blanket on a real bed. After a few moments of contemplation, my thoughts would return to what I really missed the most.

I would have given up every luxury in life, every right I thought I had, every entitlement or breath of fresh air, if only I could have had my family back and been right with the God of this universe one more time.

The trauma of what had happened pierced deep into my mind like a bizarre nightmare that wouldn't go away. My wrists were still numb and chafed from the cold steel that cut off my circulation while I was manhandled like some terrorist or bad guy being paraded through the Los Angeles International Airport (LAX). All I could think was, *This really isn't happening.* My worst fears kept taking me back to my wife and my kids. Who would take care of them? How would they survive? Would I ever see the light of day again? Or would I become a captive in this prison like in some third world country and be lost forever? I yearned for a clock or a watch or anything that could tell time. I often wondered if it was day or night. Time seemed to lose its way in that stale orange haze.

Mixed with the monotonous flickering of the lights, mumbles would occasionally come from one of the inmates. It wasn't the kind of place where conversations started easily, but with the extremely overcrowded conditions you couldn't utter a sound without everyone being aware. Most of the guys in the room were barely of legal age. The cell was filled with tattooed young men lying on concrete bunks and endlessly staring at the bunk stacked above them. Some would take the only bedding provided—a thin sheet—and cover themselves as if dead. Others rolled up the sheet in an attempt to make a minuscule headrest.

Whenever short bursts of conversation did ensue, it became obvious that the fifteen or so cell mates confined in this small abode had much in common. There were many who belonged to gangs and sported tattoos from face to toe. Some were constantly in trouble with the law, and some had no other place but this, so they smugly announced that they returned often. However, the most basic commonality was the lack of family, mainly fathers.

Some stated that they hated their fathers, while others merely reflected on a hole in their lives where a father should have lived. Most would comment that there was no father or that he was a bum. Many of these now zombielike corpses staring at the walls were intelligent and capable young men, but they couldn't break free of the pain that gripped them. This pain drove many of these guys to anger and repeated violence. Some expressed the guilt of their lives while feeling abandoned beneath their hardened outer shells. Most bore the face markings of the surrogate families they found in gangs, while others turned to drugs to hide the pain. Various prisoners would speak of their mothers briefly, but they would only sneer or look away when the conversation touched on fatherly figures.

I often think of my own journey and my father, or at least who I thought my father was. I wondered if I had more in common with these other lost souls than I was willing to admit. Mostly, I wondered if this nightmare would ever come to an end or if my true Father would rescue me.

There were few disruptions in the nonexistent routine of passing time. A guard would appear occasionally, announced by the banging of some object against the cage door to break the stillness. I'll never forget the repulsive smell that would drift through the folds of a box carried by one of the guards from time to time. I remember thinking, *What can that be, and why are they bringing it in here?* It often smelled as if something had died, only to be preserved in cardboard.

///

In a family of three kids, I was the middle child. I never thought of myself that way, since I was the tallest and eldest boy, only two years behind my sister. Although she didn't see things the same and was in no hurry to give up her birthright as the oldest child, I still saw myself as the eldest male and the leader of our sibling pack.

My brother seemed a generation away, since he was the baby, five years younger than I. My mom played the piano at church and often taught Sunday school. She was always there and took care of us because Dad always had busy church stuff to do.

Mom was the one who tucked us in at night and spent time with us. She took us to school and checked our homework. She made sure we cleaned our rooms and did our chores.

In the Southern California city where we lived, my dad was the leader of a sizable church. He was tall and slim with dark hair and a polished appearance. People loved my dad and looked up to him. He had a strong presence about him and a dynamic personality. He seemed to care about people and was always willing to stand up and speak at any opportunity. He spoke on Sundays and Wednesdays, and he even hosted his own radio show. I perceived him to be the guy who was in charge of everything. I felt important being his son. I personified him as my hero.

I grew up in the church. In fact, it seemed like we were always there, since my dad was the pastor. I was a PK (a preacher's kid), and I loved it. I didn't want to become a fireman or a pilot like the other kids when I grew up; I wanted to be a pastor just like my dad.

As a young boy I would gather my friends, and we would play church. We took turns being sick and praying over each other to be healed. I had a small band of three guys, and we played songs in the children's church on Sundays. Well, I should say I strummed a large guitar while I grasped for some resemblance of a chord on the neck of that thing. My other eight- and nine-year-old buddies attempted to keep up with the strumming while we led the two dozen or so other kids in children's church songs.

For those of you who didn't attend church as a kid, children's church was where the kids went while the grown-ups sat in the big people's church and listened to the preacher, usually my dad. I guess they felt it was easier for us to understand Bible stories with cut-out characters stuck on flannel board backgrounds than it was for grown-ups.

Church and children's church were great times in my young life. Children's church held a good-sized crowd of young and willing participants for activities such as singing along to my attempts to lead music, playing Bible games, and listening to filtered versions of Bible stories.

We were always the last ones at church to leave, because my dad had to lock up after greeting the congregation. I can remember playing in the church as a kid after service while everyone was going out. I always liked being at church. I loved all of those rows and rows of padded pews and long aisles with plenty of room to run up and down when no one was looking. However, there always seemed to be an ample supply of elderly ladies who were quick to enlighten my mom about my misbehavior. The stage was always fascinating to me as well, with its commanding view of the congregation and the pulpit, which protruded from it like a lighthouse at the end of a jetty.

Yet it was the reverence, a strong presence in the church, that I loved the most. There was something there beyond just a building. There was a spirit that was strongest when it was filled with people singing and worshipping God. When I was a kid, it felt like a warm blanket wrapped around me sitting in front of a fire on a cold, wet night. I didn't truly understand that powerful presence I felt, but I knew it was good, pure, and wonderful, no matter what people called it. I knew it was the unmistakable presence of something amazing, or someone amazing.

When I finally read the Bible for myself as an adult, I discovered a much deeper awareness of the message of the Bible than what we were taught in children's church. The whole Bible told a single story, and that story was about the presence of the spirit I felt. In children's church we seemed to focus on individual stories only in simplified ways. We learned about Noah and the ark, Moses, Joseph, and the other great characters of the Bible.

The cruel realities these characters encountered, along with the painful battles that each of them endured, were brushed over. The battles that they suffered through were barely mentioned in children's church as the storytellers quickly skipped ahead to the happy endings. Later in my life I would often wish that I too could skip ahead, but I guess my book hadn't been written yet.

Unlike the Bible stories, however, I didn't have the luxury of skipping ahead in my own story to see how things would turn out or the events and untold pain that would unfold. I'm not sure how I would have reacted if I had known what I was about to go through or the devastating events that were to take place in my life, or even if I would have been able to go through them. Yet, I don't think I could have fully understood the story of the love of a heavenly Father that the Bible told of if it hadn't been for the events of my life.

What I didn't understand at that age was the intensity of the battle that entrenched this world and that we were the prize, or often the victims of our own choices. I clearly had no understanding of the cunning evil that would be planned against me, or the power and greatness of love and grace that I would be given. I knew there was good and evil in the world, but I had no knowledge that my life would chronicle such an account of these things.

Although I didn't understand everything going on around me, I encountered some amazing things and felt that unforgettable presence.

///

An ominous shadow swallowed up everything in its path as it moved swiftly over the rooftops in a Southern California neighborhood. It darted back and forth until it reached an old house on the outskirts of town. Rusty farm equipment and broken fences dotted the grounds of the once stately, now neglected old home, where paint now peeled between the missing boards.

Shadows skimmed the earth one by one and then passed through the opening where a large door once hung. In the basement a thick, sulfurous stench filled the air. A large, hideous beast laced with bony veins over his leathery body dominated a dark corner. As Beelzebub observed the activity from his corner it seemed to become the focal point of all the other repulsive creatures darting back and forth in the shadows. A large, frightful demon cast his presence across the entrance, momentarily obstructing the moonlight. Stopping at the feet of the hideous being in the corner, the large demon bowed.

"Is it done?" came from the darkness in the corner with a breath of fiery red sulfur.

"Yes, my liege, Beelzebub. I have destroyed the leader's family, and our enemy will take a fall. The children will be handed over to me through my human accomplice, and the mother is now dead. The church controlled by the leader will take a direct hit, and his congregation will crumble. I will earn the right to torture my prey for eternity. The father will be removed from the picture, and I will take the pleasure of tormenting all of them with my legions here on this earth and devouring them in hell for eternity."

Slits of green eyes moved gradually as the hideous creature slowly turned to focus on the demon in front of him. "Do not be so confident, Chief Demon. The enemy has had legions of angels encamped around that house for years. If the man you call leader did not invite us in, you would not have been there. You have deceived him well, but you must not allow him to become remorseful and ask forgiveness from our enemy—their God—or you will lose him.

"There are others you must now worry about. Many will be praying for the three children who belong to our enemy. Their God will protect them when the prayers of his saints begin. Never forget that our enemy listens to their prayers and will send reinforcements. Your so-called 'leader,' as you call him—I believe in jest—will lose the church he once pastored. Do not let your guard down, or you will lose the pleasure of tormenting your prey for eternity . . . or worse, you could lose some of those we have already deceived. One more thing: the mother is still alive. Our enemy did not allow her death."

Chief Demon shrieked, "What?! I saw her die. I left her for dead. I took control of my human accomplice and beat her myself. I will find the leader and accomplice and return to finish this."

"It is too late. The angels have been sent. They have returned and carried her to a neighbor's home. Your human leader and accomplice are no good to you any longer."

Chief Demon scratched his talons angrily across the floor, sending a deadly chill through the room. "I will instill the shattered family syndrome that I've so often used on children of broken homes. Their father is gone from their lives, and I will see to it that he doesn't return. They will be lost for eternity. I will haunt them with this and torment them. I will delight in the taste of these little ones. I will infuse a replacement for their father and deceive them. The pleasure will be mine of torturing them for all eternity!"

Rolling burning red sulfur through the air, the hideous Beelzebub interrupted Chief Demon's ranting. "As a group you will have a chance, but as they grow they will go their own way, and you cannot be with all of them at the same time. You must choose the one you desire to pursue as your prey and assign your minions to the others. It will not be easy to conquer them now, but you must, while they are still in this physical realm."

"Yes, my liege," Chief Demon said with less vigor. "I will destroy them before they grow and separate to different locations, as you command."

The hideous creature leaned back into the shadows. "Your task is not done; you must go and help the police find your 'leader' and his accomplice. Show them no mercy now that you are done with them. Make sure they are in anguish, but do not let them become remorseful and turn back to our enemy, or you could risk losing them. Feed their ego. As we know, this has been an effective tool with them.

"I want the children and the mother to fall before they can become a threat to our kingdom of darkness." With the swipe of a talon-filled claw through the air Chief Demon was dismissed. "Leave my sight, and do not fail me in the orders I have given you."

"Yes, my liege." And Chief Demon slithered out the way he had come in, quietly through the shadows and into the darkness of night to complete what had been started.

2

Made with a Spiritual Purpose

We were all made for a purpose—it just may not be the one you thought it was.

If we find ourselves with a desire that nothing in this world can satisfy, the most probable explanation is that we were made for another world.
—C. S. Lewis, Mere Christianity

He has shown you, O moral, what is good. And what does the Lord require of you? To act justly and to love mercy and to walk humbly with your God.
—Micah 6:8 (NIV)

I'd always known that there was a God who cared for me. God was not this far-off being or mystic object that existed in some other place; he was very close and caring. Our family talked to him every day, and we would pray to him about people who were sick or going through difficult times. We saw God answer our prayers—often in miraculous ways.

The elders in our church were blessed with different spiritual gifts. Some would lay hands on people, and they would be healed by God of incurable diseases or other ailments that would go away without explanation. Doctors couldn't understand it, and at times the local newspaper would come to interview people at our church.

I've seen demons speak through people in unearthly voices as they fought to possess the person they were being evicted from.

Yet with prayer and rebuking in the name of Jesus, they eventually left with screeching and screaming, and humans would once again appear in the body God gave them.

There was a presence that appeared when the congregation gathered and began to worship—not a feeling or chill that can be manufactured, but an unexplainable exhilarating presence. It was so thick at times that it seemed to pierce through your being. It brought an unending joy and peace in a seemingly different dimension unlike any other feeling on earth. Your whole body would melt; you felt like crying and laughing at the same time. This all-consuming presence took away every fear, every worry, and every pain you'd ever known. It wasn't a foreign presence like some drug. After it was gone, it seemed foreign to be without it, as though a piece of me was missing.

I can remember as a kid thinking that I really didn't care what the Bible said heaven would be like as long as I got to be in the midst of that presence. I always hated to go home after an awesome evening of worship and experiencing this presence of God. I always felt closest to God during those evenings. I assumed that everyone knew this feeling and had felt it. No one told me about spiritual beings and the existence of good and bad spirits from other dimensions; they were just a fact of life.

One of my many fond memories of that church came from a large man who traveled around in a trailer. He would come to our church occasionally dressed as a pirate, and he would tell Bible stories. He called himself Captain Hook and wore an actual hook on his left hand. He was always accompanied by one of those dummy puppets. The puppet's name was Sharkey. Sharkey would sit on his knee and argue with him. But as Sharkey argued, Captain Hook always engaged us in adventures of Jonah and the whale and the story of Jesus feeding the five thousand hungry people with two fish.

I must admit that the hook he wore on his left hand did frighten me a little. I always wondered if he took it off at night when he went back to his trailer or if he ate with it on or even slept with it. Was he really a pirate all the time or just part time?

Many missionaries visited our church and brought stories of incredible things that God had done in their lives. They would have magnificent stories of miracles that they had seen and tales of battles they had fought with prayer. As a kid, I felt that life was good. However, I had no idea of the battles under way in my life, or the plans of a cunning enemy to destroy humans and rip their lives to shreds, including mine. I never anticipated the battles that would devastate the lives of those closest to me, or that fateful night of wicked confrontation that would disfigure me for life.

///

Click-clang! The electronic lock banged with a loud, reverberating sound as the cell door slid open to reveal a prison guard holding a box of unidentifiable food items. A chain holding oddly shaped keys clanged together by his side along with steel handcuffs and other objects that I couldn't identify. With the noise breaking the silence and that disgusting smell filling the cage, the cell came alive with inmates crawling over each other to drink in the break in the monotony.

I quickly asked, "Sir, I need to make a phone call and let someone know I'm here."

"Shut up and get back in your bunk; you do not address an officer unless you are spoken to," came the harsh reply.

"But, sir, I don't even know why I'm here. Can you at least tell me why I've been locked up?"

The officer quickly slammed the steel cage door. "Show a little respect, and maybe I'll bring food in later." The officer walked away clanging the chain of keys along his side.

The other inmates stared in disdain at me, and then at the box the guard had left outside the door. One inmate uttered, "These guards think they rule the world; what they are feeding us will probably kill us anyway." Looking at me, he continued, "How long have you been in here?"

Grasping the chance to speak to someone, I quickly let him know that I'd been there almost five days and no one would tell me why. The inmate returned a smirk of disgust before lying back down on his concrete bunk, saying little more than "typical."

Sitting at the edge of my concrete bunk trying not to hit my head on the bunk above me, I sat up to see the cast of characters that filled my vision. There were those who wanted power and control over others, those who sought approval desperately, and those who just wanted to escape their lives. A couple of them were in the fetal position hopeful this was just a nightmare that would all go away, but most of the caged inhabitants tried to play the tough guy hiding behind scarred faces.

I'd never seen so many tattoos in my life. I couldn't imagine why anyone would tattoo numbers on their face or teardrops on their cheeks or symbols on their eyelids. Behind the projected facades there was a desire to communicate, but cautious distrust limited the ability. My emotions teetered on a roller coaster between the rickety wooden rails of fear and survival, with fading hope at either end.

Mealtime was nothing to look forward to, but it was the only noticeable marker of time. This was the occasion when everyone was forced to get up and file through the steel door to receive some repugnant morsel of something that barely resembled food. The daily meals alternated between a greenish-yellow crumbly substance on a soggy piece of bread accompanied by a small frozen carton of simulated orange drink, or the next 'indulgence,' which came at what seemed like an eternity later. It was a small burrito-looking thing with runny brown meat in the semifrozen center. It came with burned microwave edges and an outer layer with a rubbery texture. The burrito-looking thing was garnished by the smallest apple I'd ever seen and a small carton of semifrozen chunky milk.

The ritual was always the same; the ground would shake from the bang of a steel electronic lock releasing the bank vault of a door accompanied by the clinking of the guard's keys. New arrivals would be thrown in with their newly appointed bunk sheet at all hours of the day and night. I assumed it was night only because the stale orange light was occasionally dimmed. Some arrived with strange smells or a stench. Others came with torn clothes or from time to time bleeding from some recently inflicted injury. After some period of time they would be called out one by one, chained to each other, and paraded away as often as the new crop would trickle in.

I wondered if I would ever be called out, or what would compel my captors to even tell me why I was there. I didn't want to play this game, and as the days went by with no communication to the outside world, I began to feel forgotten. Hopelessness began to seep in. I just wanted to go home. Between the instinct to survive and be strong, emotions would occasionally and involuntarily burst through and roll down my cheeks. I didn't know if I was going to be there for days, months, or even years. I didn't know if I was ever going to see the outside again, and I had no right to even ask my captors why they had put me in there.

One of the new tenants to occupy that small cage came late one evening, or so it appeared from the timing of our ceremonial feast followed by the dimming of the mind-twisting orange lights. He was a clean-cut gentleman much like I had been when I first arrived. I had to wonder why he was in here. Was his situation like mine?

///

Engulfing shadows crept over the sidewalks like spilled ink traversing through one hiding place after another. A gathering of shadows assembled below the shrubbery of an ill-kept yard within sight of a contemporary church of distinguished appearance. A shadow in the form of a reptile displayed its fangs in a devilish crooked grin to greet the other shadows that were gathered. Puffing out his prideful chest, the reptile of a shadow addressed the gathering:

"The plan has been executed with remarkable skill. Our Chief Demon will share the pleasure of eternal torture in consumption of our trophy the leader, as he is called. His wife is dead. Chief Demon took control of our willing accomplice and beat the leader's wife with a lead pipe in the head, then shot her."

The other shadows began to show crooked smiles of their own, and puffs of red hot sulfur steamed from the shadowy figures. Various small dark creatures echoed, "We want some of that. Yes, yes, we do."

"There is more, my malevolent friends. This victory is huge, so huge the great serpent Beelzebub may even get word of it. There are three children that would have become a threat to us and could have taken many away from the torture and suffering that we now once again will have the pleasure of inflicting. We will feast on these humans when they leave this physical world. We will enjoy the delicacy of chewing on each tasty morsel. Now they will be placed in the care of our new puppet, the leader, and his accomplice. We have conquered this once warrior from our enemy, the Light, and will savor every moment of his defeat."

The sulfurous clouds stirred in turbulent circles as the other shadows booed and hissed at the mention of the Light.

"Aw, my friends, but we are smarter and will devour our prey. The savory victory was won when we baited this leader with power and fed his ego. Like so many of these stupid humans, he fell easily. Of course it was my brilliance and advice that let our Chief Demon gain this victory. His accomplice was an easy score as well. We introduced her to the leader's power and led them both down a path until the leader gave us the keys to his home, his family, and the destruction of his church. He stopped praying to protect them and practically pushed and shoved the angels out of the way. Don't worry; I will give each of you unending turns at torturing my new victuals for eternity in savory delight."

A wisp of sound crawled from between jagged, sharp teeth of a small demon of a creature.

"What if they pray? What if the others begin to cover the children in prayer? We could still lose this battle."

A swipe of razor-sharp claws from the reptile's shadow flew through the air, followed by a deep hissing.

"How stupid do you think I am? I will be great because I am smarter than our enemy and more intelligent than you. She is dead! I helped the accomplice prepare a shotgun with a sawed-off barrel; she couldn't miss. Chief Demon fired several rounds at her head when the accomplice gave him control. There were no angels that could protect her from our strength, and the Light did not stop us. Never question me like that again, or I will send you to another realm—the Abyss, where you will be tormented!"

The jagged, sharp teeth disappeared as the smaller creature spoke quietly.

"I do wish to have my turn to torture these terrible creatures of earth, these humans. It will be joyous to see them suffer in pain for eternity as I consume my portion. I do not doubt your ability, Reptile, and I will speak more carefully in the future. I want to stay here and fight this battle with you—but if they pray, the Light will send more powerful angels."

Reptile once again puffed out his chest while pointing a dark, shadowy limb toward the distinguished church across the street.

"You must stop the prayers of the saints. Do not let them reach this place or allow them to pray together, or even alone. Distract them, find something pleasurable they like to do, or annoy them. I don't care what you do, but you must not allow them to connect with their God, the Light."

The distinguished church building did not stand alone that night. A circle of radiant, majestic beings stood with outstretched arms reaching upward. Some of the lighted beings whispered over the shoulders of humans as they walked to their cars in the parking lot. Some of the humans stopped to pray in their cars, some on their knees in the parking lot. Others went on their way as they drove away from the church. The humans who were praying seemed to glow in the darkness of the night. The lighted beings moved in great haste, seemingly urging the humans to pray.

Dark shadows slithered out of the bushes, dashing to hover over the cars driving away from the church. Some shadows settled in next to the drivers traveling without angels. Others carefully hovered over the vehicles, watching for an opening to interfere with the angelic protection. A few brassy demons darted around the parking lot seeking an opening to interfere with the praying humans, while keeping a safe distance from the majestic beings beaming with magnificent Light.

Reptile gazed on from the safety of the bushes across the street. Engulfed in the excitement of the moment, he didn't notice the unmistakable presence approaching behind him . . .

3

Something Is Wrong in Paradise

There are unsuspecting moments that define us and impact who we are, but there is also one who can give us a second chance.

And no wonder, for Satan himself masquerades as an angel of light.
— Corinthians 11:14 (NIV)

We know that we are children of God, and that the whole world is under the control of the evil one.
— 1 John 5:19 (NIV)

I was nine years old when that fateful night came. I can remember my father being in a hurry to get us to church for a Wednesday evening service. He kept saying he didn't want us to be late, which was a bit strange, since Mom usually told us to get ready. He said Mom wasn't feeling well, so she would be staying home. Mom never stayed home from church.

Dad wasn't usually overly attentive to her, and I had actually heard them arguing for the first time just days before. My dad did seem to be concerned about her that evening. He was getting her something to drink and some medication while we were changing out of our play clothes to get ready for church. Even more out of character, my dad told us to go into her room and say good-bye to our mom, which I found very odd since we'd be back in a few hours from church.

Mom and Dad had been in a car accident just weeks before. I discovered later that it was much worse than they had disclosed to us kids. Mom was using a wheelchair around the house during her recovery, but Dad said the situation was temporary and she would be just fine. She was spending a lot of time in bed resting, so I didn't see too much need for alarm that evening.

As I discovered later, the accident took place as Mom and Dad were driving home from a church banquet one evening. My dad was at the wheel of his small sports car, and Mom was beside him in the passenger seat. There was arguing in the car, and my dad swerved into a telephone pole. The car wrapped around the pole on my mom's side of the car. The impact severely injured my mom, severing her foot and crushing her leg. My mom was in the hospital for several weeks. My dad experienced some headaches after the accident, but nothing more serious.

When Mom came home from the hospital, she arrived with all types of strange equipment. They said that she needed all of this stuff until she healed. The wheelchair she arrived in made her look broken and frail, but I knew she would get better. After all, I had seen many people healed, and we still had Dad to take care of our family until Mom got better.

Life was more difficult with Mom being sick, since she was the one who always took care of us. The church pitched in, and life went on for a nine-year-old kid. I really didn't understand why Dad was always so busy and spent more and more time away from home as opposed to taking care of Mom. But Mom remained positive and assured us she was going to be okay, so there was no need to worry.

People from our church came by to help out at our home, since Mom was still recovering and Dad seemed to be so busy with "church stuff," although I really didn't know what that was. There were many times when I wondered why my dad always had time to visit other people but he couldn't stay home and visit with us. I resigned myself to the fact that this was just the way things were.

When we were ready for church and all loaded up in the car, my dad drove us there in a hurry. I was looking forward to this evening because I knew we had a guest speaker and I anticipated that Dad would sit with us for a change, which would have been a real treat.

When we arrived at the church, my dad drove up quickly to the front doors and told us to get out and to hurry so we wouldn't be late. I asked him why he hadn't parked the car. When he gave no response, I asked if he was going somewhere; he just replied that he had something to do and he didn't want us to be late. So the three of us hurried off and found a seat with some friends.

The evening service was routine. I don't remember much of it. Everything seemed normal that evening. A familiar lady led the song service, and I daydreamed my way through the guest speaker's message, imagining all kinds of wild adventures, being a missionary in a faraway land. As a nine-year-old, I had quite an imagination. I do remember that my dad never came back to sit with us.

After church all the kids hung out as usual, running around playing games. In the back of my mind I wondered where my dad was. Why wasn't he in church, and why was he so late to pick us up? Eventually one of the church families came over to my sister and me to explain that we would be going home with them for the night. They said my mom wasn't feeling well and they would be able to tell us more in the morning. I wasn't sure what to think. Dad must be really busy since he wasn't there to pick us up, and obviously my mom was still at home getting better. On the way to our friends' home for the night, they informed us that we didn't have to go to school the next morning. I wasn't about to pass that up.

By the next morning, I missed Mom and Dad and wanted to get back home. We had some breakfast, and we were ready to get going back to our house. Oddly enough, another family from the church arrived. They explained that we were going to their house for a while. A while—what did that mean? I wondered what was happening, and it all seemed very odd, mostly because no one was giving us any details or explaining what was going on. As I blindly entered a segment of my life that would engrave a scar into my memory and haunt me for a lifetime, I innocently followed.

To my delight, my brother and sister and I were told we could stay home from school for the entire week. In the beginning it was kind of exciting, almost an adventure, but it quickly started to feel strange. Something seemed odd, and I just wanted to go home. Everything seemed peculiar.

If I needed anything from our house, our friends would go get it, but I wasn't allowed to go there. We weren't allowed to watch TV or see a newspaper. I didn't normally read the newspaper at age nine, but it was still weird that we were being monitored so closely. I was a good kid. I didn't watch bad shows or too much TV, so why were these things off-limits for me now?

Simple things became mysterious, like not being allowed to attend school or even go there to get something out of my desk. I wondered what the big deal was.

I became very confused when I was asked if there was anything in my desk at school that I wanted to keep. I was then told that our friends would go get that for me too, but I couldn't go. I thought if there was something I wanted from my desk, I'd just get it when I was back at school, so what was the big deal?

Then "she" showed up.

///

This newly arrived inhabitant wasn't withdrawn or defensive like many of the others. He was angry, but with reason. As curiosity set in, I asked him how he got thrown into this dungeon. He explained his story, as unreal as it seemed. Apparently, he was a business owner who had rented a car. He told me that he had rented the car for thirty days but needed to extend his trip. He called the rental company and was granted an extension for a couple more days. On his way back to the airport to return the car, before his extension expired, he was stopped by the police in front of the rental car parking lot. He was pulled from the car and thrown to the ground then cuffed before being detained. He was being charged with grand theft auto.

I would have previously questioned the legitimacy of this story, but I had my own unanswered story of surreal circumstances to compare it with. Our exchange left more unanswered questions than it provided. Maybe I wasn't the only one lost in this terrifying nightmare.

I started cautiously asking others why they were in this place. One very large gentleman, who would normally strike fear in others, was quick to respond. Unsure of what I was about to hear, I tried to keep my composure and a safe distance as he unfolded his account.

///

Anticipating the elated time soon to come in hell and how stupid and easily played these humans were, Reptile swelled with pride. Basking in narcissistic glory, Reptile didn't notice an even bigger and darker shadow moving in behind the bush.

"Why are you here when you should be preventing the humans from praying? This battle is not going as we planned," rumbled the frightful Chief Demon.

Startled and suddenly ejected from basking, Reptile stuttered, "W-what do you mean? The others are chasing the saints, and the children are ours as soon as they are handed over to the leader and his accomplice. The leader will let us in, and you control both of them. Our minions are distracting the prayers of the saints even as we speak, so the situation is under control."

"There will be no handing over," rumbled Chief Demon. "The mother is still alive, and she is a woman of prayer herself. The others will gather around and cover her in prayer too."

Reptile quivered enough to make the leaves of the bushes shake. "What do you mean? I was there with you. I saw her dead; I mean, I didn't expect to see her after she left this physical world, since she belongs to our enemy. I had no expectation of greeting her in hell. But she can't have the kids; they are mine to destroy and feast on."

Peering at the church across the street, Chief Demon watched carefully as the large angelic beings walked through the parking lot with their humans. Turning to Reptile, Chief Demon spoke in a stern but quiet voice. "Leader opened the door and let us in, but the enemy sent an angel to carry her to the neighbors' house. He reached down from heaven and touched her. She will live. Our job just got a lot more difficult."

In an angry hiss Reptile growled, "I hate humans. I can't wait to send my humans to hell—and torture them forever. How could this have happened?"

The two stayed quietly behind the bushes until the last angelic being had left the church, and then they slithered out of the bushes and down the street.

Midmorning in an older but well-kept residential neighborhood of modest homes, two unnatural shadows hovered over a family car parked below a large tree. In the midst of the shadows, eyes seemed to glare in watch over the house across the street.

"Reptile, go in and take a closer look."

"Chief Demon, the house is full of angels, and big ones too. I can't go in there."

"Just look in the window, Reptile. The children are in there. I need to know how they are reacting so I can plan my next move. I can't let them live in the comfort of the angels. Now that their father has been deceived, there will be an opening for us to penetrate their lives. If we inject enough pain and fear, they will reject our enemy and we will have our victims for eternity. If we use the pain and execute this right, they will even blame our enemy for this, and then they will be ours. But I need to know how they are taking this news."

"Okay, but if one of those angels looks through the walls, I'm out of there."

Cautiously Reptile's shadow crept between parked cars and bushes into a vantage point that provided a view into the house. Worried adult humans talked quietly in the kitchen, often stopping to pray, while children played down the hall, seemingly oblivious to what was taking place. Reptile backed down from the vantage point without noticing a dark spot concealed beneath one of the cars. The consuming spot of darkness barely moved in the shadows of the parked cars. Suddenly talons of piercing iron appeared, freezing Reptile in place.

"What are you doing with my humans?" came a deep, unearthly voice.

"I am Reptile, and the children belong to my master, Chief Demon."

"Ha, the children look like they belong to those enormous glowing angels in there. I don't see you or your Chief tormenting anyone. You weren't even invited in; your wishful thinking is mere fantasy."

"Chief and I will torture those children for all of eternity; they are our prize to take. You don't exactly look like you've been invited to the party either."

After a short pause the deep, unearthly voice turned shrill with anger focused at Reptile.

"Don't try to intimidate me, you wimpy little demon. I am here because many evil ones darker than you have been cast out of this place and sent away from this realm. I am here because I was sent by the great evil one. My orders come from the top. The serpent Beelzebub himself knows of my mission. I am of great cunning and deceit and have a plan to lure my humans away from the Light. Don't mess up my plan, or I'll send you straight out of this physical world. I'll send you back to the dungeon without your human children, and then they will become my prey too."

Reptile retreated quickly with no reply to the more experienced demon of deceit, fading into the bushes and squirming back to Chief Demon to report.

4

Severed Dreams

The freedom to do good and enjoy its rewards cannot exist without the corresponding opposite freedom to do evil, which introduces suffering.

My God, my God, why have you forsaken me? Why are you so far from saving me, so far from my cries of anguish?

Psalm 22:1 (NIV)

Be alert and of sober mind. Your enemy the devil prowls around like a roaring lion looking for someone to devour.

1 Peter 5:8 (NIV)

There have been moments in my life that have embedded eternal memories never to be forgotten in my wounded spirit. The defining moment that carved the deepest scar in my heart and disfigured my soul came in a way that has forever left a mark. This moment will forever exist in slow motion carved into my memory.

It was late in the day, and I had been playing with my siblings in one of the rooms where we were staying. The doorbell rang, which meant little to me as I played with my sister and brother down the hall, until the lady we were staying with came into the room. She told us that my aunt Evelyn was here. Suddenly time stopped.

My mind went into overdrive. *Why is my aunt here? It takes hours to get here from her house. My aunt wouldn't just stop by for no reason; is Mom really going to be okay? Where is my dad?* I hadn't seen either of them in over a week now.

As I walked down the hall, it seemed to grow longer by the minute. With my mind racing, I could see that my siblings were becoming affected. Happy, playful eyes began to fill with fear and concern. What were we facing in the room ahead where my aunt waited? What was so important that she had to drive for over half a day to come here and talk to us?

As we arrived at the living room, an awkward silence of still air seemed to last an eternity. My aunt sat across from us on a couch trying to paste on a smile. Then she explained that we were going to come live with her. All our belongings would be sent to her house later, and we had to leave that evening.

She was going to take us to see our mom in the hospital, but Mom wouldn't be coming with us for a while. She said Mom was very ill and had to stay until she was well enough to travel.

My aunt told us that she was very sorry, but we wouldn't be able to go back to our home or say good-bye to our friends at school or at church. She kept being vague about everything while assuring us that Mom would explain everything when we saw her.

My little brother and sister started to melt into watery eyes and sniffles. I had to decide how I was going to react: What could I do? How should I feel? Do I fall apart or be strong for them? Emotions and thoughts raced furiously through my mind with no place to park. I had never felt these emotions before, and I didn't know how to deal with them. I had been on top of the world just days before, and now my world was crumbling. I didn't know what to do, and no one else seemed to know how to help me. My soul felt like it was spinning as I tried to prepare for whatever was happening. Yet, at my young age I had never experienced emotions like the ones churning inside me. I tried to prepare myself for something serious, yet at my young age I had never had a real serious talk or known traumatic emotions. I couldn't prepare myself for what I was about to experience.

The drive to the hospital was filled with silence. Emotions raced deep in my soul, igniting confusion. Although I searched and searched, I didn't know where to go inside me or how to validate what was happening. My aunt's words kept ringing through my head. "We are going to the hospital where your mother is. We have been waiting for your mom to be well enough to talk to you; that's why you have been at your friends' house for so long. After you see your mom, you are coming to live with me."

My aunt was married with three children of her own. What did she mean, we were going to live with her? We had a big home of our own in the suburbs. I had a dog; what would happen to him? What about my pet lizards? What about Mom and Dad? Were they coming with us? Time blurred into a whirlwind as if I was racing down a freeway staring at the ground watching the stripes on the pavement smear past.

We arrived at the hospital, and my fears climbed to heights I hadn't known existed. I discovered that both sets of grandparents were there. My grandparents lived halfway across the country. Police officers were waiting to meet us. A nurse introduced herself and said that my little brother had to stay in the waiting room. He was too young to go where we were going. Then the nurse ushered my sister and me into a room behind a curtain.

The room was filled with beeping machines, flashing lights, and sprawling tubes coming from everywhere, leading to a frail body lying motionless on the bed. The body was the center of the room, with seemingly everything connected to it. Hospital people in white monitored the blinking lights and machines that surrounded the bed.

When the person in the bed motioned slowly to us with great effort, I realized it was my mom. My mind got stuck in a loop like a broken record: "That's my mom, that's my mom, that's my mom" is all I could hear in my head.

Barely recognizable beneath the black-and-blue bruises and bandages, she stretched out a hand covered in hoses and hospital tape. I reached out to hold her hand, and my sister burst into tears. I stood cold still, thinking, *I'm going to get whoever did this to my mom, if it's the last thing I do.* Anger began to swell inside of me. I wanted revenge in a way I had never known before. Someone hurt my mom.

My mom began to explain. She said that she didn't want us to hate our father. I thought, *Dad, what does he have to do with this? He's my dad the pastor and leader of our church. He is the good guy that I want to grow up and be like someday.*

She continued to tell us that a woman had broken into our home and beaten my mom, shot at her several times, and left her for dead.

But there was more: my dad had planned the entire act. By the grace of God the woman had left the house presuming Mom was dead, and somehow Mom was able to escape to the neighbors' house and get help. I stood in stunned silence as she continued. The police had picked up Dad and the woman a few hours later. He would be going to jail for a very long time.

My sister's tears turned into sobbing as she burst at the seams, which ignited a flow down my face as I started to cry myself. I couldn't speak; I couldn't think. I was paralyzed from the inside out. *What will we do? Where will we go? How will we live?* My world was falling apart.

At that very moment the trusting, happy nine-year-old child died, and I became an adult with the weight of the world on my shoulders. The ill-equipped adult born at that moment was confused with ideas of grandeur about taking care of my family. Suddenly my feelings shut down and ceased to function. I became quiet and withdrawn. I sensed my sister had cried enough for both of us, and I didn't know what to feel, so I didn't. I tucked it all inside where it seemed safe and locked it away.

I started saying irrational things. I told my mom that I would get a job mowing lawns or something and that I'd take care of us one way or another. My mom kept saying that we must not hate our father. She explained that what he had done was a very bad thing that he would have to pay for, but we didn't want to have hate toward anyone.

Hate my father? I had been betrayed by the one I trusted more than anyone. My father, my idol, the one who was supposed to take care of us had betrayed me. I didn't know much about the woman who was involved. I'd seen her several times around the church but never really met her. Who was this person who had carried out the actions that my father planned? Should I hate her? Was one worse than the other? She had held the deadly weapons that bludgeoned my mom, but my father was behind the betrayal.

At that moment I felt the razor-sharp claws of evil drag across my heart, evil that my dad let in. Those claws severed my childhood and my dreams—claws that cut me deeper than I even knew was possible.

Ushering us out of the room, an official-looking lady with my aunt hurriedly moved us through a whirlwind of events to where a police officer met us in the lobby. I don't even remember what he said or the questions he asked. All I remember after that is the blue Oldsmobile . . .

///

Despite his size and a few tattoos, this giant was more gentle than fearsome. He spoke of his family and how he missed them. He told of his daughter in college and his wife, who worked at the grocery store with him. He conveyed how he and his wife had been cleaning up after hours in front of the store. They were both sweeping the store entry when his wife of twenty-five years transformed her broom into a make-believe sword and began a playful duel. In jest he accepted the challenge with his own broom, unaware of the police car coming down the street behind him. His wife quickly dropped her "sword" as he turned to see the officer—before he could drop his broom. What followed was a charge of assault with a deadly weapon.

His family didn't have the money for bail, which he was granted. He was afraid this would cost him his job and force his daughter to drop out of school, because he and his wife were helping put her through college. He also didn't know how he was going to get out of this mess.

My mind spun with bewildered perceptions of what I always had been taught by the media and those in authority around me. Weren't the bad guys supposed to be where I was? I never thought of myself as a bad guy, and I lived my life in contrast to that paradigm. I wasn't perfect, but I tried to be honest and do what was right. If this was the case, why was I here? What would prevent anyone from ending up here, lost in a bureaucratic system of misinterpreted laws and regulations with no way out?

///

Drops of blood spotted the ground, forming puddles beneath a lamppost in front of the hospital. Chief Demon perched proudly with razor-sharp talons covered in crimson. A rumbling laugh echoed through the night, gradually gaining volume until it thundered through the skies. Red and blue lights eerily flashed across the hospital walls as the leader stood handcuffed in front of the police officers and several social service workers. A social worker led a stunned nine-year-old boy from the hospital to the scene taking place in front of the hospital. After a moment of speechless staring between the boy and his father, the leader was loaded into a police car and slowly driven away. The father didn't know what to say, and the boy had no words to utter.

Standing beside him, a glowing being gently placed an arm around the boy's shoulders. Angelic beings dotted the sidewalk between officers and hospital employees. Dark growling creatures circled the scene, peering through angry spouts of steaming sulfur, watching for an opportunity to inflict even more damage. The angelic beings kept them at a distance from the humans they were shielding. Chief Demon drank in every moment of pleasure from the defeat of the leader and the scars left on the boy.

After the scene had cleared, the demonic creatures waited on Chief Demon for their next command. Swooping down from his lofty post, Chief Demon ordered the minions to the next calculated assault, and the horde of shadows howled into the night in pursuit of a blue Oldsmobile.

5

Road to Nowhere

This life is messy, but it is just the dirt we are planted in, not the garden we were made for. One day we will see the light of the garden we were made for.

Try to exclude the possibility of suffering which the order of nature and the existence of free-wills involve, and you find that you have excluded life itself.

—C. S. Lewis, The Problem of Pain

Every time you sacrifice something at great cost, every time you renounce something that appeals to you for the sake of the poor—you are feeding a hungry Christ.

—Mother Teresa

Whoever welcomes this little child in my name welcomes me; and whoever welcomes me welcomes the one who sent me. For it is the one who is least among you all who is the greatest.

—Jesus, Luke 9:48 (NIV)

An endless freeway stretched to the horizon through the central valley of California. Hours of continuous rhythm hummed through the cushions of my aunt's Oldsmobile. Headlights cast shadows into the dusk as the sky turned to a dark still night.

The road seemed to go on forever in an eternal pattern of broken lines that night. My aunt and uncle's house never had seemed so far away when we visited on family vacations. This time it was different; this time it was permanent. What lay ahead for us? My mom said she'd be with us as soon as she was well enough. What if she didn't come? What if she couldn't come?

My mind haunted me with reenactments of what happened to Mom that fateful night, when we were at church and she was at home with the assailant my dad had sent. A sketchy picture of what my aunt and Mom had told me was all I had to paint this horrible vision in my head. I couldn't cry, and I couldn't sleep. What would become of us now? How would we live?

Dad always had seemed to take care of us. He was a man of God, I thought. He had paid the bills and made the decisions. I guess none of that mattered anymore. What I felt I had to do was survive. I had to be strong for everyone now. My sister cried herself to sleep in the backseat with my little brother across her lap as my uncle navigated us into the darkness.

I needed someone to tell me how I should feel, I needed something solid to hang on to, and I needed a hug badly. But the only thing I could do was stop my feelings from flowing and tuck them away in a safe place.

I was no longer a PK. I wasn't sure who I was anymore. What would I do? Who would I become? I didn't want to be a pastor like my dad anymore. I didn't want anything to do with my dad, but I missed him dearly and a big piece of me was gone.

Questions swirled around in my head like waves tossing in an endless circle. I kept asking, *Who am I? Who is my father?* My soul kept slamming into a rocky wall only to be dragged across sharp coral that was shredding it to pieces. The questions churned in my head as I was thrust into the unknown . . .

Click-clang! The electronic lock opened with a loud reverberating noise once again as the cell door slid open to reveal a prison guard clanging keys by his side.

"Line up when I call your name; no speaking unless you are spoken to."

The militant guard began calling out names. I leaned over to the inmate next to my bunk and quietly asked where we were going. His reply was quick and swift. "Man, you never been in here before, have you?"

Once again quietly I replied, "No, and I don't know why I'm here now."

"Man, we're going to county jail, and then some of us to see the judge. I'm going to see my homies."

Not completely sure of the definition of *homies*, I lined up as my name was called. I was handed a skinny burrito-looking thing filled with mystery meat, an extremely small apple, and a juice box filled with some artificial juice-flavored drink. The inmate next to my bunk was chained up and led through the door vault. The rest of the occupants, including me, were left to walk into the cold concrete corridor between the cells.

I noticed many who seemed to know each other and made signals as if speaking a silent language. The ones signaling bore face tattoos that spread down through all revealed appendages. There were also several like me who were bewildered and didn't look like they belonged there. It wasn't an environment for conversation, nor was it a place to get any help, as phone calls apparently were available only to inmates that you would see in the movies.

After several days, with a newly sprouted beard and no shower or change of clothes, my spirit was breaking. All I could do was cry out quietly to my heavenly Father and worry about my family. Emotions raced back to when I was a child. The fears formerly tucked away fought to surface again. *What if I'm lost in this system like the others I've met here? What if I can't get out of here and work to take care of my family? What will become of my wonderful wife and children? Have I taken them for granted? Oh, God, please hear my cry and save me from this horrific experience.* A guard holding a weapon in front of the door yelled to everyone to exit the cell. He angrily slammed the cell door, leaving us in the corridor with the box of barely distinguishable food items. I immediately spotted two phones hanging on the wall. They were pay phones, but the idea of anyone having money in that place was ludicrous, since everything was stripped away during the process of being checked into these accommodations.

I thought maybe a collect call could be made. I stretched toward the phones from my place on the bench, trying to reach where they were mounted on the wall, only to find that they didn't work. I should have guessed. The condition of the phones matched the filth of the surroundings. Grunge from some unforgotten century grew on the edges of the cold walls and between the bars. What I once would have considered unsanitary to even touch I now slept on and ate from. There was nothing in that place that wasn't bolted to the floor or a wall. Everything was made of steel or concrete, almost as cold as the guards who dominated that dungeon.

I wanted to be with my family in our comfortable home. I didn't think something like this was even possible in a seemingly free country. I thought I was one of the good guys who didn't end up in places like this. Did I do something wrong? Was I a bad person destined to suffer in this life? No one seemed to be able to tell me why I was there. I prayed that my heavenly Father would find me and free me from that place.

It didn't take long before the speakers echoed through the corridor ordering the inmates to return to their cages. The hand-signaling group huddled in private circles seemingly having a confidential gathering. The resonance of the command sent everyone scattering back to their dwellings, including the confidential crew, who seemed to block all of the entrances to our quarters.

///

Angelic beings glowed into the dark traveling alongside the Oldsmobile, while others sat next to the occupants keeping guard. With tearful faces they reflected the deep wounds that had been inflicted on this family. Dark spots high above blotted out stars as they scurried through the sky well away from the travelers in the Oldsmobile.

Back at the old house on the outskirts of town below the once stately old home, Chief Demon once again passed through the opening where the large door formerly hung. In the basement the thick sulfurous stench still filling the air welcomed this large creature of darkness. Beelzebub, the huge hideous creature laced in bony veins over his leathery body waited for Chief Demon in the shadows of the room. Repulsive creatures darted back and forth in the mistiness as the darkness approached his liege. The large frightful demon cast its shadow as he stopped at the feet of the hideous Beelzebub and bowed.

"My liege, my human leader and his woman accomplice will go to prison, where I have many demons, and one will be assigned to each. The mother is still in the hospital, and the children have left my region. My minions are following them. I will prepare a plan to deceive them once we know where they end up. I have sent my top deceiver to the hospital to finish the mother as well."

From the corner of the room a cloud of red sulfur spewed into the air. "You report as if this is a victory." A pause filled the room with tension. "The mother is surrounded by warrior angels, and the saints of our enemy are praying so she grows stronger. The children will be influenced by her as they grow. Yes, much damage has been done, but they are still on this physical earth, so don't claim them as your victory yet. You will follow them to ensure they do not become a threat. You will win this battle with the human children, and they will become yours to feast on, because I have ordered you to do so."

Stammering to get the words out before it was too late, Chief Demon sputtered back, "But . . . but, my lord. I run this region, and they have fled to another. Surely there is another as evil as I that can be assigned to the children."

Looking penetratingly upon the addresser, the hideous Beelzebub ordered, "I rule this region, and you failed me here. You will hunt these children no matter where they go, and you will destroy them. Never fail me or counter my charge again."

Then Beelzebub rose from the corner. With a rush of wind he bolted through the opening where the door once hung, passing leathery wings through the walls on either side.

Beams of anger and fury raged through the slits of Chief Demon's eyes as a tirade ensued in the room. He slammed the walls, kicking and mauling any creature that got in his way. In an angry fit Chief Demon's large shadow rocketed out the opening and into the lightless night sky.

At the hospital Reptile dashed down the hall, sending a chill up the spine of those standing in the corridor. A cold deadness seemed to touch each human as Reptile passed through everything in his way. Briskly moving like a determined bulldog on a mission, Reptile raised a talon-filled claw to the air, turned the corner in front of the mother's hospital room, and almost ran square into a host of majestic glowing warriors.

Screeching to a halt with the raised claw now covering a pointy face of scales, Reptile tracked backward as fast as possible. A large angelic being grabbed Reptile by the neck before he could retreat. "Look what we have here, gentlemen." Holding Reptile's claws down while fangs burst with sulfur biting at the air, the angel spoke. "This woman belongs to the Light of this world. You do not belong here and will not be allowed to harm her anymore."

Reptile opened one eye, still shielding the other from the brightness of the angelic beings. "I see the saints are praying? Maybe we can make a deal for the woman?"

With the flash of a lightning bolt, the angel's sword flew through the air, slicing Reptile into mist. "You little deceiver, you know that guardians of the King's children don't make deals." In a vapor of red-hot steam, Reptile disappeared.

The grand being of Light returned his sword to its sheath while speaking to his fellow sentries. "There will be more of these evil creatures. I'm sure that many more powerful than this one will try to strike, so be on alert. With the prayers of the saints, reinforcements have been sent and will arrive soon. We need to encourage the humans who are praying—encourage them to ask God for a quick healing of her broken body. This family needs to be together to begin the spiritual healing process. I'm sure demons are chasing the kids as we speak. Keep everyone on high alert and encourage God's prayer warriors, and I will return after checking on the children."

One of the smaller angels reached up and placed a hand on the grand angelic being's shoulder. "These are God's precious children. The stakes are high with the evil one's plans foiled; he will be on the prowl. God be with you, my friend."

With the gleam of a smile, the grand angel spread his wings and ascended through the ceiling in brilliant splendor.

6

Whose Life Is This?

Life changes, sometimes rapidly, but never forget that this is temporary and we will never be fully at home here.

Have mercy on me, Lord, for I am faint; heal me, Lord, for my bones are in agony.
—Psalm 6:2 (NIV)

Jesus wept.
—John 11:35 (NIV)

Calm the storms that drench my eyes, dry the streams still flowing, cast down all the waves of sin, and guilt that overthrow me. Lift me up / when I'm falling, lift me up / I'm weak and I'm dying, lift me up / I need you to hold me, lift me up / Keep me from drowning again.
—*Jars of Clay*—"Flood" Lyrics

My aunt and uncle's home was the perfect size for one family, but it wasn't made for two. They had three children of their own. I loved to visit and play with my cousins, but this wasn't like visiting anymore. This time, I had a one-way ticket with no option to return to my former life.

My little brother and I slept together with my cousin in his room. Even though they did everything they could to accommodate us, I always felt like I was invading someone else's personal space.

I'm sure it must have been difficult for them to give up their rooms, though they never said anything. We were the intruders who just moved into their home one night. My cousins didn't have a lot of warning that we were coming; we just showed up in their lives. In a three-bedroom home now occupied by nine people, there wasn't space for alone time. I couldn't sort through all of my feelings and emotions, so I just kept them tucked away.

My aunt and uncle had two girls close to my sister's age and a boy my little brother's age. Everyone seemed to have someone to connect with, except me. I continued to withdraw inside, trying to control my unsettled emotions. I'm not sure I could have connected with anyone at that moment in time even if I had tried. I felt like a foreigner living in a peculiar place.

I can remember lying in bed late at night staring around the room in the shadows of the moonlight. Nothing was familiar in that strange land where I now found myself. It wasn't a dream that would pass with the morning sun or be quickly forgotten the next day. I would lie there and examine every little feature of the room from the vantage point of that small bed. I can still remember the intricate details of the little wooden characters on the dresser and the train on the floor, which had to be moved to make room for us.

I missed my home. I missed my friends and my dog, Brutus, whom I never got to say good-bye to. I longed for something familiar that I could hold on to, and I missed my mom. I felt like I was floating aimlessly on a life raft in the midst of a hurricane. Had I reached the edge of the storm? Would the sun shine once again? Or was I approaching the eye of the storm only to be followed by something much worse?

Keeping a house full of people operating was a demanding task. There were always chores to be done. I tried hard to do my part, but my emotions would often get in the way. They would try to surface involuntarily in reactions that I would have to fight off. My concentration was lost in these moments, and I would have to refocus on the present.

A couple of weeks had gone by when a large moving van pulled up in front of my aunt and uncle's house. The day that moving truck arrived at the house was an emotionally stirring one. It didn't take long for remnants of my former life to be unpacked and tightly fit into the garage.

I remember one day when there was yard work for all of the kids to help out with, but I just couldn't help anyone that day. The lure of that garage drew me like a magnet to my lost memories and dreams. My entire short life was in that space.

I stole away and crawled between the tightly packed boxes and furniture to find a cubbyhole. The familiar smells and textures brought comfort and warmth to a deeply wounded part of me. There was a connection to my soul in that garage; it was a comforting calm like the hug of a teddy bear with a one-eyed smile.

I could hear the others calling for me to come and help, but I couldn't move. I didn't want to leave that space, ever. Being in that garage gave a small piece of who I once was back again. I needed something to begin the healing with . . . or at least to let me hold onto the past long enough to remember days that were good. I wanted to remember the days that were once happy before I lost my childhood and my dad.

The day our family car drove into my aunt's driveway was the first time I encountered a glimpse of joy since that fateful day. It wasn't the car that excited me; it was the traveler who occupied it . . .

///

Once again lying on my concrete bunk after the excitement of trying to digest indescribable rations for lunch, or whatever meal that was, the story of my life played on like a motion picture in my head. Distraught about my current situation, my mind raced between the "what ifs" of tomorrow and the recollections of yesterday. The time to replay my life was in no short supply, and the material was plentiful. The hours were endless, and the answers were nonexistent.

In the middle of the silent monotony, I remember hearing a crying sound coming from the bunk next to mine. A young man who portrayed a cool yet tough exterior had covered himself in his single thin sheet of bedding and wept. From my nature I had to ask if I could help, but he quickly replied that no one could help. I told him that there was a God who cared for him, which seemed to open him up somewhat to a quiet conversation.

What he said brought home to me the hopeless reality of many who lived that grim existence. He said his father had left when he was a small child and his mother wouldn't let him come home. He had been in jail a few times before and hated it, but he had no other place to go. He was sleeping on his mother's back porch until she caught him there and kicked him out. Since there was nowhere to go and no one to direct this young man, he had to find a way to get arrested and return to this existence.

This was the only place where he felt he could fit in. The food was terrible, but it was something to eat. The place was dirty, dangerous, and scary, with no freedom or hope, but it was a place to be accepted by his peers. Sleeping on a cold concrete bunk seemed to be better to him than struggling in the outside world. He said he had tried church once but no one helped him there either. Then as quickly as the conversation had started, it ended as he rolled over and went silent. The swell of pain that just seeped through a crack in his hard exterior was once again pulled back inside to be locked away as he shut down and tuned me out.

I cried out inside once again to God. *Why am I here?* My soul ached as I thought of all the miracles in my life and how many times God had saved me. Yet I still drifted away from him and allowed mankind's original sin of pride to take hold of me. What would I do if I were in this young man's situation? I am not God. My days are not my own; they belong to my heavenly Father alone. But, who am I now?

Had I gone from one extreme to another? I recently felt I had it all and made it to the top of the world, before losing everything. After that experience I was dashed deep in depression only to climb out and scale that ladder once again. I didn't know there was a level even lower than what I had already experienced. I thought I had lost everything when my business failed a few years back, but I still had a wonderful wife, great kids, and a good job. I was on my way back up the corporate ladder when abruptly I was abducted and sent to this place.

I didn't know if I still had a job or if I'd even be able to provide for my family anymore. I didn't know what was happening to them or how they would survive. I didn't know how I drifted away from the grace that God had given me and how I felt so far from him, once again.

Despite everything he had done for me, I still had tried to take on life without him. Without his protection in my life I was nothing, and now I was in this place cut off from the world and shut out from the life God had given me. All I could do was cry out to my heavenly Father to heal my broken life and restore my soul once again.

I rolled over in my rigid concrete bunk and stared at the wall. If this was going to be my new existence, I wasn't sure I wanted it. If I couldn't leave this place or communicate with the outside world, or get help from anyone, then I felt as good as dead. All I could do was waste away while I waited, but I didn't know what I was waiting for.

///

Perched in the shadows of tree branches cast by the dim light of the earliest morning hours, a crooked being impatiently paced the darkness. A covering of wrinkled folds sheltered only by an occasional long protruding hair revealed the dark creature in the shadows. Mole's penetrating eyes darted back and forth into the distant window of a bedroom where children slept.

A large shadow of wings swooped down silently from the sky behind the wrinkled creature. Shaking the branches upon arrival, the large, powerful demon clenched on with his razor-sharp talons, frightening Mole. In surprise Mole pressed hard into the shadows, peering with his green piercing eyes at Chief Demon, and exposing his sharp teeth.

"Hissssssssssss. I don't take kindly to surprises." Looking amused, Chief Demon peered back at Mole. "You work for me now; I am now your god."

"Hisssss. If I wanted a god to tell me what to do, I wouldn't have followed the dark angel of death to earth. I am my own god." Turning to face Mole, Chief Demon billowed hot sulfur steam into the air.

"You have been ordered to follow me by Beelzebub directly. I have a very important mission that is vital to our darkest success. We could suffer much loss if we allow these human viruses to follow the Light. Don't worry—you will be rewarded. I will share the joy of feasting on these little ones with you as well."

The fangs folded back into Mole's jaws. "Hiss. I'll escort you in this, but one of the children will belong to me alone. I was told you failed in your last region, and your last sidekick was taken out by some small angel. I don't go down so easily for anyone."

With a rush of extended talons and a flurry of leathery wings, Chief Demon cornered Mole against the tree trunk. "You will follow my commands as ordered. There is a host of angels here who will take you out if I don't first, so don't tempt me. My former devotee was removed from the earth in a battle that you would not have survived."

Placing Mole back in the shadows of the branches, Chief Demon stepped back. "Yes, you can have one of the human children if you succeed, but you will have to share the rest with the other hungry minions of mine. They will be here when the mother arrives. Now, look closely through the window. There are angels everywhere, but they will thin out when the humans get tired of praying. In the meantime we will inflict enough pain and turmoil that the humans will self-destruct right in front of their glowing protectors from heaven."

Children lay sleeping as the early morning light began to stream rays through the bedroom curtains. Radiant beings stood over the small beds. The grand angelic being radiated compassion toward the small humans; then he turned to converse with his warrior colleague. "Our Father loves these little ones so much. The prayer cover is strong, and I feel the power. Have you sensed the presence of darkness yet?"

The smaller warrior of Light spoke softly as he pointed out the window. "They're in the yard watching from the tree. Can we go out there and just take them out with a sword while the prayer cover is strong?"

The grand being placed a hand on the smaller warrior's shoulder. "I wish it were that easy. Our Father of Light will let us only if his earthly children ask. We are here to protect them, and the prayer of the saints gives us the upper hand today, but we are not to interfere with their freewill choices. I know this is hard for us to understand, since we never went through this earthly birthing process that humans have to endure. Ours is to do the will of our Father, but the humans have to make their own choices, without our interference. We can act only as the Holy One directs, or I would have already flashed my sword through those trees."

7

A Warrior's Welcome

We are the seeds planted in the dirt—real life doesn't begin until we reach the Light.

But for you who revere my name, the sun of righteousness will rise with healing in its rays.
—Malachi 4:2 (NIV)

Very truly I tell you, unless a kernel of wheat falls to the ground and dies, it remains only a single seed. But if it dies, it produces many seeds.
—Jesus, John 12:24 (NIV)

The day my mom arrived at my aunt and uncle's house was the grandest family reunion ever. My mom was with us, and I felt that some small resemblance of a life could once again be set into motion.

My aunt parked our family car in the driveway and mom was slowly maneuvered into a waiting wheelchair and escorted to the house. She had to continue the physical healing for months after she arrived. She looked much better than she had in the hospital, but she still looked frail. The bandages were smaller and revealed much of the black-and-blue marks trying to mend. A remnant of our family was once again united.

She continually tried to assure us that everything was going to be all right, but she was hurting inside more than on the outside. I don't know if she was as unsure about our future as I was, but she didn't let on how she felt in front of us.

She never stopped trusting in God and leaning on him. She would tell us how our heavenly Father would always take care of us, so there was nothing for us to worry about. I knew God would take care of us, but I was broken on the inside, and the anxiety about our future still haunted me.

Mom was able to register us in a local Christian school. We didn't have any money, but someone anonymously paid our tuition, which was a miracle. I'm sure that attending a small private school helped shelter me from things I wasn't ready to deal with. I had so much to cope with that I don't think I would have survived any new issues that a large public school might have introduced.

Everything in my world was new, including my teachers, the classroom, and riding a school bus for the first time in my life. Even the place I now called home seemed surreal. I missed my old home. I kept asking myself what was going on here; was this real or was I dreaming? I couldn't fully grasp what was happening around me or this life I was now traveling through. I didn't have a good enough grasp of who I was to make any friends or allow anyone to get too close. I was no longer the outgoing young man who had led worship in children's church, and I was no longer a pastor's kid. I wasn't the boy with a plan for my future anymore. I wasn't sure who I was.

After several months my mom and aunt started a small typesetting business, since there wasn't a lot of demand for former pastor's wives or homemakers in the job market. The typesetting business came with a bunch of equipment resembling typewriters. My mom and aunt were able to work from my aunt's house while Mom continued to heal from her injuries. I didn't really know what they did, but it had something to do with typing books and magazines and different text sizes on paper.

Another great day came several months later when we met the older gentleman who would become our landlord. It wasn't the big home in the suburbs like we had, but that didn't matter anymore. The place was small, old, and creaky, but I loved it because it was our new home.

The front door didn't always close when the weather changed. The door would swell at the most inopportune times, like when we had to leave for school in the morning or needed to go somewhere in the evening. Nonetheless, Mom was able to work, and we had a place to live and call home. It had two tiny bedrooms that were just big enough for a few pieces of our furniture. It needed paint and the carpets were worn, but I didn't care; we had a home.

That two-bedroom apartment was a wonderful place. After we'd shared quarters with another family for months, the four of us in a small apartment didn't seem so bad.

Lasting memories came from my time in that apartment. It was small but appreciated. There was a row of mint growing next to the front door that seemed to be out of place, like a patch of weeds or something, but I could relate to it. The mint herbs added a wonderful smell to our apartment. I tried to nurture that strand of green growing through the concrete walk to keep it alive.

I began to experience some semblance of a life once again. The feelings still lurked deep down inside and crept out occasionally in displaced outbursts, but for the most part I was able to keep them in check, or so I thought. There were other feelings that began to haunt me as they mixed with my deep emotional scars. These new feelings generated great fear.

Every day after school my siblings and I would be home alone for about an hour while Mom was still at work. That hour haunted me terribly. A disturbing voice would whisper in my ear continually, "She's not coming back," over and over. I would perch on the counter with my gaze fixed out the kitchen window. Thoughts of being abandoned by my mom troubled me, since my dad had done it so easily. These emotions would churn until the moment she drove around the corner and I could see her coming up the driveway. Relief would race through my veins, and I could go on with life once again.

It was scary at times to know that we had so little money. There was nothing to fall back on. I never thought about money before that time. Money had been something that Dad took care of, and we always seemed to have enough. The concept of money was virtually foreign to me until this time. I began counting every penny in a swift self-education on the cost of life, especially when the pennies were all we had to count.

After Dad abandoned us, we didn't wear the name-brand clothes or shop for anything without checking to see if we could afford it first. In fact, we didn't even eat name-brand food. We shopped for the generics and discount items, but that was okay with me. It seemed a difficult but small price to pay for being together.

Mom continued to put on a positive face for us. She told us not to worry; God would take care of us. We were his children. Somehow things did seem to come together, and God did seem to always take care of us. Life wasn't easy and things didn't come effortlessly, but that same wonderful spirit I knew as a kid was still with us and now took care of our daily needs.

The amazing miracles that always came when we needed them the most—and they came often—astonished me. God endlessly reminded me that he was there taking care of me.

///

Interrupting unknown hours of monotony, the lights blasted from pasty orange to spotlight flares. A gruff voice over the speakers blared, "Get up!" and the lock on the cell door reverberated with that familiar click-bang sound. The door automatically slid open. Inmates slowly emerged from their cocoons, rubbing eyes while finding their way to the cold concrete floor. Migrating myself out the door I returned to the central corridor space, where the ceilings climbed two stories and the steel benches were bolted to the floor. I found a cold bench to sit on, and I was happy to be off the concrete bunk, though the discomfort of the steel was little to take pleasure in.

Many of the prisoners, including me, watched the room cautiously, not knowing what to expect or who to trust. Visually scouring the space, I spied a group of phones mounted to the wall tucked in a corner. Trying not to raise too much attention, I rose and began working my way over to the lifeline I thought these phones might provide me. A small spark of hope swelled as I reached the receiver, only to once again be dashed when there was no dial tone.

My pulse began to race again when a dial tone sounded on the second receiver. After agreeing to the recorded message stating that this phone was monitored and everything said would be used against me, I agreed to the dollar-a-minute-plus long-distance charges. I was able to dial my home number in Toronto, Canada. I could hear the recording on the other end, "You are receiving a collect call from an inmate in the Los Angeles Jail. Will you accept?" It was like the sound of an angel when I heard my wife answer. My exterior immediately cracked as I fell into involuntary convulsions and wailing, and tears cascaded down my face.

"Holly, it's me. I need you to do something for me."

"Where have you been, what do you need?"

After a short pause, I answered, "I need you to call our attorney and ask him to recommend a good criminal attorney. I'm in jail. They won't tell me why I'm here, and they won't give me bail. I don't know what to do. I was detained when I got off the plane at the Los Angeles Airport. I was paraded through the airport like some terrorist or something."

Through weeping on the other end, I could hear, "They can't do this to you. You didn't do anything; how can they hold you there? We have to get you out of there."

Trying to hold back the tears while standing in the midst of other inmates, I tried to reply. "I don't even have traffic tickets, let alone know how to deal with something like this. We'll need a criminal attorney of some sort, and I don't even know anyone who knows one. I need help, and no one here will help me. This place is terrible, and I need to get out of here so I can resolve whatever this is and get back to work."

Trying to hold it together, Holly quickly answered, "I'll call our friends in California so they'll know what's happening, and maybe they can help with something. I love you, baby."

Over the intercom that gruff voice once again belted through the hollows of the concrete corridor, "Return to your cells."

As quickly as I could, I sobbed into the phone, "I love you so much, Holly. Tell the kids I love them and somehow we'll get through this. Pray—please call everyone and ask them to pray." Buzz . . . the phone cut off as I tried to compose myself and dry my eyes while discretely making my way back to the chamber of endless monotony.

///

In mid-daylight a group of dark shadows perched on the roof of a home in the shade of a great oak. A breeze hid the darkness in the fluttering leaves reflected over the home. Several smaller silhouettes seemed fixed in time and space as the two largest shadows wavered in struggling gestures.

"Hisssss. Look, Chief, I'm wasting a lot of time waiting for the prayer to stop. I could have had a meal of liars or adulterers by now, maybe not as tasty as a triumph like this, but nonetheless filling," Mole spouted as the long protruding hairs on his body reverberated with each word.

Chief Demon slowly stepped around Mole, peering at the obstinate inferior. "Patience, my crony. These humans always falter, as it is their nature. When they do, we will be there to pounce, so step up the discouragement and pelt them with doubt. There is enough of a time bomb planted that something will explode in these humans sooner or later. Besides, our enemy, the great Light, will not interfere with their free will, which is our greatest asset to deceive them with. This will be more than a meal; it will be gourmet fare beyond what you are accustomed to."

Pausing to contemplate Chief Demon's words Mole scratched his chin then retorted, "The angels are still there, many of them, and some are very big and powerful. If you didn't notice, that is why we are over here. I can get a few words tossed through the window, but we are far from clenching teeth or clawing flesh from these humans. I want a tasty crumb now!"

The steam of red sulfur rose into the tree branches as Chief Demon stretched a leathery grin. "Patience, my minion, patience."

Mole glared over a wrinkly shoulder, making it apparent that the words of the new superior were ill-received.

The object of observation, the apartment next door, seemed to dance in the glowing rays of angelic beings surrounding a mom in prayer with her three children kneeling in a small living room. The accommodations were humble and the gathering modest, but the angelic joy burst through in rejoicing dance and praise to the Father of Light. In the midst of the angelic ballet, a being of Light that paled all of the other beings stood with a hand on the mother's shoulder.

8

Unearthly Phenomena

Science acknowledges unexplainable phenomena and tries to study it, but we already have the handbook that explains it—the Bible.

He performs wonders that cannot be fathomed, miracles that cannot be counted.

—Job 5:9 (NIV)

You don't have a soul. You are a Soul. You have a body.

—C. S. Lewis, Mere Christianity

Miracles were a continual part of my daily life. That presence that I'd felt when I was younger never left me. My mom became my spiritual hero as I would see her get on her knees and pray to God. She was less outspoken than my dad but much more genuine. I still saw things that would have been hard to explain by anyone who didn't know my heavenly Father.

There was another single mom in our apartment neighborhood. Her son was older than I, but sometimes we would hang out. His dad would visit him only once in a great while. On one of these rare visits his dad gave him the coolest-looking go-cart, which made him very popular among the neighborhood kids.

That go-cart was so "sweet." It had a large gas motor in the rear and sat so low to the ground that it almost scraped the asphalt. The big slick tires made it look like an open race car. It was little more than metal framing sitting an inch off the ground, with a steering wheel protruding from the front, a seat, and an engine.

There was a large cul-de-sac in front of his apartment where he would race it back and forth. Being younger than him and his other friends, I didn't get to drive often.

On one particularly hot, sticky day near dusk, my friend brought the go-cart out to the street. I just happened to be outside when I saw him rolling it down to the curb of the cul-de-sac. As he wheeled it into the street, I imagined how much fun it would be to drive. The thrill of open air rushing by as I navigated the curve of the street made me think of nothing else.

That evening someone in the apartment complex was having a party, so the cul-de-sac was lined with cars that weren't normally there. I didn't usually get to drive, since my friend thought I was too young. But this evening was special because he had promised me a turn on the go-cart the next time he got it out. So I raced over to his driveway in great anticipation.

After the motor thundered to life, my friend yelled over the sound of the go-cart and waved for me to get on; it was my turn. I climbed on and put the pedal down as hard as I could. To make the most of that ride, I steered as far to the outside of the cul-de-sac as possible. I skimmed past the parked cars as I got up to speed and rounded the corner for a fast lap.

As I got up to full speed, the wind raced through my hair. I rounded the cul-de-sac, leaning to keep the go-cart on all four wheels. I drifted wider than expected, and before I could make any adjustments, I abruptly made contact with a large trailer hitch extending beyond the lower edge of a car bumper. Four inches of unobstructed solid steel protruded about eighteen inches into my path. I didn't see it coming when that solid steel hitch connected directly with my shinbone, but I sure felt it.

The go-cart flew sideways in the air, throwing me into the street, while the back of the car lifted up and then bounced. I slid to a stop skipping across the asphalt, and then I immediately curled into the fetal position wrenched in pain. My muscles tightened, and I became stiff as a rock trying to ward off the intense agony.

Broken bones can mend, although they are excruciatingly painful, and mine was undoubtedly broken. However, we didn't have any medical insurance and could never afford a doctor to put things back together. My friends picked me up and carried me to my apartment while I screamed in pain. They didn't know what to do, so they laid me on the couch.

Thankfully, my mom was home. Without hesitation she laid hands on me and began to pray. She asked for a miracle from our heavenly Father, the one she always told me would take care of us. It was as though a peace came over me when she prayed.

I remember lying there for some time as the light of the day slipped away. I also remember the pain subsiding and a friend of my mom's coming to our apartment to look at my leg. By the time my mom's friend arrived, my leg still ached but the wrenching pain was gone and the broken bone was healed. I still have a scar to this day and a dent in the bone to remind me of that solid steel trailer hitch. However, the scar that I carry is an even greater reminder that it was my heavenly Father who put my leg back together.

God seemed to be involved in our everyday life. Not every miracle seemed as dramatic, but I was grateful for all of them. There were times when we just didn't have enough money to make it through the month, but God always provided.

There were times when we would be running out of food. Sometimes we would get up in the morning and find a bag of groceries at the front door. God always seemed to provide what we needed when we needed it, and in his own way. He always responded in new creative ways that showed me he was the one caring for us. We didn't have a lot, but we never did without.

In addition to working, Mom went back to school to complete her degree. The church we attended had a large congregation with a college on the church campus where my mom attended.

I remember college students would come to our apartment for game nights. I enjoyed hanging out with the college guys. A part of me began craving fatherly interaction, which made these times special for me. Along with the many caged emotions I carried, I didn't understand these feelings either. Nonetheless, every opportunity to temporarily fill the hole my father had left seemed to help. God became my heavenly Father in a real way, but the hole in my heart for a dad still hurt.

My heavenly Father never forgot about me or my family. I'll never forget our first Christmas in the apartment. Mom asked my siblings and me what we would like for Christmas that year. Surprisingly, we all wished for the same thing—a bicycle.

Buying bikes would be the equivalent of winning the lottery for us. We might as well have been asking for a million dollars. Nonetheless, my mom just said that we had a big heavenly Father who owned the sheep on a thousand hills, referencing a verse in the Bible stating that God owns everything.

She said our heavenly Father can do anything he chooses, so we'd have to ask him about it. She didn't say it, but I knew we clearly didn't have the money for bikes, but that didn't seem to faze her. I think we prayed more that year than ever before. We really wanted bicycles, so Mom encouraged us to pray and talk to our heavenly Father.

I saw God provide food and other things we needed, but would God really give us bikes? I think Mom started to get a little worried when she saw the faith we seemed to muster up for Christmas, though deep in my heart I knew she had tremendous faith. I believed that God could do anything, but a part of me wasn't completely sure about this bike thing. I knew God wasn't Santa Claus. We couldn't just sit on his lap and belt out a wish list like we were placing an order. He was the Creator of the universe and did things his own way for reasons we often didn't understand until later . . . sometimes much later.

Mom was at school one day when unexpectedly a man came up to her and said God had been prompting him to give her some money, and it had something to do with her kids and Christmas. And yes, it was just enough to buy bicycles. To this day, I don't know who that person was, but God does because he sent him to us.

A person had felt God's prompting and followed through. I don't know if that person will ever know the impact that had on my life. I doubt if that person knew what we were praying for or that the money they gave was just enough for the bikes, but my heavenly Father knew.

The bizarre situation I found myself in made me reflect on what life must be like in other countries and for those who were imprisoned for their faith or some other noble cause. I was stuck in that cell by captors who I thought were there to protect me and my rights as an American citizen. What had happened to the TV drama enactments where the good guys were on the outside of the bars and always prevailed? What had happened to representation or even a phone call? No one even had read me my rights; did I have any rights? Shouldn't someone have told me why I was there? How long could someone be held, lost in the system and cut off from the world? Or worse, if you fought against the system, did the government really have so much power that people could just disappear? I thought things like this happened only in third world countries ruled by dictators or tyrants. All I was allowed to do was to be silent and wait for my captors, the U.S. government, to do with me as they wished. And worst of all, my family hung in the balance. The family that I loved so dearly, who relied on me to take care of them, was at the mercy of this government.

I hadn't been to work in almost a week. By this time I was getting punchy from lack of sleep and information. I had just started a new position a few months before I was taken from the airport by my captors. I didn't know if I even still had a job.

Click-bang! The electronic steel cage door unlocked and slid open. With no intercom or sound from the speakers, I assumed it was time to wander back out into the center corridor again. Other inmates slowly came to life and migrated toward the steel benches. A small TV mounted about twenty feet up on the ceiling came to life with some soap opera or talk show in midsession.

I made my way to the phones again to find another inmate talking with his girlfriend on the phone, making arrangements for bond. I waited as others began to gather, most trying the broken phone first and then finding a cold steel bench to wait nearby. After some time passed, the conversation with the girlfriend ended, and I quickly latched onto the phone receiver, which reached only far enough to allow me to stand inches from the phone. I quickly dialed my home number and waited through the recordings. "This conversation will be recorded and used against you." Ring, ring. "You are receiving a call from an inmate in the Los Angeles Jail at a dollar-a-minute-plus long-distance charges. Will you accept?"

Within minutes the sweet sound of my dear wife lit up the line like a sweet memory. "Holly, I love you," barely left my lips, and the heaving of tears began forcing their way through while I tried to fight them off.

"Kevin, I have some news, so I'll talk quickly. I've tried calling you several times, but they won't let me talk to you. I talked to Austin in California. He drove for over an hour to get where you are, and they wouldn't let him see you. I contacted an attorney who was recommended, but after speaking to him, I saw that he seemed to be focused more on talking about his hourly rate than anything else. He isn't very helpful or encouraging, so I'm looking for another one. Kevin, this could be really bad. The attorney painted a scary picture. He said you might be in there for a long time."

Fighting through the tears, I interrupted, "But why am I in here? Can they find out anything?"

"Yes, I did find out something. It has to do with our former business, but they won't give me any details." After a short pause she continued, "I called your boss. I told him there was some confusion when you went through customs. He was concerned about you and was glad to know you were alright. He said you still have your job and to keep in touch and let him know when you get things straightened out. The way things seem right now, it would take a miracle. He said you have some vacation time they will let you use, but I don't know how long they'll be able to hold your job for you. I contacted everyone I could think of and asked them to start praying. There are a lot of people praying for you right now. I talked to your mom and my mom, and their churches are praying as well. It will be okay. I love you so much."

Sniffling through the tears, I heaved through the phone, "How are the kids?"

"Kevin, they are okay. They are praying too. Spencer and I talked about it a little, but I kept it brief without too many details—" We were abruptly interrupted by someone over the intercom system ordering everyone back to their cells.

"Holly, I gotta go. Keep praying. I love you." Click-buzz. The phones went dead.

As soon as the vault doors slammed closed, a guard appeared at the door.

"Albright, come to the door!"

Standing next to the guard, a nurse stood with a cup of pills.

///

A forest of trees circled around the edge of the apartments, forming a natural backdrop to the structures. As the sun hung low in the sky, shadows stretched over the trails like bleeding tar. In the shadows of the darkened earth, evil congregated, peering through the murkiness of dusk.

"Hiss. There are cracks in the eldest boy. He is the most vulnerable." Mole strutted as if it were completely his discovery. "I want the boy. Assign the others to your minions."

Chief Demon lectured Mole. "I have studied human behavior for centuries, and millions of humans have fallen to my deceit. The boy will have emotional problems. He will migrate to strong male figures. Put manipulative and deceitful leaders in his life, and they will draw him away from our enemy, the Light. Once he has walked away from his heavenly protection, we will attack."

Mole quickly retorted, "The enemy's spirit has been obstructing my work. I've been able to lob some anxiety into the window and occasionally get close enough to plant fear and doubt. Deceitful father figures . . . hmm. I have a few humans that could practically do my job for me. I'll have to prepare them for this mission, but they will do fine . . . Yes, I think this could work." Mole twisted the hair on his chin in contemplation of the idea.

"Mole, I planted those emotions when I destroyed his father. You can attack the boy, but I am responsible to the angel of darkness Beelzebub himself, so don't do anything without my knowing. You will continue to report like this so you don't mess up all the work I've done so far. Remember that you will not feast on this family alone, and if you blow it, you will regret that you ever knew me."

Mole shrugged those wrinkly shoulders of his and nodded as if in agreement before crawling through the forest toward the apartment complex, spitting curses.

Looking out the window, two angelic beings watched Mole scurry through the soil behind the apartment. "Our Father's earthly children have called on his Spirit, and he has been strong here. The dark ones who follow Beelzebub will stop at nothing to destroy these earthly children our Father loves. The dark side knows that the scars are deep and the children will eventually be vulnerable. Their mother's prayer cover, along with those of many other saints, has protected them so far, but as they grow and become more independent, they will be required to make their own choices. The eldest boy still harbors great pain and a void where his father once was."

The second glowing being stood at the window and then turned to observe the children doing homework at the kitchen table. "The Holy Spirit has prepared a place for the boy this summer. He will have some of that void filled for a season. He will also be protected from the schemes of Chief Demon and Mole for a while, but be on your guard, because they are sly and cunning."

In the kitchen Mole cautiously stepped through the wall while scanning the room. As he looked around the cabinets, the mother's voice could be heard as she talked on the phone.

"That's great, Dad. I think he will enjoy that. I'll look for the plane tickets in the mail."

In a perplexed stupor, Mole quickly scampered back through the wall after spotting an angel sitting on the counter.

9

Cultivating a Soul

The Father of Light weaves a tapestry of our soul in this life that we will never fully understand until we reach the Light.

But if we walk in the light, as he is in the light, we have fellowship with one another, and the blood of Jesus, his Son, purifies us from all sin.
—1 John 1:7 (NIV)

God is faithful, who has called you into fellowship with his Son, Jesus Christ our Lord.
—1 Corinthians 1:9 (NIV)

A world of healing experiences came from my summer encounter at my grandpa's farm. Through some help from relatives who worked for the airlines, my grandfather made arrangements for me to spend the summer with him and my grandmother on their farm in Missouri. The things I learned there and the imprint they made on my soul brought a wealth of healing.

Grandpa Lee was a solid man who knew what he believed and wasn't afraid to tell anyone. He was a farmer and a man who could bend the land to his will. He lived in a modular farmhouse on eighty acres with a hay barn, lakes, old trucks, tractors, and adventure around every corner.

At over six foot four inches, he had a commanding presence. But he was much more than a farmer. He was also a man of God with a passion for the Creator who made everything. When he prayed, it was in earnest with authority, and the power of God seemed to speak through him. He was a preacher who had started many churches over the years. He had retired years earlier, but on Sundays he would often be called to fill in at different country churches in the surrounding farm communities.

When I arrived in Missouri, he bought me a cowboy hat at the local tractor store. From the moment Grandpa put that cowboy hat on me, I was a farmer just like him, at least for the summer. He taught me how to drive his old Ford tractor and how to handle cattle. He tried to teach me that anything could be cured with a little salve, a milky concoction Grandpa created. I had my doubts about his medical recommendations, but who knows.

Grandma was a Sunday school teacher and the kindest lady. She brought the compassionate side to farm life. Her loving eyes were always reassuring in the midst of my deep-rooted storms when emotions would seep to the surface of my facade.

I helped her with the garden and picked fresh vegetables in the mornings before the cowboy and Indian adventures started with my cousins, who lived on the neighboring farm.

The smells of summer abounded everywhere, hay fields were as tall as my chest, cows mooed from a distant hill, and cicadas sang a concerto from the trees. For a season I was a kid again. I was up before the break of day, and I couldn't rest until long after the sun set. I learned to fish and catch squirmy, wiggly bugs to bait a hook with.

My cousins were about my age and came with a variety of handmade wooden guns and swords just waiting for new adventures every fifteen minutes. The worries of life didn't matter at that moment. There was always fresh and tasty stuff from the garden to eat, along with the best meat from the freezer, plus an occasional fresh fish from the lake.

We would sit on the deck every evening and eat dinner. Grandpa would tell stories, and Grandma would make sure he was telling them correctly. Cows would join us and chew their cud as the sun set. The farm would come alive as the insects lulled us with a symphony at dusk. As a preteen, I felt life was good for a while.

Late at night after everyone was asleep, I would drift off to my thoughts, wondering who my dad was. Now that a few years had passed, I would overlay my desires for a dad to fill the hole inside my heart. I'd dream of an illusory dad who fit the broken slot inside of me where a dad should have been. After trying to erase the pain stuffed deep inside, I would drift off in some adventure that would lead into another wonderful day of farm life.

Eventually the summer came to an end, and I returned to the apartment with my mom and siblings in California. It didn't take long before my life changed once again—this time to a place even farther away. This new home would be deeper in the forest than even I would have dreamt.

///

I moved back to the cell door, where a small opening allowed the nurse to pass the paper cup of pills.

"Take the pills!" ordered the guard.

"Can I have some water?"

"Just take the #%*@ pills," he ordered.

I didn't know what pills they were giving me, but I needed my doctor's prescribed medication to control a blood cell condition, so I took what was offered. It was very important for me to have my prescription so my condition didn't get any worse. My medications seemed to come randomly whenever they remembered or got around to it. I wasn't feeling well, but it was difficult to tell if it was from lack of medication or just my current state of existence in that place. It was probably a combination of both. Often I've wondered why God would allow me to be afflicted in so many ways through this life but he wouldn't take me home. This experience was torturous and was rapidly wearing me down.

It seemed that pain was part of this experience, but the relief that would come from death wasn't part of the plan. Lying on that dirty concrete, I wished many times I was dead and could leave this earth. I knew my family needed me, but I wasn't doing them any good watching the dirt grow in the corners of that cell. I prayed many times since then that God would use these painful experiences to help others. I guess I was looking for some value to come out of the suffering—although this was the only possible value I perceived. He knew so much more than I could ever have imagined. I may never fully understand the meaning of what I was enduring or the measure of value my heavenly Father had in mind.

After nearly a week I was losing hope in everything. The endless questions in my head often centered on what had gone wrong with our former business that somehow had landed me in that cage. Why was I hunted down and by whom? If this was some big deal, why did they leave me in Los Angeles? My business had been in Colorado, not in Los Angeles. Why didn't someone just call me or send a letter so this could be rectified? My thoughts started to become fuzzy from the lack of sleep and food. Every time I thought I would be able to drift off, the speakers lit up to announce something or to chastise someone.

As I became one with the grunge I lay in, I remembered the time I had to come home and tell my wife I had cancer. There were many other earth-shattering moments of my life that I thought were far beyond anything I could bear. Yet none of them seemed to compare with my childhood and the lifelong journey my dad had propelled me into. Although if I had known what was coming next, I might have changed my mind.

///

Perched on farm equipment surrounded by freshly baled stacks of hay in the middle of a wheat field, a shadowy figure thrashed among the sounds of cattle and chirping bugs. Reeds of hay danced in the moonlight concealing the pale appearance of the revolting creature battering on the ground. Ripping wire from bound hay bales and biting at farm animals, Mole ranted in fury, seemingly alone.

"Hiss. This Chief doesn't know anything. I am here as if some farm animals are of any prize to me. Put a leader figure in the human's life, and he will fall . . . yeah, sure. Chief has been defeated again.

I should be the leader here. I would attack head-on. I shouldn't have listened to Chief Demon. I should've been the leader myself. &#$%##."

Nearly jumping out of the shadow, Mole lurched in surprise when a deep voice rumbled from atop a haystack in the darkness behind him. "I see it is time to have another visit."

Mole's countenance quickly softened in response. "Chief Demon, I didn't expect you here in the middle of nowhere."

"Mole, I know everything you do. I am everywhere."

Quickly regaining his smugness, Mole retorted, "No, you're not. Only our enemy, the Light, has abilities like that, you twit. You are not omniscient, and it is obvious that your strategic human behavior plan has failed once again. How am I supposed to introduce someone to make this human fall if our enemy has already put someone like his grandfather in the picture? I can't even get near the farmhouse. The angels accompanying that preacher grandfather are enormous."

From atop the haystack a patronizing response stabbed through Mole's comments. "Be patient, Mole. The wounds are deep, and an opportunity will present itself. Stay at your post and wait."

Pausing for a moment, Mole drilled fiery green eyes into Chief Demon's retort. Noticeably unresponsive to Mole's actions, Chief Demon spread out his large leathery wings, blanketing the ground and blocking out the moonlight. Before Mole could respond, Chief Demon swooped down from the haystack to skim the earth while exiting the conversation in a declaration of dominance.

Mole's bare, wrinkled body dropped to the ground in aggravation. Pounding the earth in fury, Mole whispered quietly, "Hiss. I will take this human my way."

Standing in the living room of the farmhouse, several angelic warriors chatted about their assignments. "We have defended our humans from some pretty dark characters over the years. As a leader, his grandfather would take many with him if he were to fall, which makes him a big target. Yet it is still his choices that drive our direction. He is in his room now conversing with his heavenly Father in prayer while preparing for a sermon this Sunday."

"I can see that the boy has some very deep scars that will surface with time. There are some serious battles coming in his life that you'll have to help him fight."

"How is the grand angelic being? I understand he was assigned to the family too."

The smaller angel of Light warmly responded, "The grand angelic being is still with the family in California. It has been an honor to serve with him while serving our Father in heaven and guarding his little ones. I know how important it will be to keep the saints praying, because there will come a time when all of this harbored pain will surface, and that is when my human will be the most vulnerable to the attacks of the dark side. All I can do is ask the Spirit to keep the saints praying so I will be ready for the attacks that are to come."

"While you're here, we have your back. The grandfather is a prayer warrior, which is how this stronghold came about. I also understand that Chief Demon is after the child, so be careful; Chief Demon is wickedly evil and powerful."

"Yes, I've seen Chief Demon a few times, but mostly I've seen Mole. It looks like Mole has been assigned to watch the boy. Although hideously deceitful, Mole is less powerful than Chief Demon. Mole has been roaming around the perimeter hiding in the shadows, and I don't think either of them would pass at any opportunity to attack. There is no doubt that these malicious creatures are seeking to devour the boy. Reptile tried an all-out frontal assault on the mom but ran straight into the grand angelic being. With the flash of a sword, Reptile is no longer a threat to our humans."

The sizeable being, glimmering in the moonlight, nodded in agreement with the smaller angel. "There is also a change afoot back in California. The change will alter the dynamics of their lives when the boy returns home."

10

Redwood Forest

Things change, places change, people change, but God's presence never changes.

And he said: Truly I tell you, unless you change and become like little children, you will never enter the kingdom of heaven.

—Jesus, Matthew 18:3 (NIV)

As long as it is day, we must do the works of him who sent me. Night is coming, when no one can work.

—Jesus, John 9:4 (NIV)

A few years had passed since the trauma of my childhood, and although some semblance of a life had been established, the caged-up emotions of my soul lay deep inside festering like an infected wound. I had spent wonderful summers with my grandparents in Missouri that helped keep my emotions in balance and filled the missing pieces of my soul for a season.

I had a new cat that brought comfort to my solitary days. I was surrounded by my immediate family and other kids from school, but I chose to remain reclusive after returning from the farm. The introverted moments allowed me to keep the intolerable memories from seeping through the cracks in my damaged soul.

My cat lessened the pressure by sitting and listening to me for hours. Of course he was deaf, but I didn't care. The pain inside needed to be vented. He would stare at me with a great feline expression of concern. He had pure white fur and strutted like he owned everything. His name was Snowball. I always made it clear that I didn't name him, since Snowball didn't seem like a "guy" name. I guess I could have renamed him, but I never did. He wouldn't have cared what I called him.

My mom applied for a position as a women's Christian counselor just about the time she was finishing up her degree. The position was at a church in a town called Fortuna, far north of where we lived. Yeah, Fortuna . . . at first I thought it was a sandwich or something.

It was a small town about a five-hour drive north of San Francisco and south of Eureka, California. It was in the heart of the redwoods and close to basically nothing. The place was beautiful, with monster trees and massive forests blanketed with wild ferns and carpet-like bark under a canopy of boundless branches. The branches seemed to reach for miles above everything, and the ground looked like Jurassic terrain. It was easy to feel very small in the wooded areas.

We left for my mom's interview for what felt like a never-ending journey together through twisting cliff-hung roads and forests. It seemed to always be raining there. I later found that the locals didn't count the days it rained; they counted the days it didn't.

The hotel room was small and smelled like mold. It was dark most of the time, as the downpour streamed over the windows. As Mom put it, "If this is where God wants us to be, he has a purpose for it, and it is where we want to be too." I wanted never to be out of harmony with God's will in our lives, especially since he was our heavenly Father. He provided for us and took care of us.

The new church was filled with the same spirit that I had felt growing up. The people were genuine, and there were God-fearing men there who fearlessly prayed. These guys were leaders in the community and business owners who knew the God that I knew. Apparently God gave them the same message he gave my mom about the job, concurring that this was God's plan for us.

When we returned to our apartment, we packed everything we owned in a moving van. Even Snowball had his own container with cut-out holes so he could travel safely without scratching anyone.

We said our final farewells to relatives and friends, and we were off on a new adventure.

This time, moving was different. As a family of four, we were very close. Mom was with us, and we were headed to a new place, but this time we were together. We were going to a place where we knew God wanted us to be. He had made a way for us and was sending us there for a purpose . . . or in my case, for a season.

///

Abruptly disturbing my memories, the intercom belted out my name and ordered me to stand near the cell door. Thinking I was finally going to find out something and possibly get out of there, I hopped to my feet and strolled to the door. The clinking of keys preceded the guard, along with that click-bang sound of the cell door lock. However, this time the guard had heavy chains in hand. I was cuffed behind my back and escorted down a long corridor; then I was crammed into a small, crowded room filled with coarse individuals who apparently hadn't showered or shaved for about as long I hadn't.

The closet of a room held barely enough space for us to stand shoulder to shoulder. The tattoos were so close that it became apparent the letters across many of the faces were self-inflicted or carved by someone with minimal skill. Some of the inmates were crouched on the floor from fatigue, while others pressed against the dirty walls. The air felt thick, and there was little ventilation. The grime on the floor and walls seemed to penetrate everyone in the room. In this small space you couldn't think or move, and the thought of starting a conversation was out of the question for fear of disturbing one of the gang members rubbing shoulders with you. After the hour or two it took for the guard to return, it felt like a year of compressed time had been taken from my life.

When the guard did return, the moment of relief was quickly dissolved as the door opened and we saw a row of heavy connected chains laid on the floor and down the hall. As we were lined up and clamped together one by one, that familiar pain of clinching steel cutting the circulation around my wrists was followed by jerking motions as the other inmates were attached. Fighting it was futile, as it only angered the guards more and the cuffs got tighter. After an army of unshaven, raggedy men were fully chained up, we were marched down the hall to a garage with the same dim orange lights. We were loaded like cattle into a grime-filled, smelly bus.

Inside the bus there were cages separating inmates. I could only speculate why some were chained to the walls in small cages while others of us were chained together in the rows of seats. A guard sat in the front of the bus behind another cage. He was armed with an intimidating weapon that he swung while belting out orders. Solid bars had been welded over the windows. They were mostly blacked out with a slit across the top that we could peer out if we stretched our neck and shoulders. Other than twisting my head to look around, there wasn't much mobility without yanking the other people we were chained to.

The bus started its engine, and suddenly the inmates came alive and began conversing with each other and hollering as if the outside could hear them. On cue inmates began comparing offenses and blatantly announcing what they had done to get back in that place. When asked why I was there, I could only reply that I didn't really know, which brought sneers and chuckles. Several would say things like, You can't fight the system, or Once they have your number, you're done and this is your new life. All of this was less than comforting. A few inmates pegged me as a "white-collar" criminal and kept asking me to teach them how to make "real money," as they called it, in "white-collar crime." As many compared notes, the gathering began to resemble a business conference where they shared lessons learned and best practices to get away with crime. Yet many of them purposely got themselves "busted" to return and happily discussed their approaching meeting with their "family boss," who apparently lived where we were headed. The whole ordeal seemed bizarre.

The moment the bus pulled out of the dark garage, the slit above the window lit up with sunlight, sending a streak across the top of the steel bars and dirty walls as if penetrating the darkness of that place. As the others carried on like a school field trip was under way, everything got quiet in my mind. The breath of light was such a momentary luxury that it infused me with joy, only to be followed by the sadness that I might not see it again for a long time, or worse. The thoughts of my family rushed in and filled my emotions, making it a bittersweet experience. I don't know how long the trip lasted or where we traveled to, but my life somehow felt like it was coming to an end.

I recalled the things of my life and all the joy that I'd experienced in spite of the pain, the scars that marked my soul, and the healing that God had given me over the years. The surreal place I was now forced into contrasted with the life I wished I could have back. I was lost in a swirling vortex with seemingly no way out and so much at stake. I was ultimately out of control. All control seemed to be given to my new captors. I had no idea where I was headed or what lay ahead. I felt that no one could hear me, but I cried out to God my Father anyway.

Suddenly, my recollections were washed away, and the silent moment in my mind was replaced with banging and yelling. The inmate locked in the cage across from me became animated, renewing the fear that hid only slightly below the surface.

///

Burning brighter than the sun, two glowing figures glided high above the redwood forest. Descending through the clouds, the two massive angels lit every dark spot in the sky. Becoming translucent, the two melted into the surrounding environment of a narrow road winding its way through a thick forest. Reaching a small car followed by a moving van, the angels positioned themselves into formation, guarding their valued cargo.

Sitting on top of the moving van, Mole dropped his jaw, and his eyes bulged. In dismay he slowly sank through the roof of the van and into the seat next to the driver. Still fixed on the glowing creatures accompanying the car in front of him, Mole reached over and gripped the leg of the driver.

Wincing in pain, the driver rubbed his leg and then reached for a bottle of aspirin among the food wrappers and maps on the dashboard of the truck. A dark snake-shaped silhouette slithered its head from under the dash, twisting its body slowly to stay fixed on Mole.

"Ssssss. What do you think you're doing? Let go of my human and take a hike, or better yet, go find your own human." With his mouth still wide open, Mole simply raised a pointing finger toward the small car in front of them, driving back and forth through the winding forest road.

On the dash the snake creature twisted around to see what was drawing Mole's attention. After wincing, he slowly turned back, addressing Mole, "Bummer, are those your humans?"

Without a sound Mole slowly nodded his head in response.

"Who gave you this assignment? Whatever your name is, little wrinkly vice, you're in way over your head.

Either way, let go of my human's leg. I had him thinking lustful thoughts, and you wrenched him back into reality. He is probably asking for forgiveness now, so you ruined all my work today. Thanks a lot, nitwit. You can get out of my truck now too. From the looks of what's in front of us—"

Just as the shadowy snake creature was spitting out the words, a flash of light filled the truck cab, ejecting Mole. Bouncing off tree trunks, Mole rolled on the ground. Stunned by what had happened, he watched the moving truck proceed down the road with the snake creature dangling from a glowing hand out the window. A split second later the snake was dropped to the ground, where he impacted a tree trunk of his own before slithering away through the ferns. Mole gathered his wrinkly body and bruised ego before darting off through the forest.

Hours later the wrinkled and bruised demon raced over rooftops in a panic, gasping from fatigue as he dropped to the ground among rusty farm equipment. Mole got up and whisked through broken fences until he reached the stately old home on the outskirts of the Southern California town.

Passing through the opening where the large door once hung, Mole plunked his dark shadow on the basement floor only feet away from a group of large demons conversing with each other. In surprise a large winged serpent coiled back with the others. "Is it one of yours?"

A large talon stepped forward from the small crowd followed by a sizable demon peering down upon the unwelcome intruder. Tapping the sharp talon on the floor, Chief Demon articulated a gruff response.

"It is mine, and it had better have a good reason for leaving its post and disrupting this meeting."

Gasping once again from fatigue and excitement, still weary from his race to deliver his message, Mole lifted his head to speak.

"Yes, yes . . . I do. Reinforcements have arrived. Large . . . really, really big angels have been sent."

"What!!" Chief Demon screamed. Disbelief streamed through the large creature. Pausing for a moment as the skepticism steamed into anger, Chief Demon dragged his large talon across the concrete floor, leaving a deep mark. Another large demon in the group jested, "Beelzebub will have your head if you blow this one a second time."

When the steaming anger boiled to maximum capacity, Chief Demon shrieked, *"People are praying again. Stop them!* That new church of believers in the redwoods must be at the bottom of this." Swinging a large talon through the air, Chief Demon grabbed Mole's neck, sinking claws deep into the wrinkly shadow of a creature. Chief pulled Mole to his face, and burning red sulfur filled the air.

"You have been nothing but trouble, and now you have completely failed me. You can report to someone else." Chief threw Mole into the crowd of large demons, who began viciously pawing and biting at him. Unconcerned with the activity behind him, Chief Demon extended leathery wings and lifted through the ceiling with final words to those gathered. "I'll take care of this myself."

11

Submerged in the Trees

Our perspective on life would change if only we knew how much God has been involved.

Never will I leave you; never will I forsake you.
—Hebrews 13:5 (NIV)

Consider the ravens: they do not sow or reap, they have no storeroom or barn, yet God feeds them. And how much more valuable you are than birds!
—Jesus, Luke 12:24 (NIV)

Humboldt County was the place where I discovered creative ways to live indoors. Our new home of Fortuna was deep in the redwoods in the heart of Humboldt County. My bedroom window resembled a perpetual car wash in rinse cycle. Playing outside was not a good option, and cabin fever set in quickly.

With the help of birthday money from my grandfather, I was able to save enough to upgrade my ten-speed bike to a BMX bike. My new bike was a CYC Stormer. It was chrome with blue wheels and a racing plate, and I loved it. I felt free when I rode that bike. The wind rushed by as I felt in full control of everything. Riding my bike gave me a sense of freedom where nothing could hold me down.

I could do most of the cool tricks a real BMX guy should be able to do. I held the record on our block for the longest "wheelie" and the highest "bunny hop." However, riding my bike and living in Fortuna were not always compatible experiences.

The church my mom worked for found us a nice little two-bedroom house to rent. It had a large detached garage, where my siblings and I discovered we could ride back and forth in long circles for hours. Snowball would sit on the tool bench and watch attentively as if supervising. We had to clear all of the garage stuff and make sure Mom parked in the driveway, but it seemed to work.

In addition to the two bedrooms it was originally built with, the house had an extended porch that made a great guy room for my brother and me. There was just enough room for us and Snowball with our bunk beds. It wasn't insulated very well and didn't have a closet, but my limited wardrobe didn't require one, and a little cold didn't seem to bother us.

I spent many hours with Snowball talking while watching the water stream over the windows. Although it may sound like a dismal place, it brought many good memories, with the exception of the mold that would grow up the walls behind the furniture from time to time.

Our new church in Fortuna became our anchor, with great people, including a circle of praying men. Those men set an unforgettable example in the way they lived their lives. God really took care of us in that place, and he was as present as ever.

God never let me forget that he was there protecting me and watching over me. My new teacher, Mr. Fischer, was a great father figure. He was my basketball coach. Most of my seventh- and eighth-grade class had little talent, but we had a great time and actually won once in a while. Being tall for my age, I looked more intimidating on the court than most had reason to be concerned about. Mr. Fischer had his own kids but always made time and cared about his students. Although a part of my life for only a season, he was another one who left a positive impact on me.

There were bewildering things that happened in my life that could never be explained. They seemed to always come when I needed to know my heavenly Father was there the most, when I needed to know that I had a Father of my own who cared for me.

One evening I was riding my BMX bike with a couple of my new buddies. We thought of ourselves as adventurous and fearless, always looking for the next challenge to attempt on our bikes. We discovered a culvert along the edge of a road. The culvert carved a *U*-shaped slice out of the side of a mountain. The concrete edging was about six inches wide, and although it started at the street, making it easy to ride up, it protruded about fifteen feet up before abruptly curving and returning back down to the other side of the *U* shape.

Adding to the danger, a concrete pad with a steel fire hydrant in the middle was at the ground level right below the abrupt *U*-turn fifteen feet above. With no railing, an upward incline on one side with an abrupt turn at the top followed by a steep decline on the other, the challenge was to ride up one side and back down the other without stopping or falling into the culvert. If you stopped, there was nothing to hang onto or to help you regain your balance. A mere wobble or miscalculation would be followed by a perilous fall onto the fire hydrant fifteen feet below. I must admit now as an adult, I realize this was not a very smart thing for anyone to do.

After watching each of my friends balance up one side and glide down the other one by one, I decided that I needed to follow suit and succumb to the peer pressure. Swallowing my fear, I pedaled my way to the top, but apparently I didn't gather enough momentum.

At the top of the culvert my bike rolled to a stop. In trying to regain my balance, my natural reflex was to extend my leg out to push off something in the direction I was falling. The only problem was nothing was there to push off of.

Somehow my foot caught on something solid in the open air over that culvert where nothing existed. Losing my balance, I remember seeing the imminent fall to the hydrant below my foot, which was now extended into the open air. Fear suddenly drove adrenaline through my body as the reality of falling and landing on that steel hydrant struck me. Yet I pushed off something that wasn't there, regained my balance, and glided to the bottom on the other side.

In stunned silence I must have sat there for at least thirty minutes in absolute puzzlement. My buddies rode off to the next escapade while I sat speechless on my bike. I stared up into the empty space where my foot had pushed off something, but I could find no explanation. I couldn't figure it out, and no rationalization made sense other than God had reached out and firmly cradled my foot to keep me from falling. I couldn't imagine the broken mess I would have been had I lost my balance and fallen to my peril. I would have been wrapped around that fire hydrant at the bottom.

///

The guard clenched his weapon and belted out orders into the cage mere feet from me. Gripping his fingers through the steel mesh, the wild-eyed person shook violently. He screamed while focusing a stare in my direction. I jumped back, jerking the chains connected to the other inmates, but was reassured that the cage was restraining this individual. The audible sounds were undistinguishable but were clearly laced with anger about something.

The person was disheveled with long, unkempt black hair. Although this person looked like a female, he had a low, deep voice and sported a rough, scraggly beard like the rest of us on the bus. His eyes were glassy and deep red surrounded by dark lines. His shrill scream was shocking followed by an immediate retreat. Brushing his long grimy fingers through his hair in a look of innocence, he peered out the corners of his glassy red eyes. Exposing his vicious teeth, he suddenly turned to reveal a deceptive smile.

Uncertainty at every turn led me to keep my guard up; although exhausted and weary, I was still on high alert. The cages, steel bars, and vault doors never brought any sense of security. I never knew whom to trust, if anyone. The guards enjoyed antagonizing the inmates by trying to coerce them into an outburst. The inmates were a mix of society. Some were trying to survive this horrific experience much like myself. Some were professional criminals who appeared to feel at home in this dungeon, where they sharpened their skills and honed their learned trade. And others were purely psychotic souls lashing out when it was least expected, as if they were demon possessed and waiting for any opportunity to attack. I thought that this was the worst experience of my adult life and that it couldn't get any worse, but I was wrong.

///

Slithering down the street under the cover of dark clouds in the middle of the day, several shadows darted along the curb before stopping to sink into a large drainage gutter. In a cavern under the gutter gruesome creatures gathered around an overpowering presence of darkness. Vapors of sulfur stirred the air as Chief Demon pierced through each minion with the slits of burning red where his eyes should have been. Addressing the subordinates, he filled the air with a heavy, sinister presence.

"This battle is taking its toll. You have lost another demon in command. I expect this group to step it up and complete the task of destroying this family. I do not accept fear of these angels that have been sent. I will not accept that these humans cannot be destroyed, and I don't care how big these angels are! You must be deceptive and devious; you have to capitalize on their human weaknesses. I've cut a hole through this family; all you have to do is exploit it. I can't be everywhere at once; I need a new commander. Beelzebub will reward you in person if you are successful here. I need one of you to step up and take command; I need the most crafty and deceitful among you to step up and lead this assault."

From the back of the gathering a fanged head of scales led by slits of green eyes rose to the front. As the creature stepped through the horde, the clicking of four talon-filled claws scratched the floor as the silhouette of a dragon passed through the dim rays of light streaking through the grates above. "I am your new commander. I am Drach, craftier than any other in this pack."

Chief Demon took pause and focused his attention on Drach without speaking. Drach stretched a crooked grin of pointy teeth, cocking his head slightly while rising to the gutter grates above. He peered across the street through the grates while dangling his long tail out of the gutter. Drach quietly chanted, "Here, kitty, kitty."

Within moments a white cat jumped off the front porch and crouched while slowly moving toward the gutter. Drach quickly pulled the scaly tail out of sight while continuing under his breath, "Not yet, kitty. Wait for it. Wait for it. Okay, here it comes." Drach quickly taunted the cat with his tail through the grates, bobbing it like a fishing worm on a hook. "Come on, kitty. Come to evil Drach . . . now, now!" The tail danced wildly as the sound of a car approached.

Swiftly the white cat sprang into motion, moving in to pounce on the taunting lure across the street, just as the sedan reached its target. Screeching of tires followed by a thump, and the cat was launched as Drach dropped to the cavern floor in front of Chief Demon. "My Chief, I will tactically destroy this family by inflicting pain until they reject their God. I will exploit what you have started. I am your new commander."

Chief Demon stretched a grin of his own. Peering down at Drach, Chief uttered a low rumble. "I am pleased. This will reopen the scars that have been inflicted. You may earn the right to feast on these humans; you will be my new commander assigned to this family. The others will follow you per my edict."

Completing the assignment of choosing a new commander, Chief Demon rose through the gutter, casting a deep shadow below the gloom of the gray clouds. With the rush of a stealth fighter, he charged over the trees until his evil presence was no longer felt.

Reflections of gloomy clouds burst from puddles down the street as knobby BMX tires bounced from puddle to puddle. A lonely boy attempting bicycle tricks meandered in the street followed by two large glowing beings.

Racing down the road, a third angel rushed to the glowing beings following the boy. "We need to get the boy home. His mother found his cat. Snowball was hit by a car."

The other angelic beings turned in shock as the messenger spoke. The largest being reached out to the messenger. "What happened?"

The messenger hung his head. "It was Drach. He lured the cat into the street. Our young man will enter high school soon. This young man is still holding a lot of pain inside, and talking to his cat was how he often vented the pain. Chief and his minions are trying to cut at the scars they caused. We knew they would be on full attack through this time of our young man's life, but targeting the cat was a low blow."

The smaller being spoke softly as he looked to the largest of the angelic beings. "Our Father loves this young man, but Chief Demon isn't giving up easily. I know we can protect only as our Father leads, but what can we do now?"

Without pause the largest of the beings replied with authority, "Prayer cover. We need the prayers of the saints to maintain our strength in this fight. The young man must make his own choices in this place and time, where he now lives. The mother is praying, but the battle is about to get a lot more difficult."

Reaching down beside the boy, the large being whispered into his ear, "You need to go home." Suddenly on cue the boy stopped, looked around with a puzzled look on his face, and then rode off toward home.

Flashing a sword of light from its sheath, the smaller being, with increased determination on his face, began to dash away from the boy toward the gutter, only to be stopped by the largest angel.

"Our Father has not given us the okay to attack here. Remember this young man has to make his own choices. Our heavenly Father has a master plan that is beyond us, and we must not interfere with that. We will battle with the enemy of darkness to protect the boy soon enough, but only as the Father allows."

12

What Can I Hold On To?

If we look only at what we can touch, we'll touch only the surface of this existence.

Then war broke out in heaven. Michael and his angels fought against the dragon, and the dragon and his angels fought back.
—Revelation 12:7 (NIV)

I have told you these things, so that in me you may have peace. In this world you will have trouble. But take heart! I have overcome the world.
—Jesus, John 16:33 (NIV)

Losing Snowball was like losing a family member. I had friends but no one to confide in or to share my deepest hurts and pains with. There was still pain hidden below that needed to surface, and it did occasionally seep through the cracks.

Not long after I lost Snowball, Mom adopted a puppy for us. She tried to keep us focused on the positive, and she knew losing my cat had taken a toll. I think my mom could have done without another pet, but down deep she knew I needed one. Being the thoughtful and sensitive mom she was, she let us add a new member to our family. Our new puppy became a fast friend to me. Unfortunately it was difficult to confide in a puppy who couldn't sit still for more than thirty seconds.

My sister named her Mittsy. I'm not sure where she came up with that name, since the dog was a Doberman pinscher and Mittsy sounds like some fluffy little barky dog. When we got her, she seemed to be all paws. Her ears were huge, but she finally grew into them. Mittsy was a welcome addition to my life, but she could never take the place of Snowball.

Mom was always trying to find activities for us to do as a family to help keep us close. She took us camping one summer with another single mom and her kids. It gave me an opportunity to ride my BMX bike through forest trails with a friend, which I loved doing. For me it was exhilarating and gave me a chance to temporarily let go of the pain and be free. By the time we arrived at the campsite it was nearly dusk. After preparing my gear for the day ahead, I climbed into my sleeping bag and dreamt of the skillful adventures that riding through the forest the next morning would bring. During that evening in the dark of the night, an intruder came into our campsite while we were sleeping, and my prized bike was stolen.

It seemed like the pain deep in my soul never really went away; it just hung there like a dull ache that you finally get used to. Though there were times that the ache would burst, I'd let it out only for a moment or two.

When I woke up in the morning, my bike was gone. We didn't have insurance or the money to replace it; it had just disappeared like so many other things in my life. Much like my cat and my father, something I held close was once again ripped away. When the person came into our campsite late that night they stole the small piece of freedom I had from the pain that lurked inside.

Arriving at our destination, I couldn't imagine anything worse than where I had just been, but I was very wrong. Upon our arrival in another dark garage, the cages were unloaded one at a time and the inmates were escorted out of the bus by heavily armed guards. Taking short steps, we were marched into a large waiting room already packed shoulder to shoulder with others. The doors to the room where we were standing had to be pushed closed. The room was packed so tightly that you couldn't sit on the floor. If you got tired, you just let the strength leave your legs and you were held in the air by the other sardines smashed up against you.

When the doors were finally forced closed behind everyone, a belting authoritative voice yelled profanity mixed with rules to everyone in the room, including shut up and do not talk. At first, out of fear, most were silent. As the hours rolled by and the temperature of the room continued to rise, many were silent from borderline fainting. A few did pass out, and those nearest them started yelling for help, only to be met with the familiar profanity and repetition of the rules. The hours went on and on as hundreds of us were left smashed together in that human compactor. I began to feel light-headed from the intense heat and exhaustion.

After what seemed like an eternity, another set of doors were opened, and we flowed into the next room like water being released from a dam. We were immediately ordered to stand on a line painted on the floor. Several commanding guards barked more orders while making fun of the inmates. The antagonistic nature of the guards encompassed abusive slurs of every racial and sexual orientation imaginable. They instilled fear in most and hatred in some.

Everything seemed to take hours, and my captors were like the worst of drill sergeants. As we stood in line, we were belittled and mentally abused then moved from lineup to lineup and from room to room for hours on end. All dignity was stripped away from us, along with our clothes and mental capacity. We were searched in undignified ways and taunted endlessly. Those in control sought after any reason to strike out at those of us who were mentally weary and broken. The insults were unending, leaving nothing as taboo.

By the time we reached the mass showers, everyone looked like zombies, with no expression. At first a hot shower and a fresh change of clothes sounded like a good idea after the endless hours of abuse. The clothes didn't fit and came in one inmate size, but they were clean. The clothes I'd been wearing for the past week smelled horrible as I stripped down, and they were wadded into a plastic bag and toted away. I don't think I'd showered for over a week, and I was at a point where mass showering with hundreds of other guys didn't matter. I had no dignity or reserve left.

It wasn't long before the locked doors of the shower cavern held in clouds of suffocating steam, making it hard to breathe. The showers and the excessive heat, as with everything else, were controlled by the ever-present angry voices over the speakers. The momentary relief was quickly lost as the heat and humidity rose, leaving rolling sweat down my face and sticking the oversized and now wet clothing to my body. Once again the hours seemed to creep by, and some became faint. In the crowded shower cavern most sat or lay on the dirty wet floors from lack of strength. By the time the doors opened and we were ushered out by the coarse, angry captors, I was moving mentally from pure survival mode to woozy and detached.

I was a moving zombie like the masses around me. I didn't know where I was or why I was there. I didn't know if it was day or night. I didn't know where my family was or even if they were okay. All I knew was my newly assigned inmate number, which had been drilled into me endlessly by the angry drill sergeants for the past hours. I wasn't even sure who I was as I passed through that nightmare. I did know that if I were to survive in that place, I had to avoid the ones in uniform looking for a fight. Little did I know that they weren't the only ones I had to avoid; there were others who were actually in that place for a reason. There were some who wanted to be in a place like that and would feed on someone like me. There were some I had yet to encounter.

Meandering through the alley of an old neighborhood, a young man carrying schoolbooks kicked stones down the street. Movement ahead of him caught his attention as a delivery truck backed into the alley, blocking the boy's path. In the cab of the truck a burly deliveryman lit up a cigarette while a dark character sat next to him in the front seat.

"This is a good place to grab a smoke. Parking here in the alley was a good idea; your boss will never know," whispered a dragon figure to the driver. Another dark figure, unseen by the driver and filling the front seat, was preoccupied with the boy in the alley. "Crafty move, Drach. The boy is cutting between the garages toward the park."

Through a crooked, devious smile, Drach's green slits of eyes beamed into the mirror as the boy passed through his line of sight.

"Make sure he walks by the baseball field near the other boys with dads. Focus his attention toward the dads when they are showing affection to their kids. Make sure it hurts."

The two faint images of evil creatures faded through the sides of the truck. Drach's figure disappeared down the alley as the other creature raced toward a young girl watching the game with her Labrador retriever on a leash.

The young boy stopped in his tracks when the Labrador started barking from across the field. The girl tugged on the leash while an unseen spirit taunted the dog. The boy's attention was focused across the ball field, where the players and their fathers were practicing their catching skills.

The commotion coming from the dog quickly drowned into the background. The dads cheered their sons and encouraged them as the coach gave instructions from a distance. As the boy stared at the father-son activity, a tear rolled down the young man's cheek, splashing on the trail below.

From out of nowhere a large glowing being appeared next to the boy and placed an arm around him. The glowing figure leaned down and whispered peacefully into the boy's ear.

"I love you, my son. I will never leave you."

The boy slowly turned from the activity on the field and walked on his way, wiping any trace of the tears on his sleeve. The glowing being was beside him.

Two angels sitting in the stands by the other fathers focused on the Labrador. "Drach is devious, and his dark minions are evil."

The smaller of the two nodded his head. "High school starts next fall. Drach owns that place. This is going to be a tough challenge for the boy."

The larger of the two concurred. "I agree. We are going to be busy, aren't we? But the love of this boy is worth it to our Father."

13

High School

---

*Hiding from your pain only gives it strength; run to
the one who can heal it.*

If the world hates you, keep in mind that it hated
me first.

—Jesus, John 15:18 (NIV)

Do you know what I mean when I say, I don't want
to be alone. I have no fear of drowning. It's the
breathing that's taking all this work.

—*Jars of Clay*—"Good Monsters"

High school came at me like a brick. It seemed the moment I walked
onto that campus in the fall of my freshman year, my Christian
school friends scattered. I'm not sure what happened.

High school had pockets of acceptance if you were lucky to
gain approval from one of them. If you absorbed yourself into one
of the admired groups and assimilated, you were okay. If not, you
were on the "outside," or the unofficial outcast list. Some of my
Christian school friends became assimilated as part of the sports and
jock crowd. Some got absorbed into academic circles. I didn't seem
to fit into any of these.

Coupled with my mixed-up emotions, life seemed to pass by
as I wandered the halls filled with teenagers and faculty. I became
a distant observer lost in a bad movie that replayed the same scene
every day. The first year was rough as I dealt with over stimulated

seniors and their hazing, which seemed to keep the "accepted" crowd even farther away.

The only group that seemed to accept me took some getting used to. They were considered outcasts, which is how I felt, so the group appealed to me. Most of them had issues of one sort or another with their families and parents. Some were from wealthy families and some from poor, but we all had something we didn't want to face and didn't know how to deal with. There was something that haunted each of us that we wanted to escape.

Living in Humboldt County high school had an additional connotation. Humboldt country was a drug grower's capital. Being there was often referred to as living behind the redwood curtain. Drug growing was so prevalent that public announcements on the local TV channels warned viewers not to wander into the forests during growing season. It was known that many people disappeared, typically when they wandered into a grower's farm. Many of the farmers were rumored to be former military Special Forces from the jungles of the Vietnam War, who couldn't assimilate back into society, so they became drug growers in the redwood forests.

Some of my new acquaintances had grown up in that culture, and they were not just users; their families were heavily into the farming business. Things that were foreign to me before high school became commonplace in my new surroundings. I remember walking through the parking lot between classes when a guy I'd met waved me over to his car. After informing me that he was on his way to the "big city"—presumably San Francisco—for a delivery, he popped open his trunk. The trunk was completely filled to the top with what appeared to be clumpy green yard clippings. I wasn't sure if he was cleaning his gutters or if he was a drug farmer, but he sure was proud of what appeared to be dead plant remains. I didn't want to look stupid, so I gave him the thumbs-up and went on my way.

Drug paraphernalia were so common that "roach clips" and bongs were décor items on clothing and car dashboards. It didn't take long before those in my new world started offering things like a hit or toke, or other odd terms that I quickly learned had something to do with drugs. I was able to hang out with this crowd for a while because they accepted me. But I knew their involvement with drugs would become an issue for me sooner or later.

I continued to try and fit in, but I struggled with it daily. I thought it might be a wise idea for me to get a part-time job and look for another place to hang out. My mom told me our church was looking for someone to do janitorial work, so I signed up.

I enjoyed being at the church, and it kept the good memories of my childhood alive. I tried to focus on the positive aspects of life and all the great things God had done in my life since that dreadful night. Walking down the aisles of the sanctuary late at night would ignite the good memories of my childhood and the wonderful things I'd seen God do in my life. Yet there was a dark feeling that seemed to keep tugging at me, mostly when I was at school.

High school sporting events were a main attraction in our small town. It seemed to be the time when kids with dads spent a lot of quality time together. I think half of the town came to the football games. I attended just to "hang" with my new friends. They never seemed to watch much of the game. They just hung out below the bleachers, smoking and drowning themselves in alcohol while recapping their terrible family experiences. I wasn't into sports and I didn't have any other accepting groups to spend time with, so I'd listen and agree.

It was by the grace of God that I even survived high school. Many of my new friends didn't make it. Some died from overdoses or suicide, and others were killed in car accidents that often involved driving while intoxicated.

Remembering this time in my life seems like being in a dream or a bizarre nightmare. This whole chapter of my life seemed so out of character and miles from the PK who dreamt of being a pastor or missionary someday. Yet there were forces tugging on the wounded soul that I hid inside. I could feel these dark forces wrenching at me, but they couldn't clasp on. Despite the pain and darkness that tried continually to seize my soul, my heavenly Father never let go of me.

From time to time our church would have youth events. These events were great opportunities to experience the presence I had grown up knowing. It was that wonderful presence that had such a healing power to it. There always seemed to be some obstacle or another that kept me from attending. Although the distractions were often subtle, I remember one that was a bit more extreme.

It was a cool drizzly evening when a friend of mine picked me up in his El Camino. He had been riding motorcycles earlier in the day, so his dirt bikes were still in the back. We decided to bring them along. We threw our sleeping bags and camping gear in the back with the motorcycle gear, and then we headed off on the long drive to the campsite. We were to meet up with the rest of the youth group and the youth pastor at a rendezvous location in the hills. From that point four-wheel-drive vehicles would taxi us back into the camp area where we would be staying.

A few hours into the drive, we stopped at a small, quiet town to refuel. It was a one-horse town with one convenience store and two gas stations, although one of the gas stations was closed. The sun had set and it was dark, with only a few merchants open. After cruising down the main drag and noticing a few others rumbling down the street in their hot rod cars, my friend spun into the closed gas station to turn around. He wanted to make another pass down the street in low gear to really rumble the headers. I believe loud muscle cars and testosterone are closely connected.

After he quickly turned into the gas station, we heard a thump from the back of the truck. A large gas can had fallen over, causing the cap to pop off and the truck bed to fill with fuel. My friend quickly screeched the El Camino to a stop and threw the transmission into park, creating a backfire out the muffler.

I reached for the door handle and pulled the lever just as the backfire happened, and a flash of bright orange and red filled the back window. I pushed the door open to a rush of heat that singed my face as it blew by me. I could feel the scorching temperature and smell burning hair around the edges of my face. An enormous billow of flame reached thirty feet into the sky. I ran away from the blistering heat as the El Camino became engulfed in flames.

Every second seemed to move in slow motion with the drama of a still night erupting into an inferno. One entire end of the small town was lit up in a glowing fire fueled by my friend's car. A man from the neighboring gas station ran toward us with a large fire extinguisher intending to drown the flames. He raised the hose, directing it into the blaze, and braced himself before pulling the trigger. The extinguisher malfunctioned, and a few drops of white power dribbled to the ground.

Realizing that his car was going up in flames, my friend ran back into the fire to save it. He grabbed the flaming-hot gas can, which was still spewing gasoline, and threw it into the street. The can flipped through the air and landed in the middle of the road with a tail of fire chasing it. As gas continued to pour out, the street became blanketed with fire, adding to the drama of the moment. All of our camping gear and the motorcycles seemed to fuse into a blob of burning flames in the back of the El Camino.

Although it seemed like hours, the fire department arrived within minutes. Fire trucks circled the scene and doused everything in white foam, reducing the flames to a smoldering lump of fused sleeping bags, camping gear, and motorcycle parts.

After the fire department wrapped my friend's hands in giant bundles of gauze, we were able to return to the scene of the incident. The interior of the car was melted, with nothing but bare metal springs left for seating and little semblance of a dashboard. Surprisingly it started and ran, so we made our way to the campsite, leaving a trail of smoldering ash.

It was close to midnight by the time we arrived at the rendezvous location where we were to meet the other campers. Everyone had already left hours before. We were too tired to go back at that point, so we were on our own. My friend forged ahead and drove the El Camino through the hills and over big rocks down the rustic trail to the camp-site, a trek that included crossing a river. By the time we got to the river, we were beat and tired. My friend plowed through the rushing current, bringing water halfway up the doors and almost to our knees inside the car. The water did help wash away some of the sickening smoldering smell. After a rough and bumpy ride we finally found our way to the campsite, but by then we were too worn-out to engage in youth camp activities. The next morning we made our way back through the river and back home in the smoldering lump of fused gear and bare metal. We didn't stay for the youth weekend our church had planned.

My high school days brought many challenges, which at times seemed to never end, with one obstacle after another. It often felt as if something was trying to keep me away from anything that would point me back to that presence I had felt as a kid.

///

The endless nightmare just went on and on. After we were finally ushered from the shower cavern, the next stop was another overcrowded room filled with hundreds of others and a line that seemed a mile long. Fighting to remain conscious, I sat on what seemed like an endless bench with inmates sandwiched together.

Moving from stop to stop while being observed and monitored by trolling guards at every stage, I finally got to the end of the line to once again find mental abuse followed by tasteless food.

I use the word *food* lightly. I was given a slice of bread, a small tube of the size of those used for fast-food condiments, filled with a jelly substance, and another tube of tasteless peanut butter. Once again there was an apple and a small sugary juice-type drink in a carton. Feeling grateful for anything to eat, I quickly huddled and ate whatever was given to me. At that moment the gourmet food I once enjoyed on business trips or with family meant nothing. Nourishment from a small plastic tube was met with great desire from my body and broken spirit.

It felt like I was being processed for days in a mass of people who weren't mentally home anymore. I don't know if the psychological abuse and lack of sleep induced that state or if it became a coping mechanism to somehow endure the living hell. While waiting in the overcrowded rooms between the verbal abuse and taunting, I longed for sleep. My emotions swung between highly sensitive, which I fought off vigorously, and just plain numbness.

I would occasionally slip away into a daze and ponder the thin ray of sunlight that came streaking through the slit in the bus window. My successes in life didn't amount to anything anymore. At that moment I didn't care what car I drove or the neighborhood where I lived. Those priorities faded so quickly that they were mere distant thoughts fading from my mind. My family stood in the center of what was important and what I longed for. I longed for the relationships that I never had nurtured with friends. Most of all, I wondered if my heavenly Father had turned his back on me and abandoned me in this living hell.

My heavenly Father had seen me through so many things in life, but now I needed him like never before, and I felt so alone. The feeling of his presence was something that I longed for, as it would have made this experience bearable. In those long hours of endless waiting, I cried out in my heart to God over and over again, but I mostly asked him to take care of my family—my wonderful wife, whom I felt I had neglected so much lately, and the two wonderful kids I had been blessed with but saw only on weekends between business trips. If only I could see them one more time, hold them tight, and tell them how much I loved them . . . But I didn't even know what was going on outside the walls that ensnared me.

I had no idea what was happening and still no idea why I was in that place. No one had talked to me or even told me I had any rights at all. Trying to talk to any of the militant guards was strictly not an option in that dungeon. They ruled with an iron fist, looking for reasons to induce interaction that would lead to physical abuse. Thinking back to the inmate processing, I recalled a guard's comment that had left a haunting ring I would never forget and that would always strike fear in me. With a fiendish howl he had said, "Welcome to the Los Angeles County Twin Towers." I was lost in the pit of the Los Angeles County Twin Towers jail. No one was there to help or even explain why I was there, and there seemed to be no way out of the mess I was trapped in.

///

An old Ford Mustang covered in a patchwork of paint and primer rumbled past the high school, blasting everything in its path with rock music. The large mag wheels screeched to a halt by an intersection next to the high school, and the passenger door flew open. The commotion grabbed the attention of a gathering of high school teens waiting to cross the street and get to their next class.

One of the Mustang occupants pointed to a young teen and waved at him to get in. As if honored to be chosen out of the crowd and seemingly familiar with the driver, the teen climbed over the passengers to the backseat.

Unseen by the young teen were dark figures stretching an ear to ear grin in a deadly smirk. Drach reached over the driver's shoulder, whispering in his ear. The driver casually reached into his pocket to pull out a hand-rolled smoke. Leaning over the seats, one of the girls in the front informed everyone that they were going down to the river to unwind. The occupants cheered as if this was a normal midday occurrence.

Drach sat back, stretching out his claws. "It's time to close this deal, my friends."

Another demonic creature watching out the back window excitedly proclaimed, "They're behind us and following."

Placing his scaly tail around the passenger's neck, Drach smiled. "Of course they are. We have their prize, and this is our territory." Blowing a puff of steamy hot air in the young teen's face, Drach caressed his victim's head with his sharp claws. "We'll finish him off today at the river." The driver lit another joint and began filling the car with smoke. Drach continued, "I can almost taste the sumptuous feast this one will bring."

Bouncing to a stop, the Mustang skidded on the rocks of a riverbed where other teens huddled around a burning barrel. The Mustang doors flew open, and one by one the occupants rolled out and stumbled their way to greet the existing partyers. The teen in the backseat, seemingly less affected than the others, moved slightly off balance. Drach and another demonic crony nudged the young teen to the barrel where the others had gathered.

Convening far away from where the large gathering of demons circled the teens on the riverbed, two angelic creatures gathered. The larger angel pulled a blinding sword from his side and motioned to the smaller. "We have to go in. Cover me."

Pressed up against the larger angel's back, the smaller angel prepared a flashing sword. They moved toward the circle cautiously, with hissing demons circling them and swiping talons through the air. With hideous gnashing fangs, the demons lunged closer as the smaller angel prepared to engage at any moment.

As the larger angelic being moved into the circle to communicate with the young teen, the smaller angel stood at his back with sword in motion. Taking blow after blow from the angry swarming nest of demonic creatures, the angels persisted to reach the young teen. The large angel spoke into his ear, "You don't belong here."

The young teen returned to his senses and informed the others that he had to go. The others only laughed and began to fall to the ground one by one, along with the accompanying demonic creatures.

Still fighting the onslaught of Drach's hordes, the large angel spoke to the young teen once again. "Just go, now. Start walking. Don't wait for a ride; just go!"

The teen turned and started walking away from the crowd, up the trail past the scattered cars and toward the bridge to the other side of the river. Shocked, Drach let his mouth drop open. Gathering a collection of gruesome creatures, Drach raced after the boy and the angelic beings walking beside him.

Reaching the crest of the bridge high above the rushing water, the horde of malicious creatures caught up to the glowing duo and the teen. The multitude of demonic creatures lunged at the glowing beings, keeping them cornered and pushing them away from the young teen.

Drach slithered up onto the railing and wrapped his long scaly tail around his victim. "You don't belong here. You don't fit with any of the peer groups."

The boy stopped and looked over the railing while Drach paused for a moment before sinking in the dagger. "Your dad left because of you. Everything is your fault . . . yes, your fault. You don't deserve to be alive. I know how much it hurts and the pain that is inside of you, especially since your dad didn't love you at all. Look what he did to your family because of you. You are all alone and no one cares about you. Make the pain go away. You are worthless in this life and no good to anyone."

As the young teen gazed down at the rushing water below, Drach continued. "Jump. It won't hurt, and everything will be okay. Just jump. It will all finally go away."

From the midst of the supernatural brawl, the large angel yelled out, "Your heavenly Father loves you, and he will heal you. Call to him!" The teen stopped and hung his head, with tears rolling off his cheeks.

A sudden burst of light sent demonic shadows flying in every direction. Drach clenched the railing he was plastered against. In explosive anger Drach shouted into the air, "Not fair. The teen has his own free will and makes his own choices!! It is your own proclamation!! Your words can not be broken!"

Before Drach could continue, an omniscient voice of authority echoed through the sky, "When my son calls, I hear him. Don't try to twist my words. You know who I am. Now leave before I cast you into the abyss and remove you from this realm!"

Walking away from the bridge, the young teen desperately used his sleeve trying to hide the tears that were streaming down his face. Quickly retreating, Drach scampered back to the other side of the bridge. Angrily kicking rocks on the riverbed, Drach ran into one of the heavily intoxicated teens, who had stumbled away from his friends. Drach grabbed hold of the teen, making him flounder and flop on the ground like a fish out of water. The other teens and demonic creatures laughed and pointed until Drach slammed the teen's head into a rock and he passed out. Drach slid into the teen's body before the teen rose up and proclaimed in an unearthly voice, "I will have my prey." Then Drach rose out of the teen and threw him back to the ground.

14

Cruzin'

The holes in our lives were never made to be filled with earthly things.

So do not worry, saying, 'What shall we eat?' or 'What shall we drink?' or 'What shall we wear?' For the pagans run after all these things, and your heavenly Father knows that you need them. But seek first his kingdom and his righteousness, and all these things will be given to you as well.
—Matthew 6:31-33 (NIV)

The Lord is close to the brokenhearted and saves those who are crushed in spirit.
—Psalm 34:18 (NIV)

High school was taking its toll on me by my third and fourth years. I continued drifting between dealing with the gnawing hole my father had left and the longing for that supernatural presence of my heavenly Father.

My farming friends continued to invite me to their gatherings, but I drifted away from that crowd. The momentary numbness of my pain continued to be followed by a feeling of darkness in my soul.

My wheeling and dealing ventures continued to grow to support my passion for autos. Although I was known to circle the block in my own car when I was as young as fifteen, I still couldn't drive it too far until I got my license. Within a short period of time I somehow maneuvered and traded my way into a 1969 Cougar with a 351 Cleveland, high-compression pistons, and a pumped motor. If you don't know what that all means, that's okay. You have to be a motor head to truly enjoy it.

Basically, although the Cougar needed a good paint job, she was fast. The morning I passed my driver's license test, I was cruzin' the park with uncapped headers. My car made me feel free again and invincible. I was in control once again with the power of my machine. The exhilaration of being plastered to the back of the seat as the pedal went down felt like I was flying effortlessly. The front end almost lifting off the ground was elating. I always had a place to hide behind the wheel. I joined the auto club and spent most of my days building cars with my new greasy friends.

To help support my new auto habit, I somehow got a job at a fancy restaurant. I had to wear clean clothes and carry dirty dishes as a busboy, but it gave me a sense that there were others who didn't have the same struggles that I had. People were polite and didn't treat me like an outsider as long as I took care of their table. If I went above and beyond what was expected to help the waitresses, they would share their tips with me. Families would come in to eat and enjoy the evening together, including fathers. This was what I dreamt having a dad would be like. My cars took the role of easing that pain for a while, but that only lasted a season, and as with everything else, they couldn't fill the gap my earthly father had left.

I polished my wheeling and dealing skills buying and selling so many cars that my friends tagged me as someone who would most likely become a used car salesman when I grew up. For a kid with no money from a poor home, I went through a fun collection fast. My Cougar wheeled into a 1955 Chevy two-door, followed by a 1971 Triumph GT6, a 1967 Mustang, and finally my ultimate high school prize, which seemed to gain respect as I pulled onto the campus parking lot, was my 1967 SS Chevy Camaro.

With the most beautifully polished white paint and red stripes wrapping over the front and rear spoilers, the Camaro glowed in the evening streetlights. The oversized polished wheels with low profile tires sat her up just right. She was a beauty. Of course the 327 was a great motor, but as a motor head it just wasn't enough, so I saddled her with a 400 and quick-shift B&M racing shifter, backed by a 4:11 rear end. She was more than beautiful; she could purr like a kitten and fly like a rocket.

Between my auto escapades and trying to fit in, there were always glimpses of spiritual things. The presence of God was still there through my teen years. Yet the presence of something sinister and dark surfaced often. There seemed to be a spiritual battle going on, and I was somehow stuck in the middle.

I'll never forget the day I was sitting in my car at the park eating lunch when an acquaintance walked up, opened the door, and sat down in the passenger seat. She looked pale as a ghost sitting there quietly. In distress she stared fearfully at the floor. Her father went to our church. I had seen her hanging out with the "farmer" group around the school campus. When she began to speak, the fear in her voice shot shivers down my spine.

Her voice trembled nervously as she mumbled that she had been smoking dope. She said her friends told her that it was harmless. But now she couldn't stop. She went on to say that recently when she looked in the mirror, it wasn't her in the reflection looking back anymore. A hideous creature with long bony fingers looked back at her. The creature slowly waved an index finger, calling her into the mirror. It spoke to her, saying she belonged to the creature and it would never let her go free.

She turned and looked at me through bloodshot eyes and said it was so real that she hadn't slept since. She was shaken with terror. Then as suddenly as she arrived, the door opened and she walked away. I wasn't sure what to make of what she had told me. I had seen the look on her face painted on others, many of whom were silent and withdrawn.

That haunting moment brought pause to the reality of my life. Years later I heard that she had committed suicide. At the time I didn't know what to do or even why the encounter took place. I started feeling the tug of that supernatural being, my heavenly Father, in my heart again. It was as if he was calling me to chart my life in a new direction, one he had planned. I felt him calling me to flee the darkness around me, but not to fear it.

Although it was hard to shake the heavy baggage I carried, I still felt my heavenly Father with me, even when I wasn't ready to listen to him. My Father would speak to me in different ways. There were some occasions when I regretted not responding to his calling. I'll never forget an event that took place when I was nearing high school graduation.

In my last year of high school I made a few good friends, the kind of friends you would expect to stay in touch with after graduation. One of my friends was named Jay. He was a great guy, always funny and quick with a joke. We never spoke of anything serious, but we enjoyed each other's company with humor and hanging out. I woke up late one night in a sweat. I had the most vivid and real dream I had ever experienced. I was standing in front of a great being of brilliant light, and it kept saying, "Tell him . . . tell Jay about me. Tell Jay that I love him."

There was great urgency in the being's voice. This dream is as vivid in my mind today as it was then. The haunting experience of the dream wouldn't let me sleep after that. I wasn't accustomed to sharing my experiences with people, especially at high school. I couldn't figure out what to say or how to say it, so I didn't say anything.

Jay died in a car accident three days later, and I never said anything. This is one of my memories that compelled me to write down my story. Maybe this is a wake-up call to say whatever God is telling you to say, when he calls and never hesitate.

///

The Los Angeles County Twin Towers jail is like a giant beast that consumes anyone who is fed to it. It grinds their bones, chewing its victims endlessly until they are digested. All who enter are mutilated, and some are spit out but forever disfigured. Others are devoured and never see the light of day again.

After being processed I was marched down a tunnel that seemed to be deep in the earth. When I arrived at my "new home," it resembled a dark exhibit in an aquarium where the lights were low so the patrons could watch through the thick glass. It was like a zoo exhibit or a display of some dangerous wild animals. The notion that I was going to be fed to the caged inhabitants was the frightening part. The guard barked out my cell and bunk assignment, tossed me in, and then locked the door behind me. As I was being tossed I was informed that this was the medical psychiatric ward. Because I was on medication for my blood cancer, I had to be held there. My immediate thoughts drove adrenalin through my veins once again. I wondered what type of inhabitants I would encounter in a psychiatric ward of a place as terrible as this.

The main exhibit chamber was behind thick glass that allowed observation of the entire enclosure. It was a two-story space with tables and benches bolted down in the middle. The back of the chamber had two stories lined with cells that were packed with inmates. The cells were so full that many bunks were placed in the open space outside the cells. At first glance it was hard to tell where the caged rooms started and ended. Inmate bunks were strewn anywhere room for a triple-decker bunk would fit.

I made my way to my assigned cell, where I discovered a very small close sized space made for two but packed with four. One wall had concrete bunks built in. The other had a steel bunk crammed into place. There was barely enough room to pass between the bunks. Mounted to the wall near the door was a steel combo toilet sink that barely cleared the entrance.

I was ready to lay my head down and hide somewhere on that hard bunk, or anywhere that wouldn't get me yelled at or physically abused. I dragged myself into my steel bunk in that narrow cell, trying not to disturb the others who were sleeping. I closed my eyes for what felt like a second, and the intercom started blaring out inmate numbers. Trying to ignore the blasting sound and listening for my number made it unsettling. Yet it took only a minute and I was out again only to be woken once more for the same routine. This went on for hours until finally a guard started banging on the mesh glass door yelling for everyone to line up.

Scrambling to my feet, I shuffled my way to the cell lineup where the inmates stood in a line to be yelled at by the guards. After the guards made sure no one had escaped through the impenetrable fortress we were captive in, we were released to the common space in the main chamber to enjoy the hard steel backless benches. The cells were locked so we couldn't go back to the bunks, leaving us to be ogled at by our captors.

In the lineup I discovered a collection of inmates that ranged from young and timid to bold and brash. Most of them looked normal and didn't fit the stereotype of psychotic I had imagined. I wasn't ready to start making friends or anything, but I didn't feel like I was bunking with an axe murderer either. Nonetheless, I guess most people seem normal until you get to know them. In my case, this became apparent very quickly.

///

In a smoke-filled van packed with teenagers, Drach sat in the driver's seat tapping his talons on the steering wheel. Dark shadows of evil subordinates sat on the dash watching him. As a white Camaro rumbled into the high school parking lot glowing from an angel in the passenger seat, one of the minions addressed Drach. "What's the plan now? You would have had him at the bridge if he hadn't called on his heavenly Father."

In anger Drach blew steaming sulfur in his crony's face. "Don't remind me."

Staring out the window, ignorant of Drach's actions, a dark creature focused on the teen driving the Camaro. "If only you could get one of the humans to push him over the edge for you." As if a light had come on in Drach's head bringing with it a new idea, he grabbed the demon from the dash and flew through the door.

Slithering into a high school classroom, Drach stretched a crookedly devious smile as he noticed the demons accompanying the students far outnumbered the angelic beings. In a prideful fashion Drach marched up to the young man from the white Camaro and slithered around the legs of his chair.

An angelic being began to pull a sword from its sheath, so Drach moved to the neighboring table, smiling as if to say, "My bad."

Drach motioned to his evil assistant to take position by pointing to the table on the other side of the young man. Drach slithered up the leg of the chair and began whispering into the ear of the girl sitting in the chair.

Drach slowly turned his gaze toward the young man as the girl began to speak. "Hey, you. I've got a friend I want you to meet. You'd really like her. What are you doing after school?"

Looking flattered and slightly surprised, the young man looked at the girl and replied, "Uh sure, what's her name?"

The girl smiled and then leaned in. "Her name is Ronda Bronson."

On the other side of the young man, another girl piped in, "Ronda Bronson! She's evil; stay away from that—" The girl sputtered and choked for a moment as Drach's assistant poked her in the neck.

The girl selling this encounter leaned in closer. "She's not that bad. People just don't understand her, and she needs someone like you. She goes to Ferndale High just over the bridge, so you can pick me up after school and we'll head over there." The young man tried to ask another question, but the teacher interrupted their conversation to refocus the students and start the class.

15

Escape to the Desert

Life is better when you stop running from something and start running to someone, your Father.

The name of the LORD is a fortified tower; the righteous run to it and are safe.

—Proverbs 18:10 (NIV)

Consider it pure joy, my brothers and sisters, whenever you face trials of many kinds, because you know that the testing of your faith produces perseverance. Let perseverance finish its work so that you may be mature and complete, not lacking anything.

—James 1:2-4 (NIV)

I'm not sure how it happened, but somehow I acquired a girlfriend. She became angry if I did or said anything that she didn't approve of. She seemed to like me, as if fresh blood had come into her circle. Oddly enough, I felt that I deserved to be ordered around and abused. Her father was a jail guard and an alcoholic. Her mother argued with him constantly and always degraded him in public. I didn't understand the codependency of complex destructive relationships. Little did I know that the fresh blood would eventually become a savage sacrifice and that I was to become the offering.

As high school was coming to a close, a natural turning point in my life was in front of me. If I stayed in Humboldt County, the economic business opportunities were limited. I had two choices:

either I worked in the lumber mill or I became a commercial fisherman. Neither of the available choices appealed to me. Although still broken inside, I was built with a creative and driven spirit.

A recruiting guy from a small college in Arizona visited my high school and offered loans and grants to anyone interested in attending their school. One of the study majors they offered was engineering design. Although I really didn't know what that was, it sounded somewhat like a focus in the arts, only it paid better. I liked art and did well in drafting class, so I thought I had my ticket out from behind the redwood curtain. With what the graduate salaries were, I figured I wouldn't be a starving artist or a lumberjack either. So I signed on the dotted line, sold my Camaro to pay my part of the college fees, and packed what little I had.

As I contemplated the approaching crossroads in my life, I turned to my heavenly Father and fully surrendered my life to him. The struggles and the pain wouldn't go away, but with my heavenly Father I knew I wouldn't have to face them alone. Despite my own shortcomings, he never left me like my earthly father did.

I was excited to leave, even though the dependency on my mom and siblings would make the separation painful. No one ever told me that I could go to business school or do something creative with my life that actually fit the talents God gave me. My previous passion to follow my earthly father's footsteps had grown repulsive. I wanted to follow my heavenly Father, but I didn't want to be like my earthly father. Any association with him was still an infected wound.

My life had become so volatile that I became a master at controlling my raw emotions and putting on a good face. At a distance I seemed like I had it together, but I still didn't fit in. I'll never forget the high school celebration party after graduation. I remember walking in and immediately being rejected at the door. I guess I never was accepted by the "in crowd." Three days after graduation I packed everything I owned in my new little pickup and hit the road to Arizona. I felt like the world was in front of me and I was escaping the painful experiences of my past. Little did I know that geography alone never healed a broken heart; the broken pieces just went with me.

/ / /

Sitting on one of the benches visually exploring the room of steel and concrete, I noticed a bank of phones mounted to a post. I quickly walked over and started checking each phone for a dial tone. One by one I found each phone was dead. At the very last phone my heart skipped a beat as I heard that dial buzzing sound. I quickly dialed collect to my home number and waited through the long, drawn-out instructions and then the final message: "Will you accept a collect call from an inmate in the California Twin Towers Correctional Facility?"

Finally, that voice I longed to hear lit up the phone, and my mind raced a million miles away from that terrible place. The raw emotion I'd fought with adrenaline for days exploded into tears that heaved through my exterior. Holly tried to talk quickly through the tears. "Are you all right? I miss you. I have some information. I've got to talk quickly before they cut us off again, and . . . Kevin, this is going to be very expensive. This could break us. I'm selling your truck, and I called our realtor to see what can be done to sell our home quicker. I've been praying nonstop along with anyone who will pray with us. I called your mom, and she is still praying along with her church. My mom and her church are still praying as well. Your relatives and our friends from all over the country are praying. Everyone is praying."

"I found a Christian attorney online in Denver. He is more affordable, and when I spoke with him he seemed so much more sincere than the others. He doesn't know any details right now, but he does know it has something to do with our former business. His main goal right now is to get you out of there as soon as possible. He warned me to be discreet in what we say on the phones; they record everything and could use anything we say against us. His name is Terry, and he wants you to call him if you can. You've got to hang in there—"

Click-buzz. The phone went dead along with my heart one more time.

I slid slowly down the post to the floor in a crumpled emotional mess, crying out again to God. As quickly as I burst into an emotional collapse, my adrenaline capped the rushing flow and I mentally returned to my surroundings. Clearing the tears and looking over my shoulder, I slowly got up and stood momentarily facing the corner.

When the cells were finally reopened, I made my way back to my cage to find a place to disappear. When I got to the closet-sized compartment that I shared with so many others, I quickly encountered my new cell mates. It was so crowded that we couldn't all get off our bunks at the same time and fit in the cell. Some were curled in the fetal position, while others seemed to take this experience in stride by ogling the walls.

My bunk mate seemed like a happy fellow. The tattoos across his face did come across as alarming, but when we started talking, I discovered that this place was home for him. With great pride he told me details of the gang he belonged to and the terrible deeds that made them famous. With no humility he recalled the times they had made the headlines and the most-wanted list.

The name and number of the gang he belonged to were tattooed across his face along with his given gang name: Bullet Killer. He didn't know his real name and didn't care. The gang took him in when he was a young boy, and they gave him a family that he now revered as his own. I felt sorry for Bullet Killer, but this was his life. He didn't know any other way of life or probably how to survive outside those concrete boundaries.

With great delight he showed me his most recent parole denial paperwork. Just having the paperwork indicated that he had been in that place for a very long time. Possessions of any type were extremely rare, including a piece of paper. I'm not sure why he had it in his possession. He asked me to read it to him, since he couldn't read himself. Not knowing how he would react or even if he knew what was printed on the paper, I cautiously recited the parole officer's comments stating that he wasn't fit to live in society. He had committed numerous crimes and had no regard for property or human life. As opposed to anger or loathing, he seemed to revel in the life he'd led and the fame he'd gathered from his criminal actions.

His most recent offense involved robbing an electronics store and taking an armful of expensive items. According to the paperwork, he assaulted anyone who tried to stop him from exiting the store, including a police officer. Bullet Killer was proud of this. I'm not sure if his pride stemmed from the crime, which was so blatant that he couldn't have possibly gotten away with it, or from the fact that it got him back to his home. This was obviously the only home that he knew, and it provided a way of life that was predictable with some level of stability for him.

He was proud of the gang of criminals that accepted him and made him part of their family. He made it clear that his family was paramount to any end, including taking a life if he was ordered to. The daunting thing about him was the delight with which Bullet Killer could share his convictions.

Bullet Killer had a kind heart blanketed by the desire to be accepted at all cost. He gave me his very small stubble of a pencil and a piece of newspaper that he had stashed so I could write some things down. A pencil was an extreme luxury even if it was only a half inch long.

Bullet Killer was on medications, as were the rest of the inmates in the aquarium psycho ward where I lived. The guards would withhold our meds, seemingly to agitate the inmates. The longer we went without meds, the more some of us, including Bullet Killer, became distraught. His countenance of kindness would fade. Bullet Killer would start pacing the cell, flashing strange looks across his face. He would outwardly morph from an apparently normal individual into someone losing his sanity. The guards seemed to enjoy this agitation, and withholding medications undoubtedly increased tensions.

The most unnerving moments came when we were locked in the tiny crowded cells after inmates had gone without meds for an extended period. Inmates would begin pounding on the reinforced glass in the cell doors that separated the small cells from the common area. Yelling and screaming from other cages would echo through the chambers, accompanied by banging sounds and reverberating profanity. Guards would walk by the dark aquarium windows, peering in on us like some circus exhibit.

Although Bullet Killer's actions without meds were troubling, there were others who needed medication far more than he did. Others were less subtle in their ways and far less controlled. There were perils that lurked in that aquarium far more menacing than Bullet Killer, others whom I would soon encounter.

///

As the pickup rumbled down an endless freeway, with nothing more than heat waves blurring the horizon, the sun began to drift below the sphere of the earth. Vibrating sandwich wrappers danced across the dusty dashboard from the whining of a small engine as the little red Chevy Luv pickup carried an unsuspecting, tired young man.

With one leg stretched across the front seat and the other resting on the accelerator, the young man stared into the endless road disappearing far off in the distance. An occasional landmark such as an interstate sign or a tumbleweed dotted the landscape where his gaze was lost.

Unknown by the young man, an angel sat watching out the window and into the mirrors, looking for something or someone. A larger angel sat in the middle next to him, trying to keep the young man awake and watching the road.

In the pickup camper shell behind the suitcases and bags packed with the young man's earthly belongings, a band of dark minions reclined around Drach. Drach stretched out, appearing confident while bantering with a crooked grin.

"Off to Arizona. I think we got a good assignment this time. This human guy will be ours, plus I have a fondness for the heat. Granted the sunlight is not to my liking, but the heat, yeah. I can almost taste my human now, as if we were already in the midst of the flames."

Gruesome creature silhouettes danced around Drach, cheering every word with gnashing fangs and swaying talons.

At the old house on the outskirts of the Southern California town just beyond the rusty farm equipment and broken fences, shadows darted in and out of the stately old home. With the sun sinking in the sky, the shadows grew long between the missing floorboards across the basement where the creatures had gathered.

Consuming everything in its path with darkness, an enormous shadow skimmed the earth. Revealing a dark creature emitting the shadow, a pass of leathery wings swooped through the opening where the large door once hung, and then passed outstretched wings through the walls.

Blotting out all sunlight as it entered, the evil creature tucked his bony leather wings around its figure. Gliding to the corner of the basement, where a thick, sulfurous stench filled the air, the creature stopped and bowed.

"Beelzebub, my liege."

Stepping out of the corner to be visible in a dim ray of light streaking through the floorboards, an enormous being peered down on Chief Demon.

"I have not seen any of your prey in hell yet. Have they accepted our enemy, the Light, and gone to his kingdom?"

Without returning the hideous creature's peering stare, Chief Demon replied, "They are still in this physical world."

Stepping back into the darkness, the hideous creature paused in a steaming hiss.

"As I figured. Report so that you can get back to executing the orders I've given you."

"Yes, my liege. I have assigned the best of my minions to each of them while I implement my new plan. My commander, Drach, is on his way to Arizona following the eldest boy. We have a wealth of darkness that will be drawn upon from there to complete the destruction of the boy. This situation is under control."

Piercing red burning eyes stabbed through the air at Chief Demon.

"You are jeopardizing our mission on this earth. Your prey cannot be allowed to influence others for the Light. I will not accept this. You were to destroy them while they were still suffering. Increase the pressure on them; attack constantly until they fold to our will. Most of all, do not let them use this for good.

"Do not fail me, or you will feel the fury of my wrath. You are dismissed."

"Yes, my liege"

Turning from the corner of the basement, Chief Demon slowly lifted bony wings to the air before passing through the floorboards above and disappearing into the darkness of night.

16

Into the Frying Pan

Navigate life wisely, because it is easy to be led off course.

In the desert land he found him in a barren and howling waste. He shielded him and cared for him. He guarded him as the apple of his eye.
— Deuteronomy 32:10 (NIV)

. . . in the wilderness. There you saw how the Lord your God carried you, as a father carries his son,
— Deuteronomy 1:31 (NIV)

Approaching Phoenix introduced a sensation I'd not experienced before. After fourteen hours of driving, I finally reached my destination. I became aware that any exposed skin began to burn. It was too hot and dry to sweat. It felt like I was about to burst into flames at any moment. This sensation was draining, and it seemed to suck the life right out of me.

My first stop was checking into my new school. I remember standing in a line for admissions at 7:30 in the morning and my shoes melting into the burning ground. I could feel the heat seeping through my soles and out the top of my feet. I tried jogging my feet up and down in an attempt to cool them down, which made me look like I was fire-walking on red-hot coals.

Exhausted from driving all night, I signed my life away for my new education, got the address to the appointed one-bedroom apartment I would be sharing with two other guys, and melted my way down the road. This experience improved my understanding of why air conditioning was such an important feature for autos in Phoenix—which my little truck didn't have. Rolling down the window only made it worse. The air coursing through the vents or any other opening was like a blowing furnace.

Arriving at my dimly lit basement hovel, I was welcomed by a roach-ridden, dirty quarters. This struck a chord, and the term *homesick* became heartfelt. My less than tidy roommates had already made themselves at home. Dirty clothes tarnished the floor, and spoiled food sat on the counters. A 1960s hide-a-bed, apparently reclaimed from a motel dumpster, became my new sleeping space after I removed the dirty socks and gum wrappers.

With a minimum-wage part-time job at a furniture manufacturer, I couldn't afford to call long distance to my family often. The anxiety of separation and feelings of loneliness clutched me. The only way I knew to survive the emotional anguish was to stuff the feelings once again and forge forward.

I was on my own now, and I knew that I had to survive no matter what. I had no one to lean on or to turn to if I didn't make it. I worked my job into a full-time gig and went to night school. It seemed the only regular contact I had to life behind the redwood curtain, other than my mom, was Ronda. She would write often and call the pay phone down the hall from my apartment from time to time. She never had anything encouraging to say. Mostly she talked about herself and her cat. She dominated the conversation, typically giving orders. Yet she provided some connection to a familiar place. Not having that connection opened old wounds and allowed unbridled emotions tucked far below to bleed through.

It seemed just as quickly as I had acquired a girlfriend, I was engaged. Somehow I was getting married. I wasn't exactly sure how that happened, and without a father to get advice from, I went along. I didn't know how to find a good mate or anything about healthy relationships. I only knew that it gave me some kind of a connection with the familiar life I had just left.

She lived at home with her parents and had no job or money to plan a wedding, so I began sending money home to pay for the impending nuptials. I think getting married at such a young age had more to do with mixed-up emotions than anything else. Fighting the emotions became almost a full-time job in the back of my mind. Being ordered around and controlled by someone else seemed to be a welcome distraction or something I felt I deserved. It was as if some unexplained deed that I needed to be punished for lurked in the shadows.

My roommates were the typical young crazy college kids. Somehow I couldn't engage with them. The idea of having fun as a college kid clashed with the pain that still festered deep inside. It already took so much energy to just hold it all together and contain my own issues.

My new night school classmate was a great guy. We sat next to each other and talked during assignments. We became good friends. He would try to give me advice and continually tried to convince me that this whole wedding thing was a bad idea. I tried to keep myself busy with work and school so I didn't have to give it too much thought. If I hadn't needed to hide from my pain, I might have listened.

It was late one night when I arrived at school to find an empty seat next to mine. My night school classmate was gone. His life was taken while he was riding his motorcycle home from school the previous evening. He died at the site of the accident, when a lady pulling out of a restaurant didn't see him. When the announcement was made, I held the doors tighter than ever to my emotions. I locked the doors and bolted everything shut.

It was shortly after losing my new friend that I threw a change of clothes in my little truck and headed to the redwoods. Committed to school studies, I waited until after school on Friday night. With very little money and a fourteen-plus-hour drive ahead of me, I drove off with little appearance of emotion, even though I was headed to my own wedding.

I lay there on my cell bunk sifting through my memories, recounting the mistakes I had made as a young man in Arizona. The relentless screeching of useless announcements over the public address system made it difficult to converse with the others sandwiched in the small chamber. A loud buzz sounded as the cage doors opened, awakening the undermedicated occupants who shared the same personal space.

I made my way out cautiously, ready for anything edible.

Even the tube jelly and bread seemed appealing at that point. Our routinely tasteless morsels were provided, but the much-needed medications were still being withheld. I was feeling light-headed with a mix of exhaustion and adrenaline pumping through my veins where my mediations should have been. Noticing the crazy expressions on some of the other inmates' faces, I kept my distance with my meager portions while looking for a place to sit.

Spotting a relatively normal-looking guy sitting alone at one of the steel tables, I asked if I could join him. Trying to make conversation, I asked him how he was doing. Without hesitation he turned and peered at me with dilating eyes. He started ranting about how they needed more people like me in that place. He said something about how he and I were the smart ones who needed to stick together because we were the special ones.

I was puzzled and trying to understand what he was ranting about when one of my cage mates walked by. Just then his ranting turned from me to racial slurs toward the guy from my cell. The ranting intensified into screaming, verbally abusive racial swearing. The guy from my cell was a large black guy whom I'd already exchanged pleasantries with earlier. The idea of being associated with a skinhead struck me as terrifying. The guy sitting at my table leaped to the tabletop, ripping off his shirt in shreds and swinging at my cell mate.

I quickly grabbed my tube of jelly and backed away as the two of them began yelling at the top of their lungs and bumping chests in some show of superiority. The guy I had been sitting with instantly turned into a psychotic skinhead and started pushing the black guy, who was more than twice his size and in no mood to back down.

The phrases flying out the skinhead's mouth were far beyond embarrassing insults. With such profane vocabulary filling the air, I noticed everyone grabbing their food and quickly migrating back to their cell doors. Desiring to stay out of the middle of this battle, I followed suit.

It took only seconds for the event to escalate to their throwing anything not bolded down, including torn clothing and shoes. One guard armed with a weapon ordered everyone back to their cells. The only thing that seemed worse than getting caught in a jailhouse brawl would have been getting caught between a psychotic inmate and the merciless guards.

The guard maneuvered the skinhead into some sort of arm lock and forced him into his cell before bolting the door. He was like an angry hornet charging the meshed glass with his body and slamming his head against the door repeatedly. His screaming profanity changed direction to focus on the guard. Blood streamed down his face from the repeated impact of the reinforced glass and steel mesh, but it didn't slow him at all.

Back in our cell I was able to connect with the guy who had become the subject of the skinhead's wrath to reassure him that I didn't want any part of what just happened. I was just in the wrong place at the wrong time, which I'm sure is about anywhere when you're stuck in a place like the Twin Towers jail. He was very cool, and we were able to converse about his situation and how he ended up there. His story wasn't much different from mine.

The skinhead continued to yell at the top of his lungs while slamming his blood-drenched body against the cell door for hours. The guard tapped his weapon on the glass repeatedly, taunting the skinhead until he dropped in exhaustion.

I'm not sure how people could survive in a place like that for any period of time. Every turn was filled with danger and taunting by the gatekeepers trying to exacerbate perilous situations. If I was to be trapped there for any length of time, I was sure that I would forever be altered and likely never leave alive.

Perched on an old suitcase in the back of the little Chevy Luv pickup, a creature with the shadowy appearance of a frog whispered to Drach, "This is working, great Drach. I'm glad we'll get to enjoy this human together. I've never been to the redwoods. I'm sure the people are very tasty there."

Drach peered over his shoulder with burning eyes fixed momentarily on the whispering shadow. "Look, I brought you along to keep watch. Keep your eyes on that angel sitting in the front seat."

With a scowl the dark shadow glared through the rear window glass to concentrate on the passenger. "We've been in here for over ten hours, Drach. Doesn't this kid even get hungry, let alone tired?"

"I've got that covered; don't worry about the human."

"Drach, you should be pleased. This young man is walking straight into the trap you've set for him. He is as good as yours . . . I mean, ours."

Once again peering back at the silhouette of a frog, Drach puffed smoky sulfur into the air. "You have no idea how long I've worked on this kid. I almost had him a few times, so don't count my victories until we have this one wrapped up and rotting over red-hot torment in hell. This one could be a hazard to our rule here on this earth, so don't underestimate the importance of this assignment. That is why I was assigned, and you are fortunate that I selected you to assist me."

Stretching his neck to pierce his dreadful snout through the window next to the ear of the driver, Drach whispered, "Keep going. Ronda will be angry if you stop. Keep going." With a snicker he quickly retreated to the back of the truck.

From the passenger seat an angelic being tried to nudge the young man driving. "Stay awake; you're falling asleep again. Why don't you just stop and take a nap in the truck."

The young man mumbled something unintelligible and then fought to keep his half-closed eyelids open.

Drach once again stretched through the cab window. "It is so cozy in here, isn't it? Close your eyes, and everything will be okay; everything will be just fine."

In a seemingly dreamlike state, the boy slowly maneuvered the hairpin curves, avoiding the cliffs and massive trees. The angel leaned over and gently steered the small truck.

"What?! Not fair!" Drach quickly scratched his chin, thinking swiftly. "Hey, gloom frog, get out there and find a car coming the other way. Distract them so they don't see us coming down the middle of the road."

The frog shadow raced through the camper shell into the gloomy sky ahead of the trio.

Within moments, headlights of an oncoming auto illuminated the night from a curve in the distance. The Chevy Luv weaved gently down the middle of the road, safely away from the rock-faced overhang. The young man hunched over, lost deep in a dream, unaware of the impending collision. In full control without panic or alarm the angelic being steered the small pickup over the bumps in the middle of the road, jarring the vehicle and tossing the young man up and down in his seat.

Just as the man was jolted from a deep sleep, a horn blew over screeching tires. Swerving, the young man steered the truck out of the way, swiping past the other vehicle moments before impact.

Stopped in the middle of the road, wide-eyed and startled, the young man rubbed his bloodshot eyes. Then he shifted the truck into gear and started on his way through the forest once again.

The evil silhouette of a frog glided through the camper shell next to Drach. "I almost had him."

Tapping a talon on the floor, Drach turned to his inferior with a grin. "Yes, but the night isn't over yet."

The dark of night grew cold, with flecks of snow fluttering past the windshield. Welcoming warm air blew gently through the heater vents of the truck cab. The young man seemed to snuggle in the pickup seat, which grew cozier by the minute as the motor hummed a lullaby in the wee hours of the morning.

Drach reached a cupped claw up to the young man's ear to make sure he could hear every whispered word. "It is comfortable in here, isn't it? Close your eyes for just a second. That's right . . . they're getting soooo heavy . . . one more time . . . yeah, and . . . you're out."

Returning to his crony, Drach sported an ear-to-ear grin. In sheer exhilaration the frog reached out to offer a high five to his boss, only to be callously rejected.

Noticing the strange activity taking place from the other side of the truck cab, the angelic passenger observed the strange movement vigilantly. Moments after Drach slithered back into the camper shell, the angelic being took the steering wheel and pointed the truck into a median where a gentle slope came into sight. The truck recoiled from the rough gravel in the median, and the young man jolted to attention. The truck rolled to a stop. The young man shut off the engine and then returned to a curled-up position in the seat.

With the flash of a sword, the angelic being struck through the rear window into the camper shell, nearly severing Drach's tail. Drach vanished abruptly through the side of the truck, leaving the frog to fend for himself. The second swing of the sword dissolved the ghostly frog of a figure in a blast of steaming spray before he knew what hit him.

Placing an arm around the young man, the glowing being spoke softly. "Rest well. You will need it to endure the hard road you have chosen. Your Father will never leave you, but things are going to get tough very fast. Rest well, my young one."

17

Tied and Knotted

As long as there is darkness, there will be abuse. We'll never truly be free until we see our heavenly Father.

I call on the Lord in my distress, and he answers me. Save me, O Lord, from lying lips and from deceitful tongues.

—Psalm 120:1-2 (NIV)

And that they will come to their senses and escape from the trap of the devil, who has taken them captive to do his will.

—2 Timothy 2:26 (NIV)

Seeing everyone dressed up and arriving at the chapel filled me with mixed emotions. All I could think of was, *How can I disappoint them?* This thought was closely followed by, *What am I doing?* Although the thought of running continually flashed through my mind as I anticipated what would be one of the biggest mistakes of my life, somehow I couldn't. Something kept telling me to walk away . . . no, run away, and fast. I feared that if I did run, she would hunt me down and find me anyway. So I walked through the motions.

There wasn't time or money for a honeymoon, and I needed to get back to Arizona for school and my job. After returning the cheap tux and loading my little pickup to the max with her clothes, her stuff, and her cat, we headed back down the twisting forest road toward the boiling heat of the desert.

It didn't take long before she was lecturing me on her expectations. This ride was not up to her liking, as nothing else seemed to be either. The nonstop belittling and pelting insults drove me into a coma of isolation with selective hearing.

However, it quickly became more than verbal abuse as her cat acquired a parallel personality to hers and began attacking me with claws at full mast. My little pickup encompassed minimal space to maneuver, making it difficult to flee the pursuing feline. The endless hours of cruel and unusual punishment were enough for me to contemplate removing the cat's claws and teeth . . . if only I had some tools.

I tolerated the anguish in that marriage for years to follow, somehow enduring a punishment I felt I deserved. I couldn't pinpoint why I felt I deserved to be treated so badly, but I knew it had something to do with my childhood and my father. I couldn't explain it. I could only identify the emotions that drove the feelings and vaguely recognize when the feelings arrived in my life. Like a weed, the feelings were planted, and although I knew I didn't deserve to be treated so poorly, I somehow felt a need to feed the evasive weed.

It wasn't long before I graduated from school. The cat continued to attack me daily with his sharp claws whenever I entered our studio apartment. The physical scars were less wearing than the unrelenting verbal assaults from the one I had walked down the aisle with. My career started to grow, making it easier to spend less time at home. There were numerous occasions when her relatives and friends would ask why I put up with such abusive behavior, and I didn't know why.

My business pursuits took on a life of their own. I bought my first home before age twenty, then traded it for another property, and then wheeled my way into another. It didn't take long before I was living in a very nice new home in a distinguished neighborhood. I was driving a brand-new truck, and Ronda had her own vehicle and the beginnings of the upscale life she demanded.

The pain locked deep inside me never went away. The abuse didn't take it away or make me feel any better. I couldn't even enjoy the homes, my career, and the trappings of accumulating wealth, as the unyielding pain haunted me relentlessly. I pursued more and drove harder, but the shadow of my past wouldn't go away.

I found a church to attend and even tried to get Ronda to join me, but usually I went alone. I can remember sitting in the pew screaming in my soul for a dad, or something to heal my soul. I usually couldn't concentrate on the preacher or connect with the others who attended. Everywhere I went, I continually looked over my shoulder, wondering if my dad might be there. Maybe I would run into him someplace. It had been so many years at that point that I didn't know if I would even recognize him. I didn't know who he was. I didn't even know if he was still out there someplace. Even though he had abandoned me, he still seemed to hold the key that locked up all of the pain crushing me inside.

Between a career and my business ventures, I was able to survive the battering from Ronda for years. She became a shopaholic, hiding closets full of clothing and piles of credit cards from me. Her abuse gradually morphed from verbal to physical. She tried to run me over a few times with her car and made regular sport of hitting and kicking. I reached my limit when she took the dresser mirror and shattered it over the counter. The outbursts were normal, but when she came at me with a two-foot-long glass shard, it became more than even I could take.

The foundation and the walls that I had built to hold everything inside began cracking. The walls divided the pain and held a reservoir of festering wounds. I didn't care about the stuff and couldn't go on living the life I had survived with Ronda any longer. I began to fear for my life. Going home became harder than ever. When I went into the house, I had to cautiously scout the rooms, avoiding ambush until I knew where she was and what she was doing. I had to look over my shoulder at all times and plan an escape should I be attacked.

This went on for a while. I can remember one evening when I was driving down the highway through a stretch of desert not long after the shard incident. I pulled my new sports car off the road, got out, and fell to my knees.

///

Everyone stayed in their cages waiting for the yelling and screaming that accompanied the skinhead's pounding against the door to stop. Sitting on my cold, hard bed, I noticed a guy on the bottom bunk who never seemed to move. He spent most of his time in the fetal position facing the wall.

I asked what his story was. The other guys indicated that he had been there for months lost in the system. They didn't completely know his story, because he hadn't said a word for a very long time. My curiosity peaked, as I could relate to his suffering.

Before I could get very far in the conversation, alarms went off everywhere. Sirens blared while guards rushed past the aquarium window carrying weapons, obviously geared up for some sort of battle. The PA system came to life with a monotone announcement asserting that we were under lockdown. I wasn't sure what that involved until the other inmates casually informed me that a riot was under way.

Climbing back onto my bunk, I felt numb. The adrenaline rush had run its course for over a week by that point. I wasn't really sure how tired I was beneath the artificial stimulation my body had continually drugged me with. I hadn't slept for days, and now I was observing a riot taking place in front of me. It all seemed too surreal. I kept thinking, *What next? Is someone going to rush in here and stab one of us, or all of us? Are the guards going to start shooting?*

I leaned over the bunk to continue my conversation to ease the tension. "So go on," I said to the lost young man curled up on a lower bunk across from mine. Unexpectedly he rolled over and began to fill in the gaps in his story.

He was from a poor Eastern Bloc family. He came to California to pursue a dream, to find a job and then send for his family. He was arrested for a minor offense that he claimed he didn't do. He said they would release him for one thousand dollars, but he didn't have the money and couldn't work to earn it. His family was far away and couldn't come up with the money either. He couldn't afford a lawyer, and the judge didn't seem interested in hearing his story. So he'd been in jail for four months with no idea of when he would be released. He had never been in trouble before and didn't know what to do. He was essentially lost in the system, and the system didn't care.

The door lock buzzed open. A guard tossed another inmate in with us and then slammed the door behind him. There were no available bunks for this guy, so he had to stand. He then revealed a chilling story. Apparently the riot was much worse than what we had observed. Part of a building was burning, and inmates held some portion of the yard, whatever that meant. Nonetheless, it didn't sound good.

As the time crept by with little for us to do but listen to the banging sounds, I noticed some of the guys had a stash of stuff. Tucked under the frame of the bunks, some had created a space to hide their most prized possessions. I saw things like a small toothbrush, a comb, a small pencil, and a piece of used paper. I inquired about how they got their valuables. They told me if you have money, you could get anything you wanted, but everything was expensive. Assuming there was some underground black-market smuggling or something going on, I inquired again as to where and how things could be acquired. A luxury such as a toothbrush would have been spectacular at that point. I hadn't brushed my teeth in days.

Smiling, they looked at me as though I were some uneducated schoolboy; then they gave me the rundown on how it worked. Evidently the items for sale came from the guards. They sent a shopping list around. If you had any money in your account, which involved someone on the outside coming to the jail and paying the cashier, you could buy whatever you wanted. A two-inch toothbrush might cost you ten bucks. A small paper pouch of coffee might cost you fifteen.

There was no hot water—or for that matter, a cup to put it in—but the memory of a hot coffee brought my imagination alive. I could almost smell the aroma, and cold coffee from a paper bag would have been heavenly.

The picture the others painted portrayed a very different reality than the one I was living through. It became apparent that if you had money or influence, this experience would be entirely different.

I didn't know what I now looked like, as there were no mirrors. I could feel a full beard, and my eyes were sticking to my eyelids when I woke from a moment of sleep. My teeth were crusty, and I ached from the stress and adrenalin that was continually pumping through my body. My emotions continued to ebb and flow between survival and exhaustion. The activity outside of the aquarium seemed to taper off, and the occupants of the cell quietly stared at the door, waiting.

///

Rolling in laughter, mischievous creatures gathered for the regular evening performance. In the living room a young man sat on the couch fixed on a different place and time, mentally worlds away. Around the corner a lady sat at the table looking through catalogues of the latest fashions.

One of the creatures sat up, motioning to the others to pay attention to the devilish dragon creature slithering across the floor.

"Drach, do it again. These humans are so stupid!"

With a crooked grin stretching from ear to ear, Drach smirked toward his dark audience before slithering up behind Ronda at the table. He spun a noose around her neck with his tail and sunk his talons into her arms, slowly taking control. Within minutes Drach seemed to disappear as a fiendish look came over Ronda's face. She leaped to her feet and seemed to dance a jig around the table while the others looked on and roared in delight.

As Ronda slunk up to the kitchen counter, a demanding voice belted through the house. "Hey, worthless. Get in here and make something for me to eat. I've had a hard day of shopping."

The silence from the living room was deafening. The laughter stopped when one of the creatures slipped through the wall to see what had caused the lack of response. Standing next to the motionless young man, a large angel stood with sword drawn. Quickly returning to the kitchen, the dark creature shrugged his shoulders.

Casually rounding the corner from the hall, a cat stopped and froze in its tracks upon sighting the imps on the kitchen floor. Spinning in place, the cat dashed back down the hall the way he arrived, only to be pursued by one of the dark shadows.

The household feline returned moments later as Ronda casually sorted through sharp objects in the kitchen knife drawer. This time the cat did not appear to fear the dark shadows; instead his eyes resembled those of the others angrily sneering at each other. The cat turned to Ronda and spoke: "Drach, something is wrong here. Why isn't he responding?"

Scratching her chin, Ronda rumbled in an unearthly voice, "Take the kitty for a little walk and see what's going on in there."

Strutting around the corner into the living room, the cat stopped and hissed at the young man. The angel raised his sword in warning as a dark shadow slowly slithered away from the cat; then the creature stopped to dig its sharp talons into the back end of the feline, sending him screeching toward the young man.

Aggressively biting and scratching the man's leg, the cat exploded in anger as the demon looked on in puzzlement. The young man sat there motionless as if dead, staring blankly at the wall. Dumbfounded, the dark creature stared back, not noticing the shadow of a woman creeping up behind him from the kitchen.

"I said, hey, worthless. Stop ignoring me! I'm talking to you!"

As she raised a meat cleaver with one arm, the appearance of evil morphed across her face.

At that moment the angel braced his sword and yelled, "Run!" Ronda steamed across the room as life breathed back into the man and he flew out the front entrance. Trying to cut him off, Ronda darted out the side door and into her car. The man sprinted his way to the end of the driveway where his car waited, only to be met by Ronda's automobile trying to pin him against a tree and some bushes. Bobbing and weaving to avoid the hit-and-run attempts, the man managed to start his own auto and speed away.

Cursing the air, Drach leaped from Ronda's car, now lodged over a large shrub, and summoned his minions. "Go after him! She is of no value to us anymore, and he is still a threat. Do not lose sight of him."

18

End of the Rope

Stop fighting; surrender your situation and let him rescue you from it.

Do not cast me from your presence or take your Holy Spirit from me.
                                    —Psalm 51:11 (NIV)

Restore to me the joy of your salvation and grant me a willing spirit to sustain me.
                                    —Psalm 51:12 (NIV)

As I drove down a familiar stretch of desert highway at nearly sunset, the dam holding the pain in my soul cracked, and I couldn't hold it back any longer. I pulled my car off the road, walked out into the sand, and fell on my knees. With the sun setting at my back, I wept on the desert floor. I cried out to God.

"Save me! I can't live like this any longer. The pain is more than I can bear. If this is all you have for me, then I don't want it anymore. I don't want this life. If you have a plan for me, if you really want my life, take it and change it. I don't know why I do the things I do. I don't know why I feel that I need to be punished. I don't know why my father left me. All I do know is that you are the only one who can save me."

Unable to return home and face another rampage, I got back in my car and just kept driving. Neither logic nor reason ever played a part in resolving her storms. They typically went on and on for hours. In my mind I had been a million miles away that evening, which seemed to have aggravated her all the more. In anger she had grabbed a chopping knife from the kitchen and charged at me in the living room. I realized I couldn't even sleep safely in my own home anymore.

I slept in my car for the night. The next morning I rented an apartment across town, and I never returned. I called her mom to tell her that I'd left. Oddly, her mom didn't seem surprised. I paid off all of her bills, gave her everything I had, and resolved to start over, because nothing was worth staying. I left the real estate, the bank accounts, and everything I had worked so hard for.

At that moment I didn't care what anyone thought of me. I didn't care much about anything for the first time in a long time. I just knew that I had to find a way to heal my pain. Somehow the pressure of the festering wounds inside me seemed to ease. Although my apartment was bare, it gave me a quiet and safe place to exist.

She became furious. She still pursued me in anger trying to take more, but there was nothing else to give. Somehow she got my phone number and would call me constantly, screaming and yelling at me to come back or else. I let her know that I'd prefer the "or else" from now on. Somehow I felt free.

She even came to my work until finally I had to call security. She tracked down the apartment where I was living and pounded on the door demanding that I let her in several times. I had to call the police a time or two, but I wasn't afraid anymore.

It was such a strange paradox. The driven, happy person who wanted to laugh and be a kid again lived somewhere down inside me, and he wanted to come out. The person who once feared nothing surfaced through the muck and festering wounds. There was capacity to feel alive once again.

Nonetheless, gashes across my soul wouldn't mend that easily. My heavenly Father heard my cry, but the pain was far from over. I didn't know just how broken I was, or how much work it was going to take to repair the damage I'd hidden so deeply inside . . . or that I would have to learn to live with a lifetime of scars that my father had left me.

I found a small church near my apartment that became my new family. There was a support group of people dealing with issues, which was a new concept to me. Most of them were dealing with relationship issues, addictions, and other struggles life had thrown at them. They prayed to God and held each other up like family. That same presence I felt as a kid was there, and the power of that presence was strong.

I began to grow in my relationship with my heavenly Father. Exciting things started happening once more that again couldn't be explained. I could feel that wonderful presence engulfing me and a peace wrapped around me like I'd not felt before.

I remember hanging out and praying with my new friends often. I couldn't get enough of that place. It seemed I was there every chance I got.

One evening I attended a local gathering with my new friends. It was a warm evening under clear blue skies when we arrived at the large gym to hear some music and a speaker I'd never heard of before. Anticipating the strong presence I was becoming acquainted with again, I was excited to be there. I don't remember the speaker's name, but it was a powerful evening. As he spoke, he would lash out against the powers of darkness. He would rebuke Satan and his demons openly and aggressively in a way I hadn't experienced since my childhood. He spoke as if Satan was listening.

Suddenly without warning the sky cracked in thunder and went dark. The power in the building went out, and rain emptied from the skies in bucketloads. Everyone suddenly went quiet as we sat there in pitch darkness. After a few minutes the space began to fill with a cappella music of worship to God, and that presence I'd experienced my whole life was there.

Moments later the power came back on in the building as the skies cleared and glowed through the windows. We exited the building to find clear blue skies once again. Puddles in the parking lot were the only remaining evidence of the momentary torrent. No clouds were present, and the warm desert evening was once again as it had been when we arrived.

I'm not completely sure what all took place there, but over one thousand people saw what I saw and felt the presences I felt, and it was amazing. The speaker must have angered someone, or something. Inside that place the presence I'd grown to love was strong and overpowered the darkness. What an amazing time it was in my life.

I began to grow bold in my faith. One of the guys at the church needed a place to live and I needed a roommate, so he moved in. He knew my heavenly Father well. We were both bold about our faith and wanted to share it with others at every opportunity. God seemed ever present, and this presence brought life to my soul daily.

Then, when I least expected it, I was blindsided. I wasn't looking for it, but as I was moving closer to my true Father, someone else walked in to derail my course.

///

Drifting between thoughts of my family at home and my life in Arizona as a young man, I stared at the paint chipping on the wall. My mind daydreamed until suddenly the buzzer unlocked the door, letting us out into the aquarium. The signs of the riot were hidden from sight, and we were left to wander in our fishbowl.

Breaking up the monotony, I found one of the steel benches and sat down. Sitting with me at the table, an articulate middle-aged man of Hispanic origin started a conversation. He asked if I knew some Hispanic name, which I'd never heard of. I noticed tattoos on his knuckles and neck, but he was void of the typical face markings. I asked him about his background, which led to a hair-raising lecture.

He informed me that he was a mafia boss in a powerful Mexican gang. After lecturing me for several minutes on how California belongs to his people and how America stole it from them, he told me how the police raided his home. They apparently took his collection of Hummers and other expensive items along with a large stash of drugs.

Although he appeared as polished as a corporate CEO, a rough darkness edged his eyes. As I listened, he informed me in a calm voice that if someone like me came into his neighborhood, even by accident, they would take my car and shank me. After learning that the definition of shanking involved a sharp object and the taking of a life, I didn't know if this guy was for real or not.

With a hardened straight face he looked me in the eyes and told me in great detail about the first shanking he had experienced. When the man was five years old, his father had killed a man in front of him to show him how it was done. The taking of a life was an instinctive experience for him that could be performed without emotional attachment, an experience that he seemed very familiar with.

He painted the picture of life as a gang boss and *la familia*, or his gang family, which extended into prison. There were la familia that ran part of Twin Towers, so going to jail was not a loathsome thing; it was merely an opportunity to check up on the family inside. At his level in the family, he didn't anticipate being in jail for long.

If any family member wasn't doing his job, the gang boss merely ordered one of the others to shank him, and he was executed. Having control over who lived or died while running in the fast lane seemed to infuse a fearless godlike persona into this guy. I found myself seeking a polite way to exit the conversation lest I became too visible to the wrong people in that confined space.

To my relief the PA system echoed for everyone to return to their cells as the buzzers of the door locks rang. I politely excused myself and gladly made my way back to my confined space.

Seeing my new bunk mate Bullet Killer, I asked him if his gang family ordered him to shank someone he knew or even liked, would he? With a smile of sincerity he looked at me and said as a matter of fact, "Of course. I have to."

I sank into my hard bunk, nodding with a nervous smile at Bullet Killer. I once again wondered how I had ended up there and what I did that was so bad no one could tell me why I was there. I closed my eyes and cried out to God to save me. The nightmare continued with no plan of exit. What would be next? What would become of my family? Somehow I had to survive. Somehow I couldn't succumb to the darkness of the Los Angeles County Twin Towers.

///

Slithering past the familiar rusty farm equipment in front of the old stately home, Drach anxiously made his way through the outskirts of the Southern California neighborhood. Making his way past the opening, Drach timidly progressed to the basement.

A small bony creature with large horns and hoofed feet announced, "Chief Demon, I believe this is one of yours?"

Stepping out of the shadows, Chief Demon appeared slowly in dramatic fashion, revealing his hideous face with missing skin showing his sharp teeth.

The bony creature yelled in loathing, "Does Beelzebub know you are using this place for your own personal intimidation?"

In immediate response Chief Demon hissed and pinned the bony demon to the ground with his large talons. Looking down at the creature, Chief Demon puffed swirls of steaming hot sulfur toward him. "I suggest you make better use of the time you have left on this earth." Then he tossed the creature through the floorboards while turning his piercing gaze to Drach.

"My Chief, you sent for me?"

"Yes, I did, Drach. I am receiving disturbing reports about your human. I understand he is now fighting back and becoming stronger with our enemy. He is starting to affect others. Do you realize how dangerous this is?"

"Yes, Chief."

"I cannot report these losses to my liege. You must stop this now! I don't care what you have to do, but stop him!"

"Yes, Chief."

"Get out of my sight and prove to me that you are the abhorrent commander that you once said you were."

"Yes, Chief," and Drach quietly slithered up the stairway and back out the way he had come.

On a beautiful spring afternoon at a conference center in downtown Phoenix, a group of young people gathered at long cafeteria tables. As the Christian speaker wrapped up his notes, a young man greeted the other attendees. One by one the man shook hands and took an interest in each person, listening and talking with each of them.

High in one corner of the room, Drach arrived and paused to discuss his encounter with Chief Demon before changing his focus to the room.

"So what do you guys have for me here?"

"Well, Drach, while you were gone we identified a good target to mess up our human. Her name is Jade."

Immediately interrupting his followers, Drach blurted out, "What, Jade? She has an angel of her own. What are you guys—nuts?"

"Drach, hear us out. She is so messed up that even her own angel can't keep up with her. I think we'll do okay here. It worked once before with Ronda. I think we can twist his mind enough to push him over the edge with this one."

Shaking his head in disbelief, Drach conceded. "I need something quick, or I wouldn't even hear you out. Tell me more."

"Well, she is on medications, has spent a lot of time in therapy, and has a lot of baggage that we can use for ammunition. Her demons messed her up when she was a kid, and she has been fighting to face it ever since. She's got a dad issue too."

"Since I don't have any better ideas and Chief Demon is going to have my head if I don't do something soon, get down there and make the introduction. However, if this gets out of hand and he becomes a positive influence on her or anyone else, I'll send one of you out of this realm. Do you understand me?"

"Yes, sir, commander."

"I still need a backup plan. What about this preoccupation with business? I think there is something we can do with that. If we can't push him off a cliff, we'll have to lull him into a comfortable numbness and keep him distracted. Either way, he has to become useless to our enemy and cease being a threat to our kingdom."

19

Confronting the Past

Darkness has no power over those who walk with the Light.

I will give thanks to you, Lord, with all of my heart.
I will tell of all your wonderful deeds.
                                        —Psalm 9:1 (NIV)

The Lord is compassionate and gracious, slow to anger, abounding in love.
                                        —Psalm 103:8 (NIV)

At this time in my life I was meeting a lot of people and enjoying the freedom my heavenly Father gave me. I had no fear or trepidation in my shadows. The pressure and pain in my soul were masked for a season. I started spending a lot of time with one of the young ladies I had met at a church function. Her name was Jade. At first she seemed fun with a carefree personality, but as I got to know her better, I noticed a darker side starting to surface. At times she seemed to know my heavenly Father well, and at others it was as if she crawled in a hole and succumbed to a dark place. There were times when she seemed almost an entirely different person, but not violent like Ronda. She had been abused by her father when she was a child, and it left terrible scars and memories that haunted her. She seemed to be unable to break free of what haunted her.

We went to church events and gatherings where the presence of my Father was strong. I prayed for her a lot. I felt a kinship in the battles that we both fought. Yet after I had known her for a while, strange things started happening—things that once again were hard to explain. It felt like a battle was continually being waged around her with a dark presence that was never far away.

I remember one evening I had a vivid dream in which an evil spirit was trying to attack me. I didn't feel fearful as I would have anticipated. I woke late at night yelling at the demon to leave. I remember shouting, "You do not have authority over me." The odd part was after I awoke I was still yelling, and a growling noise rumbled from a corner in my bedroom. After the growling had stopped, I got out of bed and turned on the lights. I had no idea what had just happened. The presence of something evil penetrated my room with a sensation that is hard to explain but could be felt. The strangest thing was that I wasn't afraid. The feeling of that evil presence in my room was long gone, and an unexplainable peace came over me, so I went back to sleep.

Jade would receive phone calls and often messages from indescribable voices in unearthly screeching tones telling her that they owned her. Darkness in this world didn't scare me, but the scars in my own soul still held a grip on me and lurked in my background. Eventually that dark side of Jade completely surfaced. She wasn't able to break free of her past, so she cut off all connection with me and left to travel the country with a new confidant. I wondered what that whole situation in my life was about. I don't know what happened to Jade and the darkness that seemed to follow her. I wished her well, but a part of me started stirring during that time. The signs of the pain hidden deep inside me started surfacing again.

I started dealing in business ventures as I had before. I had a new home and a furniture store, and I was selling automobiles on the side while still maintaining my engineering career. I was back on top of my business game. I knew my heavenly Father, and I knew he loved me. So what was wrong with me? I began falling apart for no reason. My emotions became uncontrollable with no apparent cause. I would cry at the drop of a hat. The emotions hidden deep inside me would surface without warning, leaving cracks in the dam I had built to protect my wounded soul. Then the cracks split wide open, and the dam broke.

I became a wreck. I fell into a million pieces. I hit a level of depression that took me lower than anything I'd known up to that point in my life. I was in way over my head, drowning in an ever-festering wound that I had continually stuffed inside. My emotions became raw, and every little thing led to an explosion of feelings. I was incapable of functioning in life. I would have to force myself to just show up for work, let alone return business calls or be effective in life. I didn't know what was happening to me. My world collapsed, and I cried out once again for my heavenly Father to save me.

This time God didn't send groceries to my front door or clear the storm with the wave of his hand. He knew the depth of my pain and what I needed to start the healing. When I called out to him, he provided, but this time he pointed me to a therapy center where I had to check myself in and do the hard work involved in healing the deep scars. God used what he showed me from the small group at church to accept what I needed. My need went far deeper than what a support group could help with; I needed to go into my past with a therapist and face what was haunting me.

I still remember the day I threw my hands up in surrender. My heavenly Father put the hospital I needed right in front of me. I couldn't deny his direction, nor did I want to at that point. I checked myself into the therapy center in desperation. I didn't care if I would be branded with the stigma of a crazy person seeking professional help, as I once would have thought. All I cared about was finding a way to deal with the pain that surged through my veins. I needed to find answers to the questions that circled in my broken soul, and heal the pain at any cost.

Over the course of the next eight months, I attended therapy counseling and group sessions religiously. I discovered how God made me and that feelings are okay. I learned what to do with those haunting feelings that my earthly father disfigured me with. I anguished through each emotion as I relived my torturous childhood. I learned why I felt everything was my fault, and most of all I released the cap on the jar of my wounded soul, letting everything out. I had to relive the agony of my father leaving me and every painful emotion I'd experienced since. Therapy hurt—really bad—but avoiding it was far worse.

I also discovered that these things don't just go away and that they can't be ignored. I would have to learn how to live with the scars and reprogram how I responded to the world around me. It was the hardest and the best thing I had done in my life. I met people with scars such as mine. I discovered that there were many on this journey who were dealing with similar issues gripping their souls. I met countless others who got stuck in the therapy process and just looped through the pain but never let it go. I decided that I didn't want to go into therapy to find a crutch for my pain; I was going to find answers and heal. My journey got worse before it started getting better, but it did start to get better. A weight started to lift off of my shoulders little by little.

Then I discovered a piece of me hidden in the darkness deep below everything. I knew it was there and I'd have to deal with it someday, but I avoided it as long as I could. I had to face the source of my scars. I had to face my earthly father. I had to know who he was, since he was still out there someplace. I can't tell you exactly why; I just knew I had to, no matter what I found. But I'm not sure if I was prepared for what I discovered.

///

Staring at the ceiling somewhere between exhausted and in a dream state, unsure of the time or day, I lay on my hard bunk with Bullet Killer below me. The other lost souls who shared the small quarters were sandwiched into the bunks around me. My family and my heavenly Father were all I could think of, yet somehow when I had full access to them I had chosen to ignore them. What was I thinking? Would I ever get this life right and align my priorities where I know they should be? Would I ever get another chance to try? Would these thoughts haunt me forever?

After making a pillow out of my socks, I found the small piece of paper I had stashed, and with my one-half-inch pencil I began writing. The letters were as small as I could make them to conserve the paper I had. My paper was a page from a news magazine in its former life, so I had only the edges and various white spaces to write on. My writing curved around the existing images as I continued journaling my experience. I wrote as if I was writing a final testament to my life, in great sadness and with an uncertain future. I didn't know if I would ever get out of the mess that I found myself lost in. I didn't know if I'd ever see my wife and children again. I didn't even know if the paper I scratched the words on would ever find them, but I felt compelled to write to them nonetheless.

The jail commissary person arrived at our cell door with the coveted items the others had purchased. I'm not sure where the funds came from, but someone on the outside must have made a large donation for the meager feast. It wasn't much, and each item was shamefully expensive. It only took minutes for the others to light up as if it were Christmas morning. The paltry feast of bagged cheese puffs and Doritos chips was laid out in small pouches and delivered. The inmates plowed into the bags, sharing with each other, even smashing chips in the bag making them small enough to slide under the locked doors to share with the other inmates. While I observed the others I shared a sip of cold instant coffee from a small paper cup made from a piece of leaky paper.

Although the others tried to make the most of the moment, I couldn't. The haunting thoughts in my mind wouldn't let go for even a second. With my body beyond exhaustion and surviving on the tension that drove through me, I wanted so much to close my eyes, but rest continued to elude me. The sea of uncertainty that flooded the balance of my life, and the lives of those who depended on me kept tugging at the anchor of my distress and hung around my neck. All I felt I could do was tread water a little longer and pray for a life boat before it was too late, even if I had no clue what was going to happen to me next.

///

In a circle of chairs men and women found their seats. From the center of the hospital room some people chatted while most sat quietly contemplating or staring at the ground. Uncomfortably close, many menacing creatures slithered throughout the space, hissing at the angelic beings standing near some of the room's human occupants. Most of the humans were unknowingly surrounded by dark creatures that loomed ominously, poking and biting at them. In a large overstuffed chair a lady dressed in white held a clipboard and spoke to the people seated in the room. She marked on the board, paused, and then gave instructions to the attendees.

"Okay, let's get started, and then we'll go around and see how we are all making progress. Last session we identified and discussed issues in our childhood that affect us as adults. We looked at why this occurs and talked about baggage we carry today and how the two are connected. Becky, can you go first? I want you to tell the group how you're progressing in connecting your issues and behaviors. I'd also like us to think about the idea of facing our issues and what caused them, so keep that in mind while we go around the circle."

A jet-black creature resembling a spider gripped onto the young girl with all of its might, biting her head and digging claws into her neck. It screeched out, "I'm losing her. Someone help me here."

A large scorpion-like creature replied from across the room as he dug his stinger deeper into one of the men in the gathering, "Don't worry. You'll get her back. Just hang on for now. It's not like she's going over to the Light; she always comes back. She doesn't know our enemy."

On the top corner of a book counter, Drach surveyed the room while stretching his bony wings. He was surrounded by other demonic creatures nervously watching his every move. Piercing his burning, fiery eyes into the back of a man in the circle, Drach addressed the ominous creatures slithering behind him.

"So, the Jade thing didn't work out as expected, huh?"

"No, it didn't, Drach. We've tried to frighten him and put fear into his soul. We also tried to get him too busy with the business thing and lull him away from his Father. He is busy, but I can't say we've been that effective. He doesn't seem to be afraid of us, and Jade flaked on us as well."

Turning his burning gaze on the creature addressing him, Drach lurched and clenched a talon around its neck. "Your advice is becoming useless to me. Shall I find another more effective?" Drach's hissing fangs along with the pointed horn on his nose seemed to pulse in rage. The tightening of his grip sent the clenched demon squirming as it wrapped its tail around Drach's bony arm trying to escape.

Pulling the squirming inferior close to his coal-black pitted face, Drach scolded his minions. "I will defeat this human. There is too much invested in his fall. We have tortured and wounded his soul. We have disfigured his childhood. We have frustrated him and tripped him at almost every turn. He should be shattered in some gutter somewhere begging us to take him to hell and feast on him—not in therapy actually dealing with the issues we inflicted on him. Find me another angle; find me something *now*!!"

Drach threw his inferior at an angelic being standing near the circle of humans, and with the flash of a sword he vanished in a puff of steaming hot mist. The angelic beings stood on guard with swords ready for a battle to ensue. Drach turned to the others as one of them spoke from the back of the group.

"This might be a good time to reintroduce his father? That is what the therapist is discussing, so it shouldn't be too hard."

Drach's countenance seemed to change as the anger was replaced with a sinister sneer. He turned slowly back toward the circle of humans and scratched the horn on his face with a talon. "Yes. Yes, yes, this is good. Oh, yes, this could be very good. I could stop in and see Chief Demon while we are obliterating our human in Southern California. He'll slit his own wrist once we introduce the source of his scars. Yes, yes, this is very good."

Drach and his minions slithered to the floor to get a closer perspective on the session taking place in the circle. Standing ever ready next to their humans, the angelic beings scrutinized every move Drach made, while carefully watching the other creepy creatures in the room.

20

False Impressions

The past is rarely what we think it was.

Trust in the LORD with all your heart and lean not on your own understanding; in all your ways submit to him, and he will make your paths straight.
—Proverbs 3:5-6 (NIV)

For if you forgive other people when they sin against you, your heavenly Father will also forgive you.
—Matthew 6:14 (NIV)

It was an early desert morning when I threw a bag of clothes into my car and prepared for the most uncertain journey of my life. The sun split the horizon into an array of colors, and the rugged terrain was coming to light. Cactus and scrub brush dotted the landscape. Doubt and uncertainty dotted my memories. My past was clouded in shadows of suffering and dreams of this day. I knew where I was headed, but I had no idea what I would find, or how I would be received by what I did find. A part of me was compelled to chart this course to find answers to the turmoil in my soul. A part of me dreaded what I might find at my destination. I had to ask myself if the dreams were mere projections of the earthly father I wanted. Or was there really a father out there who loved me unconditionally? Was there really one who would take me into his family and call me son?

It took some time to find him, but I located my father still living back in the Southern California city where everything started, the city where I last saw him nearly twenty years earlier. I forced the memories of handcuffs and police officers, from that fateful night in front of the hospital, with my mom near death, out my memory. The emotions raced between the questions of why and the desire to have a father. Reason found no place in my mind or in my actions. I had to face him. I felt that I had to know if he was for real or just a figment of my imagination. And if he was real, I had to know who he was.

I contacted him before taking the journey across the desert. The moments before the phone call were filled with extreme apprehension from the instant I first started dialing the number. To say, "Hi, I'm your son," to your father whom you hadn't seen since he was taken away by the police for attempting to murder your mom twenty years ago was strange enough, but the anticipation of how that would be received would drive the awkward silence of an anxious moment. How would the conversation take place? What would I say? All I could remember about him was the double-feature movies that played over and over in my head.

The first movie involved the night he tried to kill my mom, the night he abandoned us. He was going to park the car when we got to church, but he never came back. I saved a seat for him next to my little brother and older sister. What was he thinking? Didn't he care about us? Didn't he want us, or me? I had felt abandoned for nearly two decades. I'd suffered endless torment from the painful choices I'd made without knowing why I made those choices. I had lived a life completely different than the one I felt he took from me. I was crushed when my soul collapsed, and I had to spend nearly a year in therapy. I endured a horrible marriage because I felt I deserved it. Somehow this was all connected to the one I was trying to find.

However, the second movie projected the father that I longed for, a father that loved me and cared about me. This movie started when I was a young boy on the farm. Somehow he had been looking for me and wanted me to be with him. In some odd way this was all a mistake, and he would make it better. He was the guy who wanted to play catch and teach me about life. This movie had a fairy-tale happy ending.

I dialed the number on my phone and waited. Ring. Sweat began to cover my body. Ring. Anxiety led me to question the logic of this. Ring. Somehow I couldn't hang up. Panic pumped through my veins as the words "hang up" circled the back of my mind, and I knew that at any moment this anticipated conversation that I had somehow dreaded for so long would reach the point of no return. I reassured myself with words of my therapist in my head. I didn't want to, but I had to face my fears, my pain, and the cause of the wounds in my soul.

"Hello." He answered as if somehow he had been anticipating the conversation was coming. On the phone we exchanged pleasantries and small talk with a hint of distance. A part of me felt drawn to fill the missing pieces inside me with that voice on the other end of the receiver, but could I trust in him? Could I run from the chance to mend the broken little boy that lived inside me? Which movie would play out if I did? Meeting him and getting to know him would bring one of the movies to life and would kill the other. Losing the dream of a loving father was almost as scary as facing the source of the years of pain in my soul.

Standing on the edge of no return, I agreed to meet at his house, back in that city where it all began. It might have been wiser to meet someplace neutral, but I had to know who he was, what was he like, and if there was a piece of me in there someplace. So I threw caution to the wind and agreed.

During the conversation I discovered another troubling fact that resonated with me. He had a new family. He had married the woman who held the gun and delivered the blows with the lead pipe, and he raised her kids in my place. They had married while in prison. She would be at the house as well. The logic of the situation and advice from any reasonable person would have been to take it slow and maybe rethink what I'd be getting into, but I didn't have logic. I had a need for answers to who I was and what I'd struggled against for so long. I had a hole in my heart that desperately needed filling, and I had to take a chance.

It was a long drive that filled my mind with memories, dreams, and desires all mixed together in anticipation of meeting this stranger who somehow had a grip on me. The memories of the pain moved to the background. The dreams of the father I desired flooded my mind. Who was this person? Am I somehow spiritually connected with him? Does he know my heavenly Father like I do? Will I be disappointing to him in some disturbed way? Will meeting him fill the missing pieces within me or explain them? The emotions ran deep as the miles slowly paced by.

The optimism swirled with skepticism at every stop. When I'd pause for refueling or food, my mind would try to change its direction. My thoughts kept steering me back home. Maybe he was the person the papers talked about. Maybe I was losing the father I dreamt of. Maybe I was losing my mind.

Then my mind seemed to move into slow motion when I reached his neighborhood and turned down his street. The long drive fell into the background, and it felt like an eternity had passed when I pulled up to the driveway. Seeing the home where he lived caused me to suddenly view time in extreme slow motion. The driveway felt like it was miles long as I seemingly traveled at a snail's pace. It felt like a year had passed by the time I stopped the car and opened the door to step onto the walk. Moving forward, I began to feel heavy, with each step harder than the last. There was still time to run from my fears. I could have turned around at any moment.

Finally the bell rang, but all I could hear was my heart pounding in my chest. The sound drowned out all background noise while I waited for the occupants of the home to respond. Maybe he wouldn't be home. Maybe I could just turn around and drive back the six-plus hours it took me to get there. Maybe, maybe . . . The doorknob turned, and then the door slowly opened.

A stranger stood in the doorway. He cordially invited me in while inquiring about my drive. After he introduced his wife, we sat in the living room, where he told me about his recent activities, his business, and the life his new family was living. He avoided any conversation about the past. I wasn't sure who this person was; yes, he was my father, but he was also a stranger that I could have passed on the street and not recognized. I discovered he had spent two years in prison but details of the last 20 years remained fuzzy.

He seemed to have just picked up his life and went on without me. He lived in a nice home and appeared to have a good life, but where was he over the past two decades? Why didn't he look for me? What had happened to the people of the church we left when I was a kid? Did they still live nearby? What was the screenplay of the movie in the back of my mind going to do with this? There seemed to be no sudden answers or revelations to put all of the pieces together with. I tried to understand and observe. I looked for the missing pieces where I should have fit into this seemingly unobtainable life that I dreamed of, but the puzzle didn't fit. I wasn't sure who I was supposed to be in the conversation. Was I the lost little boy running home to my loving father who missed me? Was I the observer hiding behind a wall looking for a safe exit? Or was I simply someone recognizing that I was playing with my own puzzle pieces? Could it be that my dad didn't have anything to contribute to the missing puzzle pieces of my journey to heal?

The meeting ended quickly enough, and I was back on my way home to the desert. But I kept asking myself what had happened. The visit was cordial, like visiting a distant relative, but it wasn't the height of my emotional journey. The meeting didn't heal anything inside me or change who I'd become. The meeting didn't even answer the questions that had haunted me for nearly two decades. Should I have overlooked the lack of forgiveness or acknowledgment of the missing years, or even the event that had caused all of this? I had a father, and that was all I could think of, but the realities troubled me. The grand moment had come and gone. The moment I had projected in my dreams for so long had played out with little fanfare, drama, or healing.

Maybe finding my earthly father had more to do with closure than completeness. Maybe the father I needed to find all along was the one living inside me, the one who journeyed with me through all of this mess. The Father who carried me as a broken child, and watched over my big sister and little brother, the one whom my mom prayed to and pointed us toward was my dad all along. The God of the universe was really so much more than some far away being. The journey to heal the scars was actually a journey to my true Father, my heavenly Father. He carried my mom and took care of her through all of those years as she never lost sight of him. He directed my sister on her journey to a ministry with her husband pastoring a church of their own. He never left my little brother through hard times like mine, and led him to become a youth pastor. And he led me here to find him. How could I not accept him as my dad now that I realized he had always been my Father all along, and never abandoned me?

Over the course of a few years I continued in therapy along with growing in my healthy state of mind. I went back and visited my earthly father from time to time and began noticing events that seemed odd. He still appeared as a leader, and people still loved to follow him. In addition to running his own businesses, he was always trying to start a new independent church. There always seemed to be a flock of people around him, although the size was much smaller than the church he pastored when I was a kid, and the faces of the flock often changed. After he was done with them, he seemed to always have a story to justify their "excommunication" from his circle of followers. There often seemed to be a story to justify his turning against them. He would create rumors to make them look like they did something evil and somehow deserved what was happening. The presence of my heavenly Father seemed to be missing in the middle of all of this activity. I began to feel conflicted between what I was observing and learning from my earthly father and the moral compass instilled in me by my heavenly Father.

I witnessed my dad con another local pastor into loaning him money that amounted to the pastor's life savings. The funds were to be used for some short-term business deal, but then he refused to repay the pastor. He justified it by telling stories of the pastor's immorality. Things were never black and white with him; he always lived in a shade of gray where the shade was always in his favor. He seemed to be trying to "work the system," whether it involved other business dealings or even being honest about his debts. I tried to justify what I saw and tried to project the best of him through the image of the father I dreamed of. I actually loaned him money myself for a business he wanted to purchase, knowing I didn't feel comfortable about it. As I look back, I think I probably thought it would bring approval from him.

The little things he did amounted to choices of right and wrong, not different shades of gray. These choices grated on me as I grew healthier in my own identity with my heavenly Father. I began to realize the father I'd dreamed of didn't exist in my earthly father, and my real Father was calling on me to see things for what they really were. Somehow, I couldn't say no to my earthly dad. He had a control that grew over me, compelling me to do whatever he expected.

After a couple of years I finally came to the realization that I didn't want to know my earthly father any longer. I didn't want to be like him or have him influence my life or anyone I knew. So I cut off all connection and walked away. The man I had met was very different from the dreams and desires of my childhood. I realized that only one could fill the father role in my heart. There was only one who knew my dreams and my pains, and only one who could heal me.

The dreams of my earthly father were mere projections that couldn't be met by a human. I discovered that there really is a Father out there who loves me unconditionally. There is one who would take me into his family and call me his son, and all I had to do was ask. The movie that played in my head ended when I met my earthly father. The theater in my mind faded when it was replaced with reality. I had to take the chance that I did, but I didn't have to live in the fantasy. The pain inside me was healing, and the hole in my heart was mending. A new life was springing from inside me because of the Father I already knew. My heavenly Father never left me. He had never been a stranger and always waited with open arms when I wandered away. He put me back together in a way that no one else could. Trying to fill the hole in my heart with my earthly father didn't fit. The father I sought turned out to be the Father I had all along. My heavenly Father led me through the pain on a journey to face my past and then heal it.

There is no one like my heavenly Father, my true dad, whose presence is indescribable in a truly phenomenal way. I learned that

I loved him more than I could have ever imagined, and can't wait to see him face-to-face someday. At that moment in my life things began to change as I determined to embrace my true Father.

///

Buzzzz. After barely long enough for me to drift off since the last blast of announcements over the public announcement speakers, my cell door lock opened and my number echoed against the cold, hard walls. Startled by the sound of the number that now identified me in this hellish place, slightly confused, and coming out of a moment of uneasy sleep, I jumped to my feet. I hadn't been allowed to communicate with the outside world. The phone bank was dead every time I was able to check it. I had cleaned out my bank account to acquire an attorney; maybe I was going to be able to talk with him?

The stale orange lights were still dim, giving the appearance of night within the aquarium. I waited by the door, standing on the painted lines on the floor. Everywhere I went it was drilled into me to walk on the line painted on the floor. Leaving the line became a crime deserving of jail guard punishment. In a state of mayhem I was led down several long quarters that seemed to never end, until I arrived at a series of holding rooms full of other disheveled men like myself. Some were lying on the dirty floor in exhaustion, while others huddled to themselves, merely glancing up as I was ushered in.

What seemed like hours later, after having been in numerous holding rooms, I was loaded into another filthy boarded-up bus. This time the mood was more somber, with most of the occupants barely awake. The wonderful ray of light that had passed through the slit at the top of the window in the first bus was blocked in this one. The caged occupants and armed guards were much the same as they had been in the first, in addition to the chains and wrist pain.

Upon arriving at our destination, I quickly discovered that I was in a different place than I'd been before. The holding cells were prehistorically old and dark. If ever I'd been asked to describe a dungeon, this would be it. The inmates were rough, and the walls appeared to be held together by the numerous layers of grime that seemed to have grown on every surface over decades of neglect. The holding rooms seemed just as bad, but they were better than the abusive guards and strip searches between rooms. Nonetheless, after hours of moving from dungeon cell to dungeon cell, between the guards yelling and abuse, I was finally packed into a small crowded room. This time there was a tiny mesh corner in the room that couldn't have been larger than three feet by three feet around a door.

I found a tight corner where I could lean against a wall to avoid leaning on the gang members and other rough-looking characters who occupied the same space. In the corner I met a guy who was bandaged heavily in several places and was sitting on the floor. After I learned that he had been in this room on several occasions, I was informed that this was where you went before seeing the judge. I also learned that I needed to watch my back due to the violent nature of some of the other occupants.

The gentleman I met told a story of being in the wrong place at the wrong time. Apparently his house was mistakenly marked as a crack house. One evening he was watching television in his living room when the door burst open and several Los Angeles police rushed in shooting. He was shot several times. Nothing was found in the house, and he was unarmed and left for dead. He was revived when the paramedics arrived. Now with multiple bullet wounds, he was being held in that place while an investigation took place. In the meantime he had lost his job and had no one to watch his house or make sure his bills were paid. He also didn't have money for an attorney.

I wondered what ever happened to the idea of innocent until proven guilty. Can innocent mean incarcerated until some judge decides he is ready to let you go? What about public defenders? Or was justice just for the rich, and this was all just some moneymaking venture contrived by the government?

After a while I noticed people dressed in suits standing in the caged mesh calling out inmate names—not impersonal numbers, but actual names. It didn't take long before my name was called by a well-dressed lady. Squeezing my way through the crowd, I was finally able to press myself up against the mesh just inches from another guy talking to what appeared to be his attorney.

The lady turned out to be my public defender. It was hard to hear her in the confusion of the room, with multiple conversations taking place, all within inches of each other. With inmates pressed up against one side of the mesh and attorneys shoulder to shoulder on the opposite side, conversations were hard to follow. She explained that there was some issue in Colorado, and a warrant had been put out for my arrest, making me a fugitive. I explained that I'd never been in trouble before; I didn't even have a single traffic or parking ticket. She continued to inform me that California could hold me for months while they decided whether or not I would be extradited to Colorado. They would have to evaluate the case before releasing me.

What?! I couldn't stay in jail for months; I had to get out of there. I had a job and a family to take care of. I needed to get home. She said not to count on it. They might release me if Colorado would come and get me, but she said not to expect anything. My hopes were dashed to the floor until she said she would contact my wife to see if she had any information. All I could say was "please," and I uttered the phone number between tearful sniffles.

As she left the cage, I fought with everything I had to hold it together. Was I doomed to this place? What was driving this mess from Colorado? Moments later she returned. "I talked to your wife; I told her you were doing okay. She is shaken up. In a while you'll be called to appear in front of the judge. The judge will ask if you are pleading guilty or not."

"What?! How can I plead anything? I don't even know what I'm being charged with."

"Okay, you're going to be fine, so just hold it together a little longer. You will get through this."

While I was being pushed out of the way and back into the crowd by other inmates, my attorney slipped out. Moments later the bailiff opened the door and called my name. I was led into the tight caged space and then down a corridor that opened into another caged space in the courtroom. In the new space I could see the courtroom through the bars as I stood next to the bailiff. My public defender stood outside the cage addressing the judge. I didn't really understand the legal jargon being used, and the judge had little interest in hearing me say anything, so my presence seemed almost useless.

In despair I was finally led back down the hall to another holding cell, where I waited with other inmates for hours. I waited with no answers to my questions. I couldn't even recall what the judge was asking me. I was just told to say yes or no on cue; then I was left to drown in this deadly sea of sharks.

///

A small sports car rolled away from a large Southern California home and stopped, getting lost in the dust trail from the long driveway. Pausing for a moment, the man behind the wheel dropped his head into his hands in disappointment and then looked up toward heaven. With a vroom the car shifted into gear and drove away, picking up speed as it traveled. In the settling dust a glowing being could be seen alongside the car, and another was sitting in the passenger's seat.

Perched across the street in an old barn hidden from the waning light of the day, a shadowy figure of a dragon gripped tightly onto a toolbox. Anger pulsed through the sharp talons of the sinister creature. The creature shook the toolbox violently, spewing tools from its neatly arranged drawers. Among the mess of tools strewn across the floor, a host of evil creatures darted back and forth, fearing the wrath of the dragon.

"Drach, do you want me to chase the car? I can tempt him again."

"*No!* You idiot, the angels grow stronger, and they'll just defeat you anyway."

The dragon peered with slits of fiery green eyes at his minions and hissed. "I don't get it. He was following his dad's lead. He was learning the ways of deceit and manipulation. He was ready to follow in the footsteps of ego and self-preservation. *What happened!?*"

He peered back at the house as the shadow of the day faded into the early darkness of night. Lights started shining through the windows as Drach paced back and forth.

"We are sadists; we feed on these humans because we hate them and desire to annihilate them." Stopping to glance at his minions, he continued, "We thrive on their suffering. We rule this world. This is why our leader the great serpent deceived them in the first place. They are like our enemy, the Light. They can be loving and caring if the Light lives in them—yuck, makes me puke just thinking about it!" Continuing his pacing, Drach scratched the floor with his sharp talons while speaking. "We live for nothing less than inflicting pain on these ugly and despicable creatures. Eradication is the only option I give them, but one at a time in as much pain as possible. Yes, we shall feast on them, tearing them apart slowly piece by piece with no escape from the pain. We will peel their flesh and torment their soul for eternity. And, yes, I have won this right by deceiving many humans. So why are my tactics not working now? What would the great serpent do in this case?"

From the darkest shadows a deep, angry voice rattled the barn. "Maybe you should distract him."

Shaken, Drach jumped to attention, with his peering slits of eyes growing wider.

"Yes, Drach, get him sent someplace where he can't cause me any trouble for a while. Isolate him and let him wallow in the scars I inflicted on him years ago."

Squinting, Drach cautiously addressed the presence filling the barn. "My chief, I did not know we were in your presence."

Chief Demon stepped out of the shadows, peering at the gathering. "Your tactics must he more devious. Find a weakness and exploit it. In the short term, get him out of my way. He is affecting others and damaging my grip on other victims. More important, he is impacting our kingdom of darkness."

Pausing for effect, Chief Demon let his words sink in before continuing. "He keeps calling on his heavenly Father. This is your biggest problem; you have to stop that, or you'll never be able to effectively attack."

Stepping backward, Drach tripped over a large wrench. "But, Chief Demon, we are trying."

Shaking his pointed horns in disbelief, Chief Demon raised his stretched leather wings. "I have others to deal with. You are making my job more difficult than it needs to be." Raising a sharp talon in the air, Chief Demon pointed at the dust cloud trailing down the road. "Go follow that car, and do the job I assigned to you."

Bowing in place, Drach responded, "Yes, my chief." Then he turned and skimmed across the ground as quickly as he could, followed by his dark minions.

21

Alien Sands

No ruler or king can keep God from his plans.

For the LORD Most High is awesome, the great King over all the earth.
                                    —Psalm 47:2 (NIV)

God reigns over the nations; God is seated on his holy throne.
                                    —Psalm 47:8 (NIV)

I always found it interesting how life was made of complex intertwining threads of activity as opposed to a single linear path consisting of one problem and resolution at a time. I'm glad that my heavenly Father has always understood the complex tapestry, because my life always seemed to be a tightly woven rug intermixed with the threads of battles and dark moments that were out of my control. My heavenly Father often seemed to be the only thing holding the tapestry together, and he somehow added beauty and form to what otherwise would have been chaos unraveling at every corner. Life began to be more about the thread of Light that my heavenly Father provided to light my way through the darkness, than the darkness itself that regularly stood in front of me.

Transitioning from the obsession to heal from the scars of my earthly father to the freedom of my heavenly Father was liberating. My focus began changing, and the idea of a future free of my childhood pain seemed possible. The new thread of healing God put in my life started taking me in a new direction. Although I didn't know where it would lead, I didn't care as long as he was guiding the way.

I began working on my engineering degree, and it wasn't long before I was offered a job in Los Angeles with a company that sent me to a faraway and at times very dark place. I can remember the day I packed everything I owned in a rented storage space. I parked my new 300Z in a friend's garage and, with my passport in hand, I boarded a plane to the opposite end of the earth. I was light as a feather and free from this dark world. The weight of this world seemed to lose its grip as I left the tarmac out of Los Angeles headed to an unknown hostile environment. My heavenly Father's direction was just enough to take one step at a time, but that was all I needed.

The excitement waned as the twenty-fourth hour of grueling travel passed. After a quick stop in Amsterdam followed by refueling in Abu Dhabi, the journey seemed to finally end when we landed on a lonely runway in the wee hours of the morning. Feeling exhausted, I grabbed my bag and made my way to the open aircraft door with the other passengers, only to be met with the reality that I wasn't in the West anymore.

A row of AK47-clutching soldiers made a path for the passengers to cross the runway. The path stopped at a mysterious metal building in the distance. After locating my luggage in a pile of bags that seemed to have been dumped from the airplane onto the tarmac, I carried what I had to the mysterious building in the distance. Inside the building, there was no friendly face to say, Welcome to Saudi Arabia. I was met by a stern Arab gentleman who opened my suitcase and then proceeded to dump it upside down on a table in a matter-of-fact way. He sifted through the contents with great fervor and then yelled "next" when he had finished with his task. My task was then obvious to the officer, but it took me a minute to get over the shock of seeing my belongings spread across a table before I caught on. I had thirty seconds to get my stuff off the table before the next suitcase would be dumped on the same table.

After gathering my disheveled belongings, I found a hotel near the King Fahd International Airport and settled in for a good night's rest. Although the eleven-hour time differential and jet lag took some effort to get accustomed to, my spirits were high. The traffic violation list I was given with my rental car was a bit alarming. All traffic violations came with penalties of riyals (the local currency), lashes with a cane, and other sorts of painful punishments depending on the type of violation. I found it a strange concept that the passengers would also receive the same punishment as the driver. I quickly learned that the painted lines and dividers on the road surface were merely for decoration. Locals were the most liberated of all drivers. They merely made sport of sidewalks, medians, and intersection lights. It was apparently everyone else's responsibility to stay out of their way. I later learned why.

A company attorney from the California office had been to Saudi Arabia just days before I arrived. He was there to review and sign some new project contracts. On his way back to the airport, a local Saudi man ran a stop sign from an alley and t-boned the attorney's rental car. The attorney quickly got out of the wrecked car, making it clear that everything was okay. He then stated the obvious: it was the Saudi's fault, and he was sure the Saudi's insurance would cover everything. However, the Saudi gentleman didn't see things the same way. He immediately educated the foreigner that it was his fault. When the local police arrived, they informed the attorney that the law made it his fault and he would have to pay for everything; plus he was lucky they didn't throw him in jail. They reasoned that if the attorney hadn't been in the country, the accident wouldn't have happened.

The office wasn't far from the airport. It was easy to find, since it was the only twelve-story building in town. My new office afforded me a grand view of the many shades of beige sand that blended the buildings into the landscape. The Persian Gulf added some blue to the scenery, but it still seemed to merge into the surroundings with its calm, almost motionless water.

I remember many things that were very different than those in the West. Things didn't seem to be well planned or designed, for the most part. The elevator in our building never opened level with the floor, often forcing everyone to crawl out. The stairs were not all the same height, causing people to trip occasionally. Road signs were often placed in the middle of a sidewalk at head level, creating a hazard for pedestrians. Roads didn't seem to align and often abruptly shifted, as if constructed by two different people who couldn't agree on where they should connect.

It felt like I had stepped back in time or landed on another planet. The year was different, the time was different, and the weeks were different. Thursday and Friday were the weekend. We worked six long days every week, which was a good thing, since there was nothing else to do. Other than the moving cars, there seemed to be little motion around the town. Pedestrians were scarce, and the buildings were surrounded by tall block walls. Privacy seemed to be of utmost importance to the inhabitants of this strange land. There were beautiful structures and boulevards near the beaches, but they were all completely void of people.

The guys in the office lived for their next opportunity to get out of the country for their next vacation, which came every three months. They had posters and travel brochures plastered to the walls in the offices, giving them something to look forward to. Our mail was opened and read by some mysterious government agency. They blotted ink through anything they didn't like, including photos. One of my coworkers received a photo of his family having a gathering in their backyard. The plastic cups they were holding were all scratched out; apparently the mysterious government agency thought they had some alcoholic beverage in them. The ladies wearing shorts had their legs marked out, and all of the ladies' arms were blacked out with permanent markers. The long hours of work coupled with an absence of communications from family and friends wore on many of my coworkers. The only contacts with the outside world were letters or phone calls. Letters took weeks or months to arrive, and the phone was highly ineffective and problematic to use with the eleven-hour time difference. If you did get up in the middle of the night to make a call, the odd thirty-second delays made it difficult to know when to speak and when to listen. The clicking made it apparent that uninvited guests were listening to all conversations, so you never knew if you were saying something that might get you in trouble.

There were so many things that were illegal and came with stiff penalties that it was hard to know if you were doing something wrong. Assembling for church or being a believer in Jesus was one of the most unforgivable crimes. Religious police walked the shopping areas with large sticks in hand. The shopping areas (called *souqs*) seemed to be the only place where people gathered. Public speakers mounted high on poles all over town blurted out Islamic prayers five times a day. If you were in the streets and not bowing to the east when the prayers started, the religious police would hit you with their sticks until you did. I didn't go out during the Islamic prayer times. The presence of my heavenly Father wasn't in the prayers, and I couldn't bow or pray to a stranger.

There was a spattering of underground churches that existed. I attended several times, enjoying the same presence of my heavenly Father that I'd experienced throughout my life. It was amazing to experience God with people from all over the globe whom I'd never met before, and yet the presence of my heavenly Father was the same as it was in the West. Some of the gatherings were large. Yet attending put your life at risk.

During my time in-country one underground gathering of Christ followers was raided, and people were arrested. About a dozen men from Western countries were detained for a few days and then paraded through the airport and deported. There were others who were not in the same class as the Westerners and came to a different fate. Although being beaten with a cane or whip and kept in a dungeon wasn't pleasant, the non-Western workers paid a far greater price. It was posted in the local newspaper that the non-Western workers had denounced Mohammed, which was punishable by death. Some of them ended up at Dammam Square, while others were just never heard from again. I stayed away from the square on Thursdays, even if I needed to go to the souq for any reason.

On Thursday afternoons in Dammam Square, punishments were carried out. If you were in the souq area near Dammam Square, the religious police would force you to gather and watch. Some punishments were for theft, which could cost a hand, or gazing at a woman without her *abaya* or *niqab* (her veil) could cost an eye. But the most shameful of offenses, which required beheading, was to denounce Mohammed (or in other words, accept Jesus as the Christ). There were many beheadings during my stay in the Saudi kingdom, which made Thursdays a day to avoid the souq.

Living in a class-oriented society was bizarre for someone who had grown up in the West, where "all men are created equal." The classes had many tiers. Those near the bottom could be hit by a local's car, and the local wouldn't even bother to stop. If there was a wait at a store or restaurant, they would always pick you out of the line based on your class. Women were owned property that didn't have a class and couldn't travel without a male relative. They couldn't be seen and remained covered at all times. In restaurants there was always a family section with curtains around each booth so they could unveil and eat. All the men had to eat in a different part of the establishment. Women were rarely seen and never heard from.

Westerners were second class at that time due to the Gulf War that was in progress, or we would have been much lower. It was foreign to see my newly acquired friends be treated so poorly at times just because they originated from other parts of the world. Even so, the presence of my heavenly Father was strong with many of my friends.

I was there during the first Gulf War after Iraq invaded Kuwait. U.S. fighter jets would scrape the buildings, shaking the office many times a day en route to Kuwait. There was a U.S. Air Force base outside of Dhahran not far from where I lived. I wasn't doing any work with the military at the time. I was working on gas/oil separation plants, which gave us a front-row seat to the world events taking place. The only exciting entertainment while I was there was watching the scud missiles lobbing through the skies at night. The lawn chairs would often come out as residents watched the light show streaking through the air. The missiles didn't prove to be very accurate, which was good, since we were living in the target zone. I still have pictures of myself packed away someplace in my basement with me standing next to exploded scud missiles.

I lived outside of Dhahran with the guys I worked with, in a less-developed place called Al Khobar. The streets and buildings bore the likeness of a third-world country. My one-room apartment was in a lightly guarded complex for expatriates. It was mostly populated with Europeans, Australians, and Americans. The complex was built much the same as the surrounding area. I often wondered what the architect was thinking when they put the air-conditioning units protruding at head level over the sidewalk. With no lights on the walkway, I'm sure many who lived there had collisions and never even saw the obstructions in the moonlight.

My room was a small windowless square. The lack of windows provided some relief from the piercing heat, which made Phoenix in the summer feel tepid. There were a few occasions when I was able to get out of the mundane work routine.

The office crew loaded up one morning in a bus headed to one of the project construction sites. The opportunity to get out was welcomed when I boarded. We drove for hours on endless sand-covered desert roads. Occasional Bedouins dotted the landscape between the compounds of homes. The houses were walled in with tall block enclosures. From behind the walls large castles of homes protruded out with several smaller homes appearing in the rear. When I asked, the bus driver informed me that the small homes were for the wives. The walls were for their privacy.

A few hours into the jaunt in some deserted location, the bus unexpectedly stopped in the middle of the road. Upon peering down the aisle and out the front window, I noticed cars lined up in front of a blockade. A group of armed soldiers stood in front of the roadblock. In Saudi Arabia everyone had to carry an *Agama* at all times, which is similar to a passport. It identified who you're related to, where you were allowed to travel, and other pages of information about the carrier. Traveling without an Agama was immediate cause for arrest, and those arrested often were never seen again.

The bus driver instructed us to have our Agamas ready for inspection. I reached into my pockets only to notice an empty space. My stress level began to rise as I realized that my Agama was still sitting back in my apartment. My informing the bus driver created a burst of Arabic expressions I could only presume came from distress. The driver would be in as much trouble as I would. In an animated fashion he turned and ordered everyone to be calm and not to make eye contact with the solders. He darted out the door waving his hands while riddling off words in a language I couldn't begin to understand.

Moments later an armed soldier walked slowly around the bus, peering at each occupant through the windows one at a time. My heart pounded even harder when he opened the door and boarded the bus. Not sure where our driver had disappeared to, I began to wonder how far from nowhere we were, and what was going to happen next. I focused on the seat in front of me as the guard eyed each person one at a time. As suddenly as he entered the bus, he turned and left. Hearing something that sounded like arguing outside, I waited and quietly talked with my Father asking him to keep me safe. Then the driver returned and slowly drove the bus away. I didn't know what had happened, but I knew God was involved and I was glad it was over.

In the middle of a dry desert land where men tried to ban God, my heavenly Father took care of me and walked with me daily. I saw wonderful sights like the causeway to Bahrain and biblical places like Hofuf, where few Westerners had ever been. I saw blinding sandstorms, deadly desert spiders the size of your hand, and a culture in rapid transition. But the most memorable experience was sharing the presence of God with other followers from all over the world. We professed no religion, no denominations or rituals; we just shared the same presence and knew the same Father. My heavenly Father, who welcomed me into his family, knew me long before I knew him. My new friends were part of that same family and knew him as I did. Being part of the same family brought instant camaraderie, even in the most distant places on earth.

Eventually I was led into a series of holding cells, again with different inmates in each. Many of the rooms had old pay phones mounted to the walls, but none of them seemed to work. There was nothing to do during the waiting, only time to think. Talking with the others was always done cautiously based on the conversations I'd had so far. The walls just seemed to close in slowly, hour after hour after hour. A sense of relief finally came over me when I was moved into a corridor and chained up for the bus ride to somewhere; anywhere would have seemed better. At that moment I had become numb to the abusive guards. I just thought about my journey through life and mentally blocked them out.

The bus ride was uneventful and quiet. Most occupants were absorbing the bad news they had received from the judge. Many were crying, some had a look of disbelief pasted on their face, and a few seemed unfazed, as if this was just another daily routine.

Back at the Twin Towers jail, I walked through the in-processing routine deadened to the environment that surrounded me. During the yelling and humiliation my mind looped the words of my public defender: "You could be in here for a while." I had stood before the judge, and still no one would give me any answers. I was told that I was a fugitive, but I had no idea why. I don't think I was ever really arrested; no one read me my rights or explained anything. I was just cuffed and taken away. If I had been put in prison for some noble cause, I could have handled that much better, but my family were now suffering and the only thing I could remember doing was getting too busy. I had ignored them and my heavenly Father lately, and I had not been the husband or dad I should have been. I remember surrendering to God once again and asking him to forgive me for the way I'd been. I begged of my Father to please help me if there was any way I could get out of there. I wanted him to hear me, and most of all I wanted to feel his presence again.

Upon returning to the cell block behind the walls of the unbreakable glass that was referred to as the aquarium, I decided to make one last attempt at the phone bank on the wall. After I'd checked the first couple of phones, my hopes were waning. Then one of the phones had a dial tone! I dialed my home number as fast as I could. I waited through the recordings, and then Holly's voice filled my ear. I did everything I could to hold back the tears while she talked. "Kevin, our attorney has been talking to the Colorado district attorney, and I have some information."

Eagerly pressing my ear against the receiver, I could hear her continue. "This whole ordeal does have something to do with our company when we went bankrupt. A former client of ours apparently filed a complaint against you. It was the Harrigans."

"For what? They owed our company money when it went under. They stiffed us for over a hundred grand. How can they file a complaint against me? Besides, although I was the president, I was an employee of the corporation."

"They are claiming that one of their subcontractors didn't get paid. I'm being told that according to the law, apparently we have no claim against them for the money they owe the company. The government acquired all of the company stock in the bankruptcy, so they own everything now. However, if any of the subs didn't get paid, the owners of the corporation are liable."

"But we paid the subs."

"Unless something got missed in accounting when the business closed? The accountant was let go abruptly along with everyone else."

"This doesn't make sense. What do they want? Do they want money?"

"They are angry, and it sounds like they want more than money; they want you to suffer."

"But what did I do to them?"

"Kevin, it sounds like the crash in the economy forced them into bankruptcy too, and they're blaming you for it."

"That's crazy. How much are we talking about? I have to get out of here so I can go back to work and at least start making money to pay this debt."

"It's not that simple. The amount is about $15,000, but the Harrigans want a million dollars and then they will agree to drop the charges."

"What? They are crazy. Who do they think I am? We don't have a million dollars. We are barely back on our feet from bankruptcy ourselves."

"Kevin, I don't know what to do. Our attorney is trying to work with the district attorney to get you bail. All we can do is pray. I have asked everyone I know to pray. This is going to take a miracle."

Click, buzz. The phone went dead, and I dropped the receiver in shock.

///

"This is your captain speaking. We have just left Saudi air space." With a cheer, passengers immediately flung off abayas and niqabs, revealing their fine clothing underneath. The liberated occupants began ordering drinks all around. Flight attendants unlocked the liquor cabinet and roamed the aisles with bottles of champagne and mixed drinks.

In the dim evening lights of the plane cabin, a dark, sinister creature resembling a dragon sat in an empty first-class seat. Hideous creatures crawled over the plush leather seats and floors between the passengers. Slithering through the seats, a creature with the head of a bird, the scaly body of a lizard, and the face of a dog crawled into the seat next to Drach.

"Drach, we've had a good stay here in Saudi Arabia. Aren't you worried about our human going back to the States after Chief Demon said to keep him away from there?"

Looking smug, Drach flashed a hateful sneer. "I don't think so. This is only a temporary thing. It is a technical detail, and that is all it is. Our allies are working on the renewal of his work visa to keep him in Saudi Arabia. He'll be back in a month or two."

"How can you be so sure?"

"Humans are not as smart as we are. It is his heavenly Father that keeps getting in the way. We are no match for him. So keep the human away from his Father, and we'll be fine. This paperwork thing is just a minor hiccup."

"But, Drach, he did manage to avoid us in that gathering of believers, even after we tipped off the mutaween (religious police) about that underground gathering of Christ followers who worship our enemy, the Light."

Growing angry at the comments, Drach peered with his burning eyes at the dark creature sitting next to him. "I told the mutaween where to find him, and he was supposed to have been there when they raided that place. It was a mere issue of timing. That's all it was. Once he returns, we'll get him. Don't worry. I have many friends in the Middle East, and his God is not welcome there."

"No offense, Drach, but what if this causes a problem back in Southern California?"

Furious, Drach shredded the seat cushion with his sharp talons. "I will have this human! I will have him arrested for his faith in our enemy when he returns to Saudi Arabia! I'll have him beheaded at a minimum, which should please Chief Demon. But mark my words, I'll greet this human in hell if I have my way."

"Yes, Drach. I didn't mean to upset you."

The dark creature leaned over the armrest and gazed down the aisle away from Drach. Looking down the aisle toward the general seating in the back of the plane, he saw the glow of an angelic being standing in the aisle with sword drawn, causing him to shiver. Fighting off the shiver, he growled ferociously from the safe distance of the first-class cabin. Then he turned around and started biting the passenger in front of him as the passenger rubbed his neck in pain.

22

New Life

The simple joy of experiencing our heavenly Father
comes through humble faith like that of a child.

But those who hope in the LORD will renew their
strength. They will soar on wings like eagles; they
will run and not grow weary, they will walk and
not be faint.

—Isaiah 40:31 (NIV)

Give thanks to the Lord, for he is good; his love
endures forever. Some wandered in the desert
wastelands, finding no way to a city where they
could settle. Then they cried to the Lord in their
trouble, and he delivered them from their distress.

—Psalm 107:1, 4, 6 (NIV)

After many months in a place where standing for what you
believed, what you knew to be true in the core of your soul, was
punishable by death, I pondered what was important in my life. I
had a renewed vision of life and a lack of trepidation about what
lay ahead. The worries of this life were miles from my mind. My
return to the West would be for a couple of months while my
two-year work permit was being approved. I would then return
to the spiritual wasteland I just had left. Living and walking daily
with my heavenly Father gave me new life and a freedom from the
pain I used to carry.

After a short stop in Holland, I was en route to Los Angeles, where I would wait. But God had other plans, plans beyond my wildest dreams that I couldn't have anticipated.

I had sent a letter ahead of me asking a friend to pick me up at the airport, but when I arrived no one was there. *Odd,* I thought. I got a cab to my friend's house, where I'd left my car. When I arrived, there was a For Rent sign in the window, and the home was empty. A little freaked out, I walked to a hotel for the night, but I couldn't sleep. At 2:00 a.m. I was wide awake, with my body clock in another time zone. I wandered the streets of Pasadena talking with my heavenly Father and asking him to lead me, and to get my car back. I asked him to direct my life and take me where he wanted me to go next.

When the sun finally showed its face, I called the number on the For Rent sign. The landlord met me at the house where I'd left my car. He was quite surprised when he opened the garage and there sat my 300Z with a note that read, "We had to move for my job." To my delight I was there just days before the new renter took the house. I had transportation, and most of all I had my heavenly Father leading the way, so off I went.

God put my life back together over a period of time and then filled me with a joy I'd never experienced. Things that would have stressed me before seemed less important. With my heavenly Father leading, things seemed to fall into place in often unexplainable ways. Shortly after returning I found a great apartment, got involved at Lake Avenue Community Church, and met some friends. The company I worked for didn't have a position for me in the States, so I didn't have a job, but God provided. The money I'd saved while I was in Saudi Arabia was enough to carry me through that time. I spent time relaxing and going to the gym and the beach, and I hung out with my new friend, Austin, from church.

Austin was a rugged, construction-savvy guy with a kind, creative heart. Having a lot of similarities in our personal backgrounds, we instantly became good friends. We formed a bond of friendship that would resurface years later at a very crucial time in both our lives.

I became very involved with my church for the summer. I was a big kid for a season and had fun in everything I did. I felt emotionally healthy for the first time. My Father gave me a freedom I'd never experienced before.

Something else happened during this time in my life, something that I wasn't expecting. It was a Saturday night at a church singles social event where they selected members from the audience to play the dating game. I was selected along with several others, which seemed like a fun idea at the time. The event was engaging, and somehow I won, but someone in the audience really caught my attention. I ended up talking with the person in the audience immediately after the event. We talked nonstop for the rest of the evening, as if no one else was around. Before we knew it, everyone had gone home and we were still sitting there.

The people who had to close up that evening finally interrupted us. They told us that everyone else had gone, and it was getting late, so we needed to leave as well. I hadn't noticed the hours that slipped away or the others leaving while I enjoyed the company of my new acquaintance.

Holly was emotionally stable like I had become, and we loved spending time with each other. It was strange and wonderful to have a best friend who knew my heavenly Father like I did. At that time I had joined the social committee for the singles group at Lake Ave Church. I needed some help and she was willing to join the team, so together we planned elaborate events and promotions for the singles in the group. It was a memorable time in my life that I would never forget. Several other friends had joined the team, including my good friend Austin. It was a spectacular time in my life.

Some of the group activities that we had planned became annual events even after I had left the group. A couple of the events included an elaborate ballroom dance called Moonlight Serenade and a holiday event called Christmas Around the World. This event involved people first gathering at the church parking lot, where five vans waited. Everyone picked a van they would ride in, not knowing the destination or what was coming next. Each van went to a different home or place where they interacted with people performing a live drama or skit about a different place in the world. After twenty minutes the vans would leave their destination and move on to the next interactive performance. At the end we had a large participant and cast Christmas party.

We reenacted a secret underground church celebrating Christmas in a hidden room, a poor family demonstrating a grateful attitude despite their situation, and a wealthy Western family focusing only on the gift aspect of Christmas, along with several other scenarios. It took large blocks of our time to dream up, plan, and execute these events. Holly and I realized we both had a great time doing these together; we enjoyed creative ventures and the fact that we had a lot in common.

As a nurse Holly worked long hours but only a few days a week, which gave us lots of time between the times she was on duty to plan events for the singles group. We'd have wonderful dinners in Old Town Pasadena, hang out at the beach, and explore. We loved going Rollerblading on the Strand down at Venice Beach. Some days we'd take the top off the 300Z and hit the road exploring for hours on the Pacific Coast Highway.

I had a circle of friends, but Holly found a special place in my life. On my thirtieth birthday Holly surprised me with a hot-air balloon ride over San Diego. Conversation was easy and so enjoyable. I purposely scheduled quiet time to be with my heavenly Father daily, and she completely understood and encouraged it. My Father took care of me continuously in so many ways, proving that he loved me.

I was eventually offered a job by another company in downtown Los Angeles. They gave me a grand office on the thirty-third floor, with views that seemed to go on forever. Everything seemed to be going wonderfully. I felt like I was dancing through this life, which once had been filled with so much turmoil and pain. The wounded soul that once lived in the festering depths of my spirit hidden behind the walls of my past had been freed. The scars remained, but the pain no longer lived in the darkness. I no longer felt haunted by my history but felt optimistic about my future. If only I could have lived the rest of my life in that moment—but God wasn't done with his plans for me yet. I had much to learn and journeys to take for reasons I wouldn't understand. My past now belonged to him, and I was enjoying my present, but life comes with an unpredictable future that can't be navigated alone.

Then, when I least expected it, the "phone call" came. It was the call that I originally had been waiting for, but now dreaded.

The call struck conflict inside of me when I was told my two-year extension in Saudi Arabia had been approved and I would be going back shortly. What would I do? The job in Saudi Arabia came with great financial benefits and a reunion with my fellow underground believers. If I stayed, I would have to deal with the fact that I didn't have a very good track record of being in long-term relationships. Although things were great at the moment, I didn't know what the future held. It had taken much longer than I had anticipated for the call to come, and I'd almost forgotten about it at that point. Holly had become such a big part of my life. Fear of making a wrong decision or a mistake that I might regret surfaced in my mind. The fear of ruining the wonderful life I'd so enjoyed with her over the past several months danced in my brain.

I'd been emotionally messed up for so long. But God had done so much in my life. I felt his presence right where I was; did he really want me to return to the desert? I asked him once again for direction in my life. I asked him to show me what I should do and where I should go. If he was leading me back to that wasteland, I would have to trust my Father and go. It wasn't all about the financial benefits or career advancement. I had learned that it wasn't about location or the things of this world; it was about my heavenly Father. After all, the future was in his hands, not mine.

If I returned to Saudi Arabia, Holly would not be coming with me, and I couldn't expect her to wait two years or more for my return. After spending a lot of time talking with my heavenly Father and meeting with my pastor, I felt the answer was clear. The answer would lead me down a new path in my life. The questions were serious ones that I had contemplated deeply, and I knew what I needed to do next.

It was another Saturday evening much like the night I met Holly. It was nearly a year after we had met when a friend of ours asked her to meet. The meeting came because they needed to talk about something, something serious that I couldn't do alone.

///

After what felt like minutes of restless sleep, I heard the public address system start blurting out announcements again. Somewhere in the middle of the muddled sound, I heard my inmate number blasted one more time. Not sure if I was dreaming or in some sort of cloudy haze, I slid off the bunk and made my way to the door as quickly as possible to avoid the wrath of the guards. Waiting on the painted line near the reinforced door, I could hear the clinking of keys preceded by a guard who unlocked the aquarium door. My cell door shook the dirty walls as it slammed open.

I was ordered to once again follow the endless painted lines on the floor down corridor after corridor through the stale orange light until I reached the familiar rows of holding cells. Once there I was ushered again into one cell after another. Other inmates spread across the concrete floor in exhaustion while waiting their turn in the next cell rotation. Eventually I was ordered to the hall with the rows of chains. After completing the process of being bound to another gang member covered in tattoos, I entered the boarded-up bus. The feeling of being cattle going to slaughter once again filled my mind as we were herded into place and caged into compartments.

The drive was barely memorable, as my brain seemed to go in and out of consciousness. The strip-down interrogations in the hallway once again came with the routine abuse and humiliation before I was ushered into the familiar small room with a meshed cage around the door. I remember trying to pray but being unable to get past "heavenly Father" before the words got lost someplace. Finding a dirty concrete bench to sit on I leaned my head against a wall discolored with filth and grime, and I must have drifted off for a few moments. I suddenly noticed the room had emptied to a small crowd of guys. Most of them huddled on the other side of the small room and surrounded a younger version of the familia leader I had met earlier. One of the Hispanic young men came over to me and said, "Hey, homie, what size shoes are those?"

Coming out of my daze and unclear of the purpose of the question, I quickly replied, "Eleven."

The young man walked back over to the crowd. Then the crowd seemed to open, with the leader sitting in the middle and everyone staring at me. Too exhausted to fully contemplate what might be going on, I just stared back. Another older member of the Hispanic gang approached me slowly, moving as if he was hopping on one of his legs in some strange walk. He looked at my jail shoes, and then his eyes pierced straight through me. He spoke with a heavy accent while pointing to the man in the middle of the crowd behind him.

"You need to show respect for Borracho, he *calaca*. He needs your shoes."

Rubbing my eyes, I looked up at him from my bench and replied, "What am I supposed to wear?"

"You're a wood. You can wear his shoes."

Looking at what the man in the middle had on his feet, I saw shredded, worn-out prison shoes. Feeling exhausted and cranky, I looked back up at the Hispanic man in front of me and simply said, "I don't think so."

The man threw up his arms almost as if in shock at my reply. He backed away slowly, simply uttering, "No respect . . . *trucha*."

(Unsure of the words, I later learned what they meant: trucha was prison gang slang for warning or watch your back, Borracho was a term used to describe a specific gang in prison, calaca meant murderer, and wood is what they called a white guy.)

As he was backing away, my public defender entered the mesh-caged corner of the room with an officer and called my name. Leaning into the mesh, she told me that my attorney in Colorado had worked a deal with the district attorney, and he was helping me get out of the Los Angeles Twin Towers jail. I had to call him as soon as I could to discuss the details. However, I had to go before the judge again to solidify that the State of California was going to let me go. I recall asking her why California would hold me in the first place; I had no issue in California. It seemed that my issue was in Colorado. She didn't respond to the question.

I was then escorted down the hall to the caged portion of the courtroom, where I stood next to the public defender in front of the judge. After hearing the public defender explain what the Colorado district attorney had asked for, followed by some political wrangling that I didn't understand, I was returned to the holding room that I came from. I wasn't completely sure of what had taken place, and all I could think about was finding a working phone to find out what was really going on.

My thinking changed quickly after the guard left and I realized the gang members were still behind me in the room. Thinking that I might be going home soon and desiring to live to see another day, I turned and walked up to the leader. In surprise the others stepped out of the way. I took off my shoes and handed them to him. With a big smile he removed his old shoes, traded them for mine, and simply said, "respect."

Walking back to my concrete bench, I noticed my public defender enter the mesh cage and call for me. "Kevin, do you have someone who can bring the money to the courthouse? They'll need a $60,000 check or bond before releasing you. If you don't show up in Colorado in three days, they'll keep the money."

My heart sank once again. "Sixty thousand dollars? I don't have $60,000. Even if I did have that kind of money, I live in Canada. How would I get it here in time to get out and get to Colorado in three days?"

"We may have a problem; you'd better call your attorney in Colorado." As she turned and left the room, all I could think of was how in the world I was supposed to call anyone from here.

///

In a dark parking garage tucked underneath a tall apartment building, something darted between the shadows of the parked cars. Indistinguishable figures threw silhouettes against a concrete wall as a maintenance worker flashed his truck headlights in their general direction. Stepping out of a company truck, a man in coveralls squinted in disbelief and then cautiously approached the potential intruder, or hint of a specter, in the corner. With skepticism he rounded the parked cars, noticing the shadows darting around. The shadows seemed to be on their own without a light source to generate the dark spots. As he slowly crept closer, a cold chill came over the man as the silhouettes seemed to stop in place. Almost motionless the maintenance man reached slowly for a large wrench on his tool belt.

A dark creature covered in stretched leather from pointed horns to a pointed tail, with claws like a leopard's, hung from the garage ceiling watching the interaction. Suddenly, it dropped from the ceiling, with fiery eyes hovering above the red outline of a mouth lined in pointed teeth protruding from a skinless skull. Filling the peripheral vision of the maintenance man with large bony wings, the creature lunged its face inches from the man's. Amid a hiss and a burst of red-hot vapor, the maintenance man went limp and fell to the ground in sheer terror. The creature circled the man, gnashing its teeth in a fearsome growl.

"Hey, play with your own human. You're here to report on what's going on with my human's paperwork. Why is it taking so long to get him a work visa? He is getting out of hand here, and I need to get him back to Al Khobar."

Speaking in slow, deliberate bursts, the creature turned its ribbed neck to face Drach. "I hate these humans. I can possess this one and attack your uncooperative victim if you'd like. I haven't been out of the desert for over two hundred years. The humans here don't seem so tough to me. If you appeared to them, I'm sure they would fold as this one did."

Shaking his head in annoyance, Drach stared at the creature. "You have been in the desert too long. The problem humans do not frighten so easily, and the presence of our enemy, the Light, is strong with them. Appearing to them only drives them closer to him. Now, answer my question and be on with your business."

Pacing closer to Drach, the creature retorted, "My, my, aren't we getting cranky; this human must really be getting under your scales. From where I'm from, we don't let our humans push us around."

"From where you're from, there aren't many angels either; the presence of our enemy is much stronger here."

Taken aback, the creature sat like a dog on its hindquarters. "Yes . . . I've felt their presence here. It has been a long time since I've felt this much power of the Light. I assume the angelic beings follow your human too?"

"More than you know. My human keeps calling on his heavenly Father every time I push him. I need to draw him away or distract him to make him vulnerable. The only other thing I can do is remove him from this physical realm before he does any more damage. Now, what is taking so long in Saudi?"

The creature shook his head in bewilderment and gazed at the ground. "Every time our Saudi Arabian humans send the paperwork, it gets lost or misplaced. It has been an effort to keep them filling out the paperwork over and over. I had some of my wraiths follow the paperwork, but they didn't return; there's no telling what mischief they got into. So tell me, what do you have planned when you get him back to Saudi? Beheading? I love the human torture at Dammam Square."

Losing interest in the conversation, Drach watched the driveway while replying, "Something like that, if not worse."

The creature gripped onto the maintenance man and seemed to climb inside of him. The man's eyes popped open, and he immediately got up and started walking away. Then he turned to Drach with a wink before getting into the truck.

As the truck drove out of the garage, a 300Z sports car drove in and found a parking space. The glow of angelic beings stood guard as an unaware couple stepped out in a carefree fashion and unloaded Rollerblades and beach gear. The two paused for only a moment and then went on their way to the elevator.

The hissing of creatures from somewhere in the shadows quietly rippled through the garage. In anger, Drach dragged the sharp hook on the tip of his wing down the side of a new luxury automobile. Tap, tap, tap. Startled by the familiar tapping of a talon on the ground, Drach froze, still scratching the side of the car.

"I am hearing reports that are not favorable."

Tucking his hook into his wings, Drach slowly turned with trepidation. "Chief Demon?"

"Yes, it is I. The human I have assigned to you has not fallen from the Light. He still walks this earth, and he is influencing others. Do you have any other bad news to give me?"

"Well, Chief Demon, he has a girlfriend who—"

Interrupting Drach, Chief Demon butted in. "Who also has her own strong angels? She also knows our enemy, their heavenly Father. I fail to see any reason to gloat in this fact."

"Yes, Chief Demon. I am working to get him back to Saudi Arabia, where our allies are strong. I am also working to get him away from this girlfriend. I will have him removed from this earth, even if I do not gain the pleasure of feasting on him in hell."

"You give in too easily, Drach. You must be deceitful, devious, and filled with pure hatred if you want to succeed. You have one more chance. I cannot afford to allow this one to affect others. Lull him into a false sense of security and pacify him. Keep him from talking to his heavenly Father, and do not allow him to discuss his heavenly Father with others. Do you understand?"

"Yes, Chief Demon. I will succeed with this victim as you have commanded."

Chief Demon smiled through the rotted skin on his face in a condescending manner before fading into the parking garage wall.

Drach shook the pointed horns on his head, scratched the horn on his nose, and then melted through the elevator door in pursuit of his victims.

23

Cruise of a Lifetime

The greatest gifts of this life are the things that last beyond this life.

Enter his gates with thanksgiving and his courts with praise; give thanks to him and praise his name.

—Psalm 100:4 (NIV)

For the Lord is good and his love endures forever; his faithfulness continues through all generations.

—Psalm 100:5 (NIV)

My friend was a friend of Holly's. She drove Holly to the Lighthouse restaurant, which was a favorite of ours on the pier in Long Beach. They sat down at a table overlooking the ocean and prepared to have a conversation about something serious, unknown to Holly. Holly innocently walked into the meeting with no knowledge of the outcome or the depth of contemplation that went into it.

After conversing with Holly for a few minutes, my friend excused herself for a moment. To Holly's amazement, I stepped out of the crowd and sat down across from her with a rose in hand. I told her that the rose was for her and that we had someplace to go.

Not sure what to think of the events at hand, she followed me as I led her down to the water along the pier. Our friend and her boyfriend had changed into captain and crewmate outfits and stood next to a small Boston Whaler boat. Puzzled, Holly stepped aboard. At first the small motor didn't want to start, but after a few tries it fired up and we all putted through the marina. I wasn't sure what she was thinking at that moment, but she kept looking at me with a puzzled smile. The ride was pleasant, and the early evening weather was perfect with clear skies and a warm breeze. The conversation was quiet, with Holly shifting between enjoying the view and being perplexed at what I was up to.

It didn't take long for her to realize where we were going. My friend the "captain" was a member of the marina yacht club in Long Beach. We glided next to a forty-five-foot motor yacht, which I had reserved for the evening, and tied off the Boston Whaler. Still mystified, Holly boarded, and the captain and crew member disappeared to prepare the vessel. Holly kept asking what I was up to, but the anticipation and suspense building up was too enjoyable for me to let on. We cruised out just beyond the Queen Mary and dropped anchor as the sun was setting over the Long Beach marina. We felt miles away from everything on a calm, still night sitting in the harbor far away from the hustle of the city and all alone in our own world. The captain and his girlfriend, the first mate, were busy preparing dinner on one of the other decks. Slow dance music drifted through the night air as I asked Holly to dance. The white lights I had strung along the deck sparkled as we danced to a romantic song.

We talked some but mostly enjoyed each other's company. When it became good and dark, I asked her to follow me to the top deck. From the top deck we could see the lights of the city shimmering across the water. In the twilight we were greeted with a candlelight dinner for two. The evening seemed beautifully perfect. With the confidence that my heavenly Father granted me, I got on one knee and asked her to share the rest of her life with me and my heavenly Father—just the three of us. And she said yes. Of course I told her later if she had said no, she would have had to swim back, but I was just kidding. We sat there for hours enjoying the wonderful surroundings and the beauty of God's creation.

I would have liked to say that we lived happily ever after and everything was perfect, but life doesn't seem to work that way. I continued to learn that fulfillment is never fully achieved in this life. Life is truly a journey, and I was still on top of the world at that moment, but the journey wasn't over. Taking this journey came with no guarantees or promises, except that I wouldn't have to walk it alone as long as I walked close to my heavenly Father.

Holly and I were married by my grandfather. I love my grandfather. He was in his mideighties, so it might have been a good idea to have a second pastor assist with the wedding. He forgot a few names and confused a few statements that left a formal evening wedding rumbling with laughter, which wasn't part of the plan. Noticing that he was holding his Bible upside down during the ceremony didn't add to our confidence. Anyway, we forged forward with great embarrassment after the caterer didn't arrive and we had to send people to a local grocer to find a cake. Nonetheless, the wedding is just where a marriage starts, not the marriage itself.

We bought a quaint Old World bungalow home in Pasadena. We adored that home. It was a wonderful place to start making memories as husband and wife. The house was built in 1927 and was full of character. It was filled with aromas from a beautifully mature rose garden around the home. We would stroll through the roses and the fragrance of blooming flora in the cool of the evenings. Our passion for architecture and homes was excited by the craftsmanship and character of our first place together, and the life our heavenly Father had granted us.

It wasn't long before God gave us a son. The greatest fear, anxiety, and love ever imaginable came in that little bundle of blue blankets. The idea of being a dad came with great excitement and trepidation. Without a fatherly role model, I felt I was winging it most of the time, which often struck fear in me. What if I got it wrong? What if I screwed up this little boy's life like my dad screwed up mine? How could I ever be a good father since I didn't know what that looked like? But my heavenly Father was teaching me what a father was. He walked with me daily, continually carrying me as I stumbled through life. Late at night when I would hold my little baby boy and rock him back and forth, I could only pray that my heavenly Father would lead me and teach me to be a good dad. Most of all,

I prayed that I would be able to introduce my son to my heavenly Father someday.

Life changed dramatically as our family grew, and it wasn't always easy, but it was worth every lesson, every moment of laughter, and every tear that we shed together. My heavenly Father continued to be with us and care for us. I remember when we started feeling an unexplainable tug in our soul. We both felt that God was leading us out of the Los Angeles area. Events seemed to happen quickly. The project I was working on for my employer was finishing, and we felt God was sending us somewhere new, but we didn't know where or when.

Holly and I talked about the situation and the uncertainty of the unknown that lay ahead for our family. We prayed for the power to let go and allow God to show us what he wanted. The next day, my boss offered me a new position and asked if I'd be willing to go to Denver. I'd never been to Denver, but I wanted to be open to wherever God might be leading us. It was a Friday. I said I'd be interested, but I'd need to discuss it with my wife. His response was quick. "You'd better go home and talk to her now. We need you there on Monday."

Our beloved house sold in four days. Everything fell into place. The movers showed up, packed everything, and drove away. It seemed as if we blinked our eyes and then we were sitting in a new home in Colorado. I had a new team at work, and we lived in a new neighborhood. We found a new community of friends who knew my Father like I did. God had prepared not only our leaving, but also a place for us where he had sent us.

After living most of our lives in warm climates snow was still a mysterious wonder to experience. Then one very early morning, it must have been 2:00 a.m., Holly woke me and asked me to come over to the bedroom window. A bluish shimmering hue illuminated the air as a blanket of pure white covered our whole neighborhood. It was an unbelievably beautiful sight.

As I look back on that time in my life, the struggles and issues we dealt with in normal daily life seem to vanish. The memories bring to light the beauty I'd been granted in my life. The relationships and family God gave us rose far above the acquired things. It wasn't long before our family grew again. Another mystery came wrapped in a bundle of pink this time. We were blessed with a beautiful baby girl. She was gorgeous. I remember standing next to my wife's hospital bed with my son beside me, holding my little girl for the very first time. My heart skipped with joy as I realized that I'd become a father, a dad, once again. Once robbed of my own childhood, I was now entrusted with the lives of two little ones who would depend on me. Even though I feared my own past failures, I knew there was nothing greater than being a dad and leading my own children to know their heavenly Father.

It seemed like an eternity before I returned to the aquarium. I'd checked every phone accessible and heard nothing even resembling a dial tone as I was moved from holding cell to holding cell. In the aquarium I quickly made my way to the bank of phones and started working my way down the row until I finally found one with a dial tone. I dialed my home phone number, agreed to all of the outlandish terms and obscene charges, and then finally I could hear ringing and a voice on the other end.

"Kevin? Is that you?"

"It's me—"

"I have to talk quick before they cut us off again. Our attorney in Colorado is going to help us. He's a Christian too. He is praying for you as well. The district attorney sent a letter to the Los Angeles court asking them to release you, but you have to be in Colorado by Monday morning. I talked with our friends Teresa and Elgin in California. I wired the money to them for your bail, and they are going to the Los Angeles courthouse to pay it."

"Where did you get $60,000?"

"What? The Colorado district attorney agreed to $6,000, and we get it back when you show up at court in Colorado. We'll need that money back so we can pay our attorney fees. Who said anything about $60,000?"

"The public defender in Los Angeles said the judge set my bail at $60,000."

"How can they do that? . . . I'll call our attorney again. Everyone is praying. We're going to get you out of there."

"I love you, Holly, more than I ever realized, and all I want right now is just to be with you and the kids."

"Kevin, our friends Austin, Teresa, and Elgin keep trying to see you in the jail, but they are turned away every time. They're not letting you have any visitors."

The lights of the aquarium changed to dim orange as the announcement over the speakers blurted out, instructing us to return to our cells.

"Kevin, I'm really scared. I don't know where the money for all of this is going to come from, and the house won't sell. Our realtor is completely puzzled. The other homes in our neighborhood are selling quickly. Everyone says we're priced below market value. Everyone seems to love the house too, but we're not getting any offers. I don't know what to do. I was able to sell your truck; we're going to need that money too."

"Holly, I've got to go. They are going to cut us off—" Buzz, silence.

///

In a large new home scattered with empty boxes and kids' toys, a mother busily unpacked dishes while watching the children. A little boy played with trains on the polished wood floors. A baby girl slept quietly in a crib seemingly safe and sound, while soft Christian music played from the radio. A glow from the fireplace radiated in the darkness of the night as a light snow gently fell outside. In the driveway a large German luxury sedan tracked through the snow on its way to the garage. The father stepped out of the car, carrying a pizza box in one hand and a briefcase in the other. He closed the door with his hip and made his way through the garage, around an array of boxes, and an obstacle course of toys. Standing guard at the door, large angels stood with swords drawn. Through the living room window the family could be seen clearing some space and huddling around a makeshift table of boxes to give thanks for the dinner.

Posted in the shadows of a snowbank in the front yard, a dark creature stared through a bay window into the living room, watching the family.

"Drach, can we go inside? Maybe hang out on the ceiling or behind the couch or something? It is miserable out here."

The dark figure turned to the voice coming from the shadows of the snowbank. "*No!* We'd never get past those angels."

"Well, I don't think we're doing a lot of good out here, Drach."

The bony horn on the top of Drach's nose leaned out of the shadows, bordered by burning green eyes. "Shut up, or I'll throw you to the angels myself. The prayer cover is too strong right now. We haven't even seen the inside of this new home yet, so we don't know where to safely gather."

"Then what is your plan? Do you want us to just sit out here in the snow and watch this family slip through our grasp? We continue to throw temptations in there, but it doesn't seem to be very effective while we hang out here in the shadows."

A sudden burst of snow fell next to Drach and startled him into a defensive stance. As the swirling white powder settled, a large talon emerged. Slowly looking up at the hideous creature, Drach began to feel dwarfed by the large wings and horns outlining the peering eyes focused on him.

"Chief Demon, what a surprise. What brings you to Colorado?"

"Drach, your followers are losing faith in you, as am I. I am not hearing good reports of your progress. The plans you have laid to ensnare your victim have not materialized, and I cannot afford failure any longer."

Grasping Drach by the neck, Chief Demon lifted him off the frozen ground to his eye level. Fixing his glare on Drach, Chief Demon spoke through the torn and rotted skin on his face. "I am reassigning you elsewhere. This victory appears to be out of your reach. A prize such as this seems to be beyond your ability, so I have summoned another."

Flailing his tail back and forth, Drach grasped for words. "But Chief Demon, I want this prize . . . I can do this . . . I . . . I . . . ."

Maintaining his grip as he slammed Drach back to the ground in a burst of frozen powder, Chief Demon sized up the minions gathered in the shadows and then motioned to them to follow him as he flew through the night, clutching Drach by the neck.

In a large basement nearby, the hideous creatures gathered amidst others already assembled in the dark red glow of a furnace. Holding Drach's head to the ground beneath his large talon, Chief Demon stood in control of the room. The other sinister creatures nervously heckled each other under the dwarfing shadow of Chief Demon. Chief growled a deep rumble that vibrated throughout the basement in order to grab the attention of those assembled. Then he addressed the gathering of hateful deceivers slithering across the floor.

"I have decided that this failure has gone on long enough. This victim of ours has now joined forces with another follower of the Light. He carries what he has learned from his prayer warrior mother to the next generation. Yes, torturing and feasting on a prize such as this for all eternity would be a sweet thing to savor. However, losing our deceived humans, or even worse, losing another generation, is intolerable."

In the dead silence of the room Chief Demon tapped his sharp talon on the concrete floor. Tap, tap, tap.

"This has risen to the attention of Beelzebub himself."

Letting the gravity of his statement sink in, Chief Demon panned the room. Then he continued.

"You are all here because there is a gathering of humans that must be brought together, in order to be torn apart. In the midst of success your humans will be introduced and used to destroy not only the human family that I am after, but many others who will rally around him. The most vile and deceived humans that you control must be involved to execute this properly. Then you must turn them against the one I am after. They must reflect your loathing behavior as you control them in this plot. Promise them the world, appeal to their greed and their sick desire to be like God—the desire we deceived them with from the beginning."

Once again for effect, Chief Demon tapped his talon on the concrete floor as the others eagerly absorbed the fiendish plan being unraveled before them. Tap, tap, tap . . .

"Drach will be assigned to another problem human. My new plan of treachery will be led by a local who is a master of deception. He has deceived many in the earthly human desire for achievement. He is one who has numerous human victories already awaiting his feast in hell. He understands the line between having money and the love of money, and he has many human accomplices at his beckon call. He will be your new leader."

From the shadows another large creature draped in a dark cloak stepped forward.

"I give you hatred wrapped in deception. I give you Sham, your new leader."

The cloak was removed, unveiling a fiery red creature that stood next to Chief Demon. It had the body of a human wrapped in large chains, the legs and feet of a goat, and four twisting horns of blazing embers that appeared to be crawling from his large skull. His face was made up of burning eyes and a large mouth of pointed teeth. As the cloak fell to the ground, large torn wings of charred skin rose above him. In an unearthly voice that echoed through the unfinished space he spoke.

"I am Sham. Deceiving humans who achieve success and earthly wealth is my specialty. I am an expert in the American way of success. This human being who has become a problem to our kingdom of darkness must fall, but he will not deny his heavenly king simply because we lob suggestive ideas at him. We must replace his focus on his heavenly Father with the wealth and pleasure of this world. We must distract him while he thinks he is successful and then lure him away and into our trap. This will require a plan of dishonesty."

Walking around the room like a master motivator polished in the skills of persuasion, Sham continued his executive sermon.

"Our little human will become wildly successful in earthly pursuits. We will not stand in his way. In fact, we will help make this happen. Our goal is to introduce other humans who will appear to support him. These humans will appear as the source of his success and take all the credit for the gifts his heavenly Father will grant him. They will work their way into his life and affirm how great he is."

Listening intently, the audience fixated on the flaming red horned creature as he moved in for the key of the message.

"Then we will pull the rug out from under him when he least expects it. When everything falls apart, the humans we put around him will turn on him, making him question his belief in his heavenly Father. We will crush him and cripple others who follow our enemy. We will taunt the humans we control and arouse their anger, and then we will turn it against our target. In centuries past we would have had him surrounded with torches and pitchforks, but now we have learned how to prolong the torture far longer. And you, my followers of iniquity, you will rejoice in the inflicted pain and suffering. You will feast with me in this celebration of a fallen human. You will join me in this conquest as we stamp out the Light of their heavenly Father in one more human being."

Met with cheering and gleeful hissing, Sham strutted back to Chief Demon's side before concluding.

"We need to round up your greediest and most self-serving humans. I need you to bring them to me and introduce them into this situation. We must make sure they are strong willed. They must be skeptical and well deceived by our darkness so they will not easily be affected by our victim."

Infused with excitement, the room full of sinister creatures erupted. Biting each other while filling the room with steaming sulfur, they danced back and forth. Leaning toward Chief Demon, Sham whispered, "I got this."

Leaning back, Chief Demon peered into the burning red face of Sham. "You'd better. I evoked your services for a reason; now impress me." In the excitement of the commotion, Chief Demon faded into the darkness and rose through the basement ceiling, with Drach in his clutches.

24

Losing the Summit

When life is good, praise God; when life is bad, praise God. It's not about life—it's about praising God.

. . . I am in deep distress. Let me fall into the hands of the Lord, for his mercy is very great; but do not let me fall into human hands.
—1 Chronicles 21:13 (NIV)

If you are really a product of a materialistic universe, how is it that you don't feel at home here?
—C. S. Lewis, Encounter with Light

Time ticked away, and I continued to climb my career ladder while dabbling in sideline businesses. I felt a great obligation to provide for my family, as well as to be a good husband and father. Somehow these two things conflicted at times. We moved a couple of times around Denver, wheeling and dealing homes, until I reached a career plateau. Sometimes the kids would come to the office with me on weekends and run the halls and play while I worked. I remember playing tag and writing reports simultaneously, which in some odd way seemed to work for a while. Later we would camp out at one of the remodeling projects I was working on, and sometimes we would stay late into the night or end up just sleeping over at the house. I would get up early and stay up late every day. I was buying fixer homes and flipping them, often a couple at a time. I had a truck and trailer loaded with tools and supplies. I'd leave work and go straight to the next project and work late. Our family photo album typically had the kids in hard hats or playing around one of our construction projects.

My sideline business had surpassed my career abilities. We flipped so many homes that it was time to move on from my career and run the business full time. I quit my job and created a plan to build a company, sell it, and retire—whatever retirement meant. I hired my first employees and formed a new corporation that I named after Holly. Holly and I took the war chest of reserves we'd built and started building our first custom-home neighborhood.

I remember driving away with my first multimillion-dollar construction loan, thinking we were going to either make it or go under, though you never really think the going under part is a real option when you make statements like that.

The homes we built got bigger and bigger, as did our staff. We became the fastest growing high-end-design build firm in Colorado. We were building spectacular seven-thousand-plus-square-foot custom homes for professional athletes and wealthy business owners. We built a fabulous dream home overlooking the city, with a view of the Rocky Mountains, for ourselves. I found myself being interviewed in the media and hanging out in my own home with Bronco football players and other celebrities.

I felt that I had achieved everything the Western world viewed as success. I had access to anything I wanted. I lived in a mansion on the top of the hill and drove the best of the best. We vacationed in the Caribbean and ran a successful company. Even though I seemed to be on top of the world, I began to struggled again. I continually felt there had to be something more fulfilling than just achieving more success. Holly and I were burning the candle at both ends, working endless hours. We had a good-sized staff, but there was always something that needed our attention. I had so much, but was this what my heavenly Father was calling me to do? I was working fourteen hours a day, seven days a week, which left very little time to spend with my Father or my family. Holly and I sat down one day and evaluated where we were and decided it was time to make a change. The business had much more success ahead of it, but we didn't feel like it was what God had called us to do.

We prayed to our Father and asked him to change things. I honestly thought that would involve selling the business and taking the early retirement package I had planned. I wanted to spend more time with my family and invest my time in something more lasting than material wealth. We sold our home to a Denver Bronco wide receiver and bought a more modest home to live in. We had two companies looking at our business to purchase, and I planned on taking a year off to cruise across the country in our motor coach, but God had other plans. Wealth was part of my journey but not my destination. God answers prayer, but sometimes it involves a desert experience like that of Moses, or worse, Job from the Bible. Often the plan has more to do with us than the circumstances we are praying about.

It was 2007 when the unthinkable happened. We had done our risk analysis and tried to plan our business risk conservatively. When the banking crisis hit across America, everything suddenly changed. Banks stopped lending, and many folded. Our business was heavily tied to the banking business. Construction projects required construction loans, which our company would acquire and hold for a short term while the project was being built. These projects also required a permanent or long-term loan that the bank would give the new owner once the project was completed. We had several multimillion-dollar construction projects under way when the banking crisis swept across the country. Our clients couldn't get the financing to close on the finished projects, and we were not equipped to carry the construction loans for extended periods.

When the crisis hit, our buyers had no choice but to walk away from the projects, leaving us with expiring construction loans that we could neither service nor pay off. Our loans were secured against a large portfolio of land, commercial properties, and homes, which became almost worthless overnight. Property values fell so fast we couldn't liquidate anything. Our potential business buyers quickly walked away. Holly and I drained every dime we had trying to make payroll and service debt until the well went dry.

That wasn't how it was supposed to happen. I once again cried out to my heavenly Father in anguish. I had worked and planned so hard to achieve the wealth of this world. I had good intentions and worked hard to take care of those who trusted in me. His ways were beyond my understanding, and I hadn't spent the time with him to know where he was leading us. All I could do was surrender to him and blindly trust, because all other options had been taken away.

Memories of that time still haunt me. I can recall telling the staff they no longer had a job. I tried to explain that it had nothing to do with them and that I appreciated the work they had done for the company. I remember crying in my truck in the parking lot as they packed their stuff and drove away. Everything seemed to fall into a bottomless chasm. I continually asked myself why, what could I have done differently, and what did I do wrong?

I will never forget the day I had to walk into a meeting with my bankers—the day I had to tell them that I wouldn't be servicing the loans any longer. With my perfect credit and history of ridiculously high credit lines, it was unfathomable for them to hear this from me, and painful to say. All I had to offer them was the devalued properties back; I didn't have anything else left. My company always had been known for paying our subs early and being a reputable company to work for. Almost overnight the lawsuits filled the mailbox, and the world seemed to turn on me. The phone started ringing nonstop with angry threats from people and businesses we'd bent over backwards to help in the past. Now the only thing anyone wanted was the very thing we no longer had: money.

Some employees stole what they could from the company before leaving, either out of anger or greed. The bank sold off what they could at less than half of the construction costs and a fraction of the former market value. Within a few short months, the once touted grand builder celebrated in the local media became an object of scorn. The reports and editorials transformed the praise to blame, heralding how things could have been done better as if this crisis had been foretold.

I remember cleaning one of the last properties before giving it back to the bank. There wasn't any staff left to help, so I was there alone with a broom and cleaning supplies when I noticed the TV news vans parked out front. I already felt like a failure, and now I was cornered. I would not only be ridiculed by the over stimulated media, I would have to face them and hang my head publicly on live TV.

I stepped out the door headed for my truck with supplies in hand only to be met by rushing cameras and microphones. Questions about local construction and the market falling apart flew, peppered with questions about my company and what I could have done differently. I humbly stared at the ground and asked if I could just get in my truck and drive away. I told them I had just lost everything and let my staff go, so this company was done. As they filmed everything, I slowly drove away.

I fell from the top of the hill to what felt like the bottom of the pit within a few short months. I lost the many high-profile friends I had acquired. Those who always came with an open hand when they needed something now mocked me. What hurt the most was being helpless to repay my lenders and investors, whom I'd come to know well. We had friends who had invested in property projects, and they got hurt as we did. Our friends turned to strangers overnight and abandoned us. The weight on my shoulders was more than I could bear. We were about to lose the home we lived in, and I literally didn't know how I was going to feed my family. I questioned what kind of father I was. The word *failure* was stamped on my forehead in a public way, but most of all it haunted my own mind. I started selling our furniture, lawn tools, and anything else we had to feed my family.

Although I thought I was at the end of my rope, my heavenly Father still provided. I would run an ad for the strangest stuff—like two bags of cement mix that I found behind the garage, a door knob, a chair, etc.—and someone would always come and buy it. We didn't eat elaborately, but we didn't go hungry. We were able to pay the electric bill and keep the heat on. I had no job, no work, and nowhere to go when I got up each morning. But there was time to spend with my wife and kids, and most of all, my Father—lots of time.

Since we had signed personal guarantees on some of the company debts, we were forced to file personal bankruptcy, total liquidation.

Darkness seemed to circle me on all sides, but my heavenly Father never let go. He would bring moments of encouragement when things seemed their darkest. The stuff all went away, but he never abandoned me. The emotions of shock, fear, and anger all took their course, but he patiently waited and cared for us one day at a time. When we were starting to run out of stuff to sell, I started getting calls to interview for jobs in my former engineering profession.

I was being flown around the country interviewing for job positions, which all seemed to go very well. We began to get excited about some of the locations and would take each opportunity into prayer, asking for direction, and then each door would close. We really didn't know why. Then there was a call from a company in Toronto. We'd never been to Canada, and although it didn't sound that appealing, I wasn't about to turn down an opportunity to provide for my family, so I went for the interview.

It was a cold, gray day when I landed in Toronto. All I could see out the cab window was bare trees and gloomy high-rise buildings between the sleet and occasional snow. It seemed more like a major city than the frozen tundra speckled with polar bears that most Americans perceived Canada to be. I walked through the interview without much of an effort on my part to sell myself, thinking this wasn't the place for me, with or without the polar bears.

When I returned to Denver, Holly and I prayed again about the different job possibilities. Shortly after we prayed, all of the possibilities closed tight, one after another, except one: Toronto. The position in Toronto swung wide open, and I was offered the job. Somewhat shocked, I started asking my heavenly Father if this was really where he wanted us to go. Although it wasn't our first choice, it apparently was his, and his reasons are always far beyond my understanding. So we waited through the work visa process and then went through the routine of packing what little we had left in a truck and headed north in blind faith.

Our truck was full, including a family of four and two dogs. We had all of the paperwork that was needed to cross the border and a map to our new rental home. And once again, God had given us enough for the journey, but the rest involved trusting in him. The journey across the United States was hopeful and optimistic as we headed into a new life with little more than faith in our heavenly Father. The job he had provided stood ahead of us, and our family would be starting over. We knew very little about Canada, and I was the only one in our family who had been there, even if it was just for a brief interview and to get my new job started. Life was taking a new turn. We had struggled to survive for nearly a year after losing everything, but he always made a way.

It took a couple of days on the road to reach the border. My first experience was unlike anything I'd expected. The U.S. customs side was militant and demanding. The officer yelled at my little girl and me, and then held us in a parking lot with our truck until they got around to letting us leave the United States. The experience was just a little better than the one I had in the Middle East many years before. On the Canadian side of the border we were met with smiling, cheerful faces as the customs officers asked about the dogs while looking at our paperwork. They seemed to welcome us as if part of the family. Tensions were low and casual, which came as a welcome surprise. The drive from Detroit to Toronto revealed a beautiful country that I'd never expected, with more vegetation than frozen tundra and polar bears.

The company was very good to us. We had to watch every dime, as we had no reserves and found things to be expensive, but we had a life together as a family. Our first winter was brutal, and everyone kept telling us it wasn't normally that severe. However, chipping the ice off my drive in blocks to get the car out was a new experience, as were many other things. Milk came in strange plastic bags as opposed to the U.S. gallon jugs. Gas, or petrol, came by the liter, and we had to learn the Celsius temperature system. The signs were in English and French, as were the TV channels. The people were pleasant and the seasons beautiful. The villages along the water front and thick green forests between the neighborhoods were magnificent. The cities were clean and felt safe. People didn't hate us or blame us for everything; they just let us live our lives and be part of their community.

Back in the States it seemed everyone came out of the woodwork and wanted to find a way to sue us in hopes of getting money from us or our former company insurance. One perpetually angry couple who had purchased a beautiful home at a very low price continually tried to badger us and the company insurance carrier for money. Their claim was around the basement being three degrees cooler than the rest of the house, of over seven thousand square feet, in addition to a number of other similarly ridiculous claims. Another sub said someone promised he could paint three more homes. He wanted to be paid for the work he didn't get to do even though the company was out of business. An architect who had stopped by the office a year or more before and dropped off some really poor house plans, without being commissioned to do so, wanted to be paid a premium for them even though we never looked at them or had any interest in using them. Our once trusted broker forged paperwork to get liens on property the bank was selling to get money from the liquidation sales. A former client took control over his own construction project when we closed the business, only to keep the bank's construction money instead of finishing the project. We also found out that some of our former employees were taking kickbacks from subs and suppliers. We never sued anyone, although we were told we should. We forgave debts when others fell on hard times or made mistakes. Everyone seemed to become scavengers, out to get anything they could at any cost. Moral value and ethics meant nothing, and we became the carcass everyone wanted to clean scraps from.

I began to realize that there were many reasons God had taken us to Canada. The distance made it difficult for the angry mob in the United States to badger us. Some of the companies I had interviewed with were beginning to let employees go as the economy in the United States continued to decline.

The schools in Canada were great, and our kids were accepted by the other students, as many of them were from foreign countries as well. The health system turned out to be much different from how it was portrayed in the United States. The Canadian health system seemed very efficient and accessible from our experiences.

Another reason my heavenly Father sent us to Canada became apparent more than a year after we arrived.

During a routine checkup my doctor found that I had white blood cell abnormalities. He then informed me that I had leukemia, a cancer of the blood. The doctor referred me to a specialist immediately. When I told Holly what they had found, she burst into tears. Being a nurse, she knew it could be very serious. After some research on the Internet, I too felt more worried about what this might mean. I had an appointment two weeks later to see a specialist, but at that time I had no idea if I had chronic lymphocytic leukemia (CLL) or acute lymphoblastic leukemia (ALL). The first is a slow-growing cancer; ALL is a fast-growing cancer that usually comes with a two-year life span after diagnosis.

The following two weeks often found me taking long walks at lunch contemplating the possibilities. I had no fear of leaving this earth, but I worried about my family who would be left behind. I wrestled with how they would be taken care of and provided for. I reflected on the time I spent building my business and achieving the success I'd recently lost. What did I give up with my wife and kids in the process? I finally came to the peace that it wasn't me taking care of them in the first place, and my Father had given me another chance. My heavenly Father had been there all along. My time with him became more valuable than anything else.

I can remember that life looked different during my walks. The grass and trees seemed to glow in vivid colors. The sounds of bugs in the fields came alive, though I'd hardly noticed them just weeks before. The scurry of cars and people that seemed in such a hurry to go someplace of importance now faded into the background. A sense of peace came over me and followed me through my days.

My oncologist at Credit Valley Hospital was excellent. After my blood was skillfully drained on a repeated schedule, it was determined that my leukemia was CLL. With a slow growing cancer I had been given more time on this earth. It would probably catch up to me at some point, but it would likely be years away. I was so grateful to be able to see my kids grow up, and to be able to be there to take care of them. Yet somehow the noise and scurry became visible again. The songs of the bugs and the vivid vegetation began to fade into the background.

We tried to return to the United States a couple of times when opportunities became available, but the doors kept closing. We loved living in Canada, but we wanted to return to our country of origin. This thought lurked in the back of my mind and kept me from setting roots where my heavenly Father had planted us. Miracles continued despite my focus often drifting from where he was pointing.

The lease on our rental was ending, and our realtor said we should think about buying a home. The market was very good in Canada, and a mortgage would be cheaper than rent. Thinking that buying a home was impossible, I made the call to a mortgage lender with little expectation. Somehow after just a year in Canada, we had developed great credit in our new country, and with some effort we were able to scrape together the minimum down payment. Although this was a miracle in and of itself, it was a good market in Canada and homes were not cheap, so we needed an even bigger miracle to find a home. But these things never seemed to be an issue for my Father.

Our realtor showed us several homes, but we were outbid on all of them as the prices went far above what we could afford. We asked our heavenly Father if he really wanted us to stay in Canada, then our realtor found the deal of the century. With homes typically receiving multiple offers as soon as they went on the market, often making it a bidding war, it seemed strange to find a nice home for a price we could afford. My expectations were low at best, but our offer on the home was accepted. In a miraculous way, our Father gave us a nice family home in a neighborhood that we could have never afforded. We had just enough money to get into the home, and we didn't have to deal with the bidding fanfare.

We discovered that many others wanted the home but didn't learn about it until it had already sold. The new home was close to work, and the schools were wonderful. It was a great place to live. God knew what we needed. We didn't need a mansion or a fancy place to reside anymore, we needed a home for our family.

God continued to open the doors at every turn and provided for our needs one day at a time. It would have been great to say I had learned well and life went on happily forever after. But life is messy, and perfection doesn't come until we get to heaven. However, I wish I could have seen what was about to hit me next, because what I had just walked through paled by comparison.

///

Climbing onto my steel bunk in the claustrophobic cell, I laid my head down on the hard surface desperate for rest, and gaining none. Bullet Killer paced the small space in front of the door, murmuring something over and over again. I seemed to drift off for a few minutes before the public speakers lit up again, blurting some undistinguishable sounds. Then I heard my inmate number once more. After remembering the abuse other inmates took for not responding when called, I slid off my bunk one more time and made my way to the door. While I was standing at as much attention as I could muster, a guard arrived and escorted me down a different corridor than I'd traveled before. This corridor led to an elevator. I was taken down several floors to another dark cavern, where I waited in a row of benches with several others. These benches were in the middle of a room where we were told to straddle the bench and each other as tightly as possible. A large court-like desk was elevated at the end we all faced. Guards circled the benches, watching those of us sandwiched together in the middle. We were called up to the desk one at a time, given some paperwork, and then ordered to the next room. The following rooms were much the same, with long waits and paperwork, and then we moved on. At one stop I was given a bag with my inmate number on it. Inside I found the clothes I had arrived in. We were ordered to change and return the inmate outfit.

Although my clothes stank, it felt good to shed the jail garb. At one station I was given an envelope with a receipt in it. It was for the money they had taken "for jail charges" out of the cash I had on me when I arrived. I was then given my cell phone, my wallet, and my wedding ring, which I now cherished more than ever before.

Finally after hours of stations and rooms, we were lined up with a finger-print desk on one side and a holding room on the other. The rooms were separated from the outside world by a single door. One by one we were finger-printed, told to sign another form, and finally allowed to enter the exit room on the far side. I could hardly believe that I was going to see the outside world again. After I had signed the final form that was pushed in front of me, I was told I'd need to see the cashier at the court clerk outside of the jail to actually get any of my cash back. I had cash with me when I arrived and wanted to get whatever was left back, but I wanted to get out of there more than anything else, so I signed whatever was put in front of me. Finally they let me enter the exit room to wait with the entire group to be released.

When the last person was processed, everyone waited in great anticipation, until the guard at the desk made an announcement.

"If your name is called, you need to return to the first room."

Fear ran through me. They seemed to have made so many mistakes; what if they didn't let me leave? What if this was all a cruel hoax? One guy in front of me heard his name called. As he entered the other room, he was handcuffed and taken away; then another was called with the same result. After a few moments' pause while a group of guards seemed to stare at a computer screen, my heart almost stopped. I heard my name. In great discouragement I made my way to the other side to await the worst.

A guard approached me and then escorted me to the desk. I thought I would crumble into a million pieces. The person behind the desk pointed to the finger-print board and told me to stamp it one more time. As he inspected the completed stamp, my heart pumped with adrenalin that I didn't know I still had in my body. To my amazement he pointed back to the exit room and ordered me to get back in line. A glimpse of hope sparked inside me as I returned to the second room. Within moments a loud buzzing sound preceded a slamming noise, and the door opened to the outside world. The men raced out the door with conversations about finding the nearest bar or scoring something new. I simply stepped out into the darkness. I embraced the wee hours of the morning and breathed in the wondrous dirty air of downtown Los Angeles. I was free . . . for the moment my soul soared. I was free . . . or was I?

///

A sharply dressed man in a business suit and carrying a black travel bag boarded a shuttle at the Los Angeles International Airport. Two angelic beings followed him onto the shuttle and sat across from him.

A dark shadow skimmed the crowd of airport travelers before darting into a crowded corner and morphing into an attractive young lady. The young lady picked up a travel bag from the baggage carousel and made her way to the shuttle.

In the back of the shuttle a dark cloaked figure sat surrounded by sinister shadows watching the man and his glowing guardians. A voice from one of the shadows whispered. "Hey, Sham. Ya think Chief Demon is going to show up soon? Everything you've thrown at the guy seems to get deflected by his Father of Light, our enemy."

The figure seemed to utter words without movement. "I learned centuries ago that plans have to be adjusted as you go. His heavenly Father got him out of the mess we put him in before I could lower the boom on him. But this new development in California will work nicely."

"Sham, those angels that his Father has sent have continually been a problem for us. Even those former clients we badgered him with about that basement temperature thing couldn't seem to break through that protective layer he seems to be carrying around with him. We had strong control over those people too. What's the plan? And why are those angels allowing us to sit so close to him?" The shady figure reached up and pointed to the lightly glowing beings on the shuttle.

The young lady boarded the shuttle and found a seat near the man in the business suit as the driver pulled away from the shuttle stop. The lady subtly looked toward the back of the shuttle and winked at Sham; then she turned and smiled at the man.

"Well, my ominous apprentice of malice, if you notice, those angels are getting weaker. Our victim is getting too busy to spend time with his heavenly Father, so his prayer cover and protection wane. We will reintroduce the idea of the success he once had. We will be able to use it to lure him. He is human, and without his heavenly Father he is vulnerable."

The man exited the shuttle and made his way to a rental car counter. Sham drifted past the angelic beings to the clerk at the counter. Sham focused the clerk's attention on a high-end expensive sports car, and then he whispered in the clerk's ear, "This one is available in inventory. Your customer looks like a good choice for first-class treatment. Give it to him."

As the clerk stared at the computer screen, he addressed the business traveler. "Since you're one of our star customers, I have a nice upgrade for you."

Peering out from under the hood of the cloak, Sham looked at the angelic beings and shrugged his shoulders with a smile.

The young lady standing behind the angelic beings faded into the wall when no one was looking.

As Sham and his cronies climbed into the backseat of the car behind the angels, Sham's apprentice whispered into his ear, "What are you doing? Why are the angels allowing this?"

Patting his apprentice on the shoulder, Sham smiled with a face full of pointed teeth through the shadows of the cloak. "Watch, my menacing inferior, and learn from the master."

At the hotel Sham darted to the counter and started whispering in the ear of the clerk. The man in the suit handed the keys to the valet and strolled through the grand lobby. The two angelic beings followed until the young lady appeared at the entrance blocking the angels path. Crossing her arms she focused on the angelic beings and shook her head, preventing them from following the man. The beings backed away and stood on the curb, watching while discussing the situation.

"Where has the prayer cover gone? This has created an opening, and Sham is stocking our human. I'm feeling the loss of strength, as our human's Father doesn't seem to be invited here."

"Once again, we can't interfere where we are not invited. Our Father has given him a freewill choice. Sham has found a way to get to him. We'd better gather the saints and prepare them for battle. We need the prayer cover if we are going to gain strength. Sham is evil, and he will strike hard when he does. Our Father still loves this one, but he will be hurt badly if the prayers of the saints do not intervene, and quickly."

"I'll round up the others and urge them to get their saints praying."

One of the angelic beings rose up the side of the building while the other darted away into the sky.

Following the man down the hall to a large suite, one of the shadows addressed a question to Sham. "I don't understand. We have him right here by ourselves. Why don't we oppress him or attack him?"

Unveiling his fiery twisted horns from the hood, Sham aimed his burning eyes at the man. "Because he will call on his heavenly Father, and we will be defeated. If we lull him to where we want him and slowly draw him away, he will become more and more vulnerable. Then we'll attack hard."

"Oh . . . good plan, Sham."

"No, it isn't just a good plan; it is why I have so many of these humans awaiting me in hell. I also have something special planned for this one. Our sinister cronies back in Colorado are working on something that will hit him like a bomb, when he least expects it. Keep him busy and focused on himself and his work. Don't let him talk with his family, and especially his wife. She could foil everything if they resume praying together. Find a good property investment deal or two. He is familiar with these, and it will eat up more of his time and attention."

Slithering between the overstuffed chairs and couch in the living room of the hotel suite, the sinister creatures casually continued their conversation.

"Sham, how is this different than what we tried to do after crushing his business and turning everyone against him?"

Removing his cloak and stretching the torn bony wings, Sham shook his fiery, charred horns. "My followers, I have saved the best for last. I have taken control of the most self-absorbed angry human client from his previous business and combined him with a conveniently misplaced subcontractor's invoice that will be divulged to the authorities. Our human victim sitting here in luxury is being crafted into an international fugitive. An innocent mistake will be manufactured into an inescapable disaster of deadly proportions. This crash will take him to places that will make the last one seem like child's play. This crash would destroy any human, and this one is as weak as the next. He will be lost so deep in the system that his only friends will be the humans I own. My humans will eat him alive, and then I will not only remove him from this earth, I will feast on his soul."

Morphing from a shadow on the couch, a young lady with a bittersweet voice replied, "I want a bite of that too."

Smiling in arrogance, Sham scanned his followers before he unveiled the next step of his plan. "My plans are almost ready, my vile followers. We need this dreadful human to remain distracted and absorbed in everything this world has to offer a little longer; then we will spring the trap at the next border crossing."

Hovering outside the window of the top-floor hotel suite, a lone angel watched the man working away on his laptop while talking on his cell phone. The angel bowed in place, calling out to the God of the universe. "Oh, heavenly Father, this little one needs your protection badly. He needs you to draw him closer to you. Don't let him ignore you and lose focus of what this life is all about again. Oh, Father, the evil one plans his destruction while we wait. I know this is not the path you have for him; please let him see it before it is too late. Please intervene; please intervene soon."

25

Shock Waves

---

*Those who think they have full control of their own
life have not calculated the cost.*

I consider that our present sufferings are not worth
comparing with the glory that will be revealed in us.
—Romans 8:18 (NIV)

Everyone comes naked from their mother's womb,
and as everyone comes, so they depart. They take
nothing from their toil that they can carry in their
hands.
—Ecclesiastes 5:15

A few years in Canada went by, and an opportunity at work
came up. The opportunity was a new position with the company
I worked for. It involved working with North American offices,
which included those in the United States. I could be based out
of the United States or Canada for the position. Thinking of my
own ambitions, I quickly jumped on it. I began traveling between
Toronto and Los Angeles about every other week, often stopping at
other office destinations in between.

I began feeling empowered and in charge again. I started looking
at investment property and filling my time with long hours. Work
at the office was demanding and took my time away from my family
and my Father. My illness began to slow me down, and I began to
feel tired more often than I had in the past, but I forged forward
as if nothing had changed. I lost all perspective of who I belonged

to, who I really was, and who my God was. The vivid colors of life were replaced with a fast life focused on the things of this earth. I was distracted with my new life. I charged straight into it with little regard for others or the input of my heavenly Father. I was ready to charge out there and fix things on my own. I was going to do things better and respond to the questions of failure that still lingered in the back of my mind. My focus was lost. God focused on things that last forever, such as family and relationships. His focus and the focus of this world collided in my heart, and my perspective was lost.

We decided to move back to Los Angeles, so we put our home in Canada up for sale and started looking for a place to live in California. Our realtor assured us that with a hot market and the right price, the house would sell fast. Immediately the house was flooded with potential buyers, who all loved it. However, for some strange reason no one wrote an offer. A month went by with several showings each day, but no offer. If I had been listening to my heavenly Father, I might have known why he wouldn't let our home sell and that he wasn't done with us in Canada.

As I raced farther and farther away from God's plan for me, my life began to accelerate to a feverish pace. It was like staring at the world from the center of a merry-go-round spinning in circles. I should have been watching the direction the road was taking me. My Father sent friends and my wonderful wife to question where I was going and what I was doing. But when I took the wheel to steer on my own, my Father didn't force it away. He just stood by and let me make my own choices, and then waited patiently for me to crash. He never left me. He was preparing a way to restore me before I even called out to him for help. Then, when I did crash, he gently picked up the pieces once more.

It was a Friday morning when I boarded the Air Canada flight to Los Angeles. U.S. customs seemed rougher than usual, with grilling questions followed by an escort to the flight, which although odd didn't seem entirely out of character for the border agency. The five-hour flight was filled with thoughts of the day's meetings that I needed to attend and the business awaiting me at the Los Angeles office. I had no idea what was about to happen or the battles the evil one had won in my life. I was too distracted to see them. I simply steered straight into that storm at full speed.

Although my thoughts were absorbed with the full agenda that awaited me in Los Angeles and my week ahead, I did detect an odd announcement from the captain over the speakers after we landed. He stated that a second passport check was being made and everyone should remain in their seats.

Moments later police officers rushed down the aisle and stood over my seat. They asked my name, and then they asked for my passport. They didn't ask anyone else for a passport, and they surrounded me as if they were waiting for me to arrive. After examining my passport they became more authoritative. I was ordered to accompany them down the aisle, and more officers stood just beyond the exit door. Puzzled and confused, I followed their orders. I was pushed up against the side of the walkway and frisked before my wrists were clenched in steel cuffs behind my back.

I kept saying, "What is this all about? Am I under arrest or something?"

The officers talked among themselves, holding a piece of paper and examining me. "We have a warrant for you. It says here that you're an international fugitive. That is all we know; you must know what this is all about."

"*What?!...*"

As I stood in the early hours of the morning, my emotions were raw and exhausted. The questions ran deep, but I couldn't begin to fully comprehend them at that moment. As I made my way to the cashier, I quickly noticed that the neighborhood they had released me into wasn't much better than the neighborhood I had just left inside jail. As low riders drove by blaring music backdropped by walls of graffiti, I suddenly realized that I stood out like a sore thumb. I was wearing the business clothes I had on when I arrived at the Los Angeles airport, although the beard and disheveled look probably fit in better than I realized. I walked briskly down the dark sidewalk with the realization that I had stepped into the unknown with no idea of what was coming next.

When I reached the court cashier building, I was surprised they were open before dawn. It felt safe enough to stop and make a call in the building, so I anxiously called Holly. This time there were no messages, outlandish charges to agree to, and no one recording my conversation with that endless clicking sound.

"Holly? I'm out." I began to weep tears of joy and uncertainty.

"Oh, baby, I can't believe how many miracles it took to get you out. I can't believe all of the things that have happened. I can't tell you all of it right now. I'll tell you more when I see you in Colorado. Elgin will be there in twenty minutes to pick you up."

All I could do was stand there with silent tears in the first light of the morning.

"Kevin, I have to tell you one more thing. It is truly a miracle that you are out. The extradition paperwork had been prematurely signed and processed, and it needed to be reversed. The bail was also set incorrectly. Remember that clerical error about the bail requesting $60,000? It was supposed to be $6,000. Our attorney happened to know the district attorney from previous cases, and he felt comfortable enough to speak with him and ask him for a favor. The district attorney wrote a letter requesting that the paperwork be reversed. He also wrote a letter clarifying the correct bail amount of $6,000. That never happens. If it hadn't happened, you could have been in there for a very long time. God has been answering prayer, and the attorney he gave us was the right attorney. God has been working on the district attorney as well. Our Father is in control here, and he will see us through this."

I turned my face from the street as a low rider drove by, slowly thumping rhythmic vibrations through an open window with a tattooed passenger peering out. I wiped my face with a sleeve and nodded in agreement as Holly continued.

"Kevin, you must be in Colorado on Monday morning, which was part of the arrangement. You have less than twenty-four hours to get there. Our attorney said the warrant won't be removed until you see the judge in Colorado. You can't go to the airport to get your luggage; you can't rent a car or get on a plane or use your credit card. If you do, there's a chance you could be picked up and arrested again. The fugitive warrant is still active."

"Holly, how am I supposed to get there? I can't walk halfway across the country in less than two days. Plus, I'm so exhausted I wouldn't even know where to start."

"You can stay at Teresa and Elgin's for a few hours this morning. Then they are going to drive you to Barstow. My mom is leaving from Arizona right now, and she will meet you in Barstow and take you to Colorado. I'm making arrangements to fly to Colorado and meet you after you get there."

In a surreal daze all I could say was, "Okay, thank you."

"Elgin will be there shortly, and we'll talk after you get some sleep. You must be exhausted."

"I am."

I hung up the phone and went to the cashier booth. At that moment I couldn't feel anything. My body went numb from the void of adrenalin in my veins. I tried to mask the exhaustion coming over me and went into autopilot. The cashier was behind thick glass while I stood in the open with a few strange characters lingering around. The lingering loiterers casually watched her count out what money I had. Then they watched me slip it into my pocket. After collecting my money I felt vulnerable standing there with an envelope of cash in downtown Los Angeles at 3:00 a.m. Looking around, I tried to stay observant of my surroundings while standing in the open. I didn't want any trouble, and if there was any, I didn't want to see any police at that moment either.

However, my other senses started to rise. I was starving. I found a vending machine in the corner and purchased a Pop-Tart. It was the sweetest-tasting thing. At that moment it was better than any steak dinner I'd ever eaten. Every bite was wonderful. It wasn't a tasteless tube of jelly or mystery meat burrito. I wasn't typically a big Pop-Tart fan, but at that instant I had become one.

As I was finishing my Pop-Tart, Elgin drove up and I quickly got into his minivan. I was surprised he even recognized me. I was dirty and smelly, and I hadn't shaved for over a week. I had a beard and frumpy hair. When I sat down in the soft seat and heard a friendly voice, I lost it. The façade I hid behind for protection came down, and the emotionally raw tears heaved from my soul as the exhaustion flooded my face. The days of pent-up emotions erupted down my cheeks, and all I could say to Elgin was, "It was bad, really bad." The sun broke through the morning darkness on the horizon, and through the streaming blur of the tears it was the most beautiful thing. When I arrived at Teresa and Elgin's house, they had prepared a bed for me, where I slid into comfortable covers with a pillow for my head, and I collapsed from the fatigue.

///

Screech . . . smoke rose between the squealing commercial airline tires touching down at the Los Angeles International Airport. Waiting in the concourse windows, dark shadows stood around a sinister cloaked figure that eagerly anticipated the arrival of their unprotected victim.

Over the sound system in the plane the captain announced, "Please remain seated. Customs agents will be coming through the cabin to do a secondary passport check." Like a sheep oblivious to the impending slaughter, a man sat patiently reading e-mails on his phone. Before the door could open, the sinister cloaked demon stepped in. Filling the cabin with darkness, the red horned creature focused two burning eyes on the man reading his e-mails; then he pointed a dark red finger down the aisle. In an unearthly hollow voice the creature chided a bright glowing being standing behind the man. "I don't believe you were invited to this party. *Get out!*" Appearing through the darkness of the creature, two police officers rushed down the aisle and grabbed the man by the arm. They hurriedly ushered him down the aisle and threw him up against the walkway wall.

"What is this all about? I don't understand. Why are you doing this? Did I do something wrong?" the man cried out in shock.

Throwing him up against the wall again, the officers frisked him and then paraded him through the terminal, with little more uttered than, "We have a warrant for you. It says here that you're an international fugitive. That is all we know; you must know what this is all about."

The man continued to reply, "I have no idea what is going on. Why are you doing this?"

In a small room the man was cuffed to a bench while one officer stood guard from the hall. "All I know is that I have paperwork stating that you are an international fugitive; that's all I can tell you."

Puzzled, the man inquired, "Am I under arrest or something?"

The officer only repeated his earlier statement.

Angelic beings stood at a distance as a horde of hideous creatures wrapped in dark leathery skin gathered to mock the man chained to the bench. The large red horned creature with burning eyes stood in the middle of the horde. The enormous evil creature stepped forward, spreading torn bony wings in the face of the man; then it gnashed rows of sharp teeth at him while blowing steaming sulfur into his face.

"Finally, I have conquered you . . . you pathetic little human. I will dismantle you one painful piece at a time. I hate you." Looking over his shoulder, the creature stretched out a bony arm with long fingers topped by sharp fingernails and pointed at the angelic beings. "They can't help you now, my prey. You are mine, you pathetic loser. I plan to enjoy every tasty moment of your eradication."

The laughing of the hideous red burning creature echoed through an unearthly realm while two men from the Los Angeles sheriff department arrived and bound the man. They paraded him in chains through the masses in the airport to an awaiting police car. Cutting the circulation in his wrists, the cuffs clamped tighter as the man was crunched into the back of the car and whisked away in a spectacle.

People stopping to watch the commotion couldn't fathom the surreal activity taking place next to them, just out of their realm. Demonic creatures darted from counter to counter while following the large demon throwing flames through the air. The evil being strutted through the center of the airport corridors with massive wings of torn leather spread. A cold darkness was felt by all as he passed, sending a chill through the humans nearby.

In the police car the man asked the officers, "Can you tell me why I'm here? Was I arrested? What did I do?" The officer could only reply that there was a fugitive warrant out for his arrest. "Excuse me, sir, what will happen with my luggage at the airport?"

"That's the airport's issue; you'll have to deal with that later."

Laughing hysterically, the large demonic creature clenched onto the police car. He was followed by a horde of dark shadows howling in the full daylight as the squad car entered the Los Angeles freeway.

At the police station the man was stripped of everything, including his wedding ring. The reality of the situation broke as the man began to weep. "I need to let someone know I'm here. I need to make a phone call."

"They'll deal with that at the jail. They have pay phones there."

"Please, sir, I need to let my family know where I am. I live in Canada. Can I please make a call from my cell phone?"

26

Midnight Run

God is in control, even when we can't see him at work.

When you pass through the waters, I will be with you; and when you pass through the rivers, they will not sweep over you. When you walk through the fire, you will not be burned; the flames will not set you ablaze.

—Isaiah 43:2 (NIV)

For our light and momentary troubles are achieving for us an eternal glory that far outweighs them all.

—2 Corinthians 4:17 (NIV)

When I woke up, the room was dark but the bed was soft. The plush blanket that covered me and the pillow beneath my head were luxuries I had dreamed of, but now cradled me. I got up and opened the curtains to sunshine everywhere. The light of day brought the world alive in vivid colors again. There were pencils on the nightstand just casually left there. This prized possession that I had longed for just days before was now abundantly available. My good friends had laid out a change of clean clothes from Elgin's closet. In the sorrow of the unknown journey that faced me, coupled with the joy of the moment, I wept. There was no one yelling at me and no public announcements blasting orders. It was just quiet, and a peaceful space surrounded me. I took a hot shower, shaved off my beard, and brushed my teeth for the first time in over ten days. My hands shook from the trauma and the weight of an uncertain future that rested on my shoulders.

After the utmost pleasure of hot coffee and a wonderful breakfast, Teresa and Elgin and I set out on the long drive to Barstow, where I would meet up with June. Along the way they told me of the endless hours Holly had worked to get me out of jail and the miraculous things that had taken place. Holly had contacted numerous people from all across the country to pray. They informed me how I still had my job and somehow I had just enough vacation time to cover my absence. They told me of the times they had gone to the jail and were not allowed to see me, and the many other events that had taken place while I was locked away in that dungeon. Teresa and Elgin were careful to keep me out of sight along the way, since the warrant for my arrest was still active. Although I was never really arrested in the first place, I think I was officially detained, but it felt like I was just taken and held against my will without explanation.

We drove for hours through the desert. It was late at night when we arrived at the rendezvous place in Barstow, where June was waiting for me. She had driven from Phoenix to meet me and transport me the rest of the way to Colorado. We had ten hours ahead of us to get to Colorado, but we were very tired, so we stopped for a few hours of sleep. I remember the uninterrupted slumber without the fear of what my cell mates might be capable of. The weight of the world lingered around me, but I was out of the horrific place that had engulfed me for what seemed like forever. My future was incredibly uncertain, but I knew my heavenly Father was still with me.

The next morning the passage through the Rockies with June revealed more miraculous tales of people praying. She shared how God had provided our attorney, who was a Christian, and how there was just enough money to pay for fines and deposits. Holly had called and spoken to my boss about the situation, and he agreed to let me work from their Denver office temporarily, and then their Los Angeles office until I was able to return to Canada. I felt overwhelmed by the seemingly unending puzzle that had come together to paint this picture. I also felt shell-shocked and terrorized, but my heavenly Father was there, and I took comfort in the fact that he was in charge.

We rolled down the hill into Denver early Monday morning as required. The passage through the desert and over the Rockies was over, but the road I had yet to travel was just beginning. I had to stay in Denver for over a week, but God provided for my job and my family. I couldn't afford to live in a hotel, but God had moved my sister and her husband to Colorado shortly before my arrival. My sister and her husband were from California as well. They had never thought of living in Colorado prior to their most recent move. However, my heavenly Father positioned them along their journey to cross paths with mine at this time. My nephew was away at college, so they happened to have a spare bedroom for me to use.

My brother-in-law was the pastor of Journey church in Windsor, Colorado. The people of Journey church embraced me and prayed for me as my journey intersected with theirs. They stood with me along with the many others around the country who were praying, and they cared for my needs.

I didn't know how I was going to get to the office in Denver or back to the office in Los Angeles. I didn't know how I was going to get around without a car, but my heavenly Father did. When we arrived in Colorado, some friends of the family happened to be in town from Arizona. They just happened to be passing through and asked June if she would accompany them on their trip back. With her traveling back with them, she needed someone to take her car back to Arizona, and I needed a car to get to the office in Denver for a week. However, I needed to get the car to Arizona, and I needed to get back to Los Angeles eventually so I could get back my job. That dilemma also had been figured out for me. I couldn't afford anything, because we needed everything we had to pay for legal fees and court costs. Plus, I had no idea how I was going to live away from home and support two households, but God did.

Upon returning to Arizona, June flew to Toronto to stay with our kids so Holly could be with me in Colorado. God had touched so many people's hearts and composed a symphony of events, with me sitting helplessly in the middle. It wasn't my doing or control of the situation this time. I had no power to do anything, as my control was completely taken away. Yet my heavenly Father organized everything and provided in ways that were far beyond anything I could have done.

When Holly arrived in Colorado, it was like being reacquainted with the most precious gift God had blessed me with. The one that I felt I had neglected the most stood by me through the hardest of times. At the initial hearing in Colorado I was handcuffed once again and booked at the county jail; then I was released on my own recognizance without bail. I learned that one of our previous clients, the Harrigans, had spent an enormous amount of time trying to gather any information they could for the district attorney to use against me. They pushed the case with the district attorney in an angry vendetta. I couldn't believe the perception they created of me and the charges filed against me. They had painted a picture of my fleeing the country to avoid the situation. My living and working in Canada didn't help the appearance of the situation. The charges originated from a misplaced invoice in our accounting department. The invoice arrived at the office when the doors of the business were closing. The fact it was an honest mistake didn't matter, and the threat of spending years in prison hovered over me. The worst part was the attack on my character and the values that I tried so hard to live by. I was painted as a criminal, one of "those" people I never dreamed I would become, and now I was labeled as one and understood how it felt.

Since our former company no longer existed and I was the principal shareholder, the charges of the crime fell back on me. Holly was also a shareholder. It was an absolute miracle that she wasn't charged as well. The thought of that still chills me with the realization that our children would have been in Canada with no one to look after them. The Harrigans wanted money, and they felt that this was their way to get it. If I had any money, I would have paid anything to get this weight off me, but the legal system doesn't work that way. Once it becomes enmeshed in the courts, it's a long, drawn-out process with no room for mercy. The Harrigans wanted a million dollars, as if that was even a real possibility.

I felt trapped in something I didn't know existed. I was cornered with no options to resolve the situation or try to correct it. The Harrigans wanted blood—mine. I wasn't allowed to go home and be with my family in Canada. I didn't have a place for my family to live in the United States, and I didn't know what the future would hold. I wondered if I'd ever be able to go home or see my family together again. The weight on my shoulders felt unbearable, and the stress pulsed through me constantly as I contemplated the events of my life and the very real possibility that I could be going away for a long time.

Living day to day became my ordinary way of life. I survived from one miracle to the next, with my heavenly Father providing just enough for one day at a time. A wonderful couple in Arizona gave me a used little truck. I didn't have to ask for the pickup truck; God just touched their heart and it was provided. The only catch was, the truck happened to be located in Arizona and I had to go get it, which was also where I needed to go to deliver June's car. Arizona was also on my way back to the office in Los Angeles, and I had no idea how I was going to get there before the truck was provided. God put the truck right where I needed to be, when I needed to be there, and he provided for me.

///

In a dark control room at the Twin Towers jail, several guards sat around drinking coffee while laughing at the inmate stories of the day. Dark characters darted through the shadows in the corners, seemingly dancing and laughing. A large red horned demon rolled on the ground in creepy delight, spitting puffs of smoke into the air. Standing up and slapping a guard on the back, he looked over the monitors showing an inmate being kicked on the floor by a guard. Another monitor captured an inmate being beaten by a gang member. Sham looked over his shoulder, addressing the shadows in the corner.

"I love this place. These are my kind of humans. I'll be meeting these guys in hell when I'm done with them here, and then the torture will really begin. In the meantime, this is great entertainment."

"Hey, Sham, what's your plans for that problem human you threw in here for Chief Demon? Are you going to shank him or what?"

"Oh, yeah, I'll shank him all right. But first, I'm wearing him down. I want his soul. With time he'll curse his heavenly Father, and then I'll shank him and greet him in hell at the same time. I can't wait to hear Chief Demon's applause as I tear into his victim."

One of the screens filled with Chief Demon's hideous face before he stepped through the screen into the room. Momentarily one of the guards shivered, and then did a double take at the monitor screen as Chief Demon's reflection faded. Standing in the control room, Chief Demon appeared disappointed at the other sinister occupants.

"Chief, good to see you, my ominous cohort. I presume you are here to congratulate me and gloat in my glory as a master at my craft."

Tilting his horns to focus all of his attention on Sham, Chief Demon condescendingly asked, "Where is the human that I assigned you to?"

"Now, Chief, we can share this prize together in hell as soon as I finish him off. Remember, I got this one for you."

"Sham, once more, where is the human I assigned you to?"

"Chief, look. I have this under control. He is tucked away safely next to Bullet Killer. I have blocked any bail, and I've made sure his paperwork keeps getting lost. This victim of ours is lost in my system now. Did you see that wonderfully vicious riot we started? Those humans are—" Abruptly interrupting, Chief Demon stopped Sham in his tracks.

"My victim is in Colorado at his sister's house. You do remember her, don't you—the pastor's wife?"

"Chief, that's impossible. We've been checking on him. How could he have gotten out? How could he have gotten there so fast?" Reaching down, Sham clutched onto two evil characters and threw them at the door. "Get down to the aquarium and do a visual on his cage, *now!*"

Chief wrapped his stretched leather wings around his hideous figure and shook his head. "He is not there. My sources watching his sister's home in Colorado have already reported on his whereabouts. The Colorado district attorney helped negotiate a release with the Los Angeles County court. Where were you during all of this?"

As his burning eyes bulged, Sham began to raise his squealing unearthly voice. "That doesn't happen; it never happens. District attorneys don't work with courts to get prisoners out of jail."

The shadows in the corners stopped dancing and started scurrying out of the room as Chief raised his voice to a rumble. "His new attorney helped arrange this, probably one of the only attorneys between here and Colorado who is also well connected with his heavenly Father. Oh yeah, the Colorado court is letting him out on his own without any bail either."

"But, Chief Demon, how did he even get there? I made sure the warrant was still active. I checked it just this morning. Someone would have picked him up and brought him back. Plus, he is an international fugitive. They can't let him out without bail; they shouldn't let him out at all."

Sham began backing into the shadows as Chief Demon angrily continued, "There was a caravan of heavenly believers who relayed him across the country. And, he still has his job. They are going to let him work from Denver for now, and then return to Los Angeles so he can provide for his family while he's awaiting his court appearances."

Pressing up against the concrete wall, Sham squeamishly shrugged his shoulders. "The saints must be praying. We were blinded."

Spreading his wings and reaching toward Sham's neck with his sharp talons, Chief Demon pointed a talon between Sham's dimly glowing eyes. "Go get him before I turn you over to Beelzebub for your failure."

27

Anguish of a Soul

When life goes bad, hold on and pray; then pray again, and don't stop.

. . . we also glory in our sufferings, because we know that suffering produces perseverance; perseverance, character; and character, hope.
—Romans 5:3-4 (NIV)

You intended to harm me, but God intended it for good to accomplish what is now being done, the saving of many lives.
—Genesis 50:20 (NIV)

After a week of meetings and drifting through the legal system with a heavy weight now firmly affixed on my shoulders, Holly and I made our way to Arizona en route to Los Angeles. I had no clue how or where I was going to live now that I would be living in Los Angeles, as opposed to just visiting on temporary business. Life seemed to take place one minute at a time with little regard for the future, since I didn't know if I even had a future. The details of the journey seemed to flow together in a preplanned way, even though I had no idea what was coming next.

Other than the underlying stress of the situation, the drive to Arizona was wonderful. The skies stretched forever over the rock formations as we drove through Four Corners. The desolate beauty was striking in brilliant desert colors. The time spent with Holly was amazing, when just hearing her voice was the joy of my life just a week before.

After reaching Arizona, we dropped off June's car and proceeded through the desert with the little pickup to Los Angeles. I didn't know where I would stay in Los Angeles or how I was going to live. I didn't know how I was going to make it back to Colorado for the upcoming court appearances. I didn't know how my fragile state of post-trauma was going to hold up, but my heavenly Father already had my way planned ahead of me.

Shortly after arriving in Los Angeles, I had to take Holly to the airport so she could return to Canada to be with our kids. They were still in school, and I couldn't uproot them and bring them to California when I didn't even know where I was going to live. I missed them dearly, and seeing Holly leave was heart-wrenching. With no clue of what was coming next or how bad things could get, I didn't know if that would be the last time I would get to see her. With the picture that was painted for me by the legal system, I feared that I would be going to jail for years, leaving my wife and kids all alone. We still had our home in Canada for sale. There were still many daily showings and everyone loved it, but there were no offers, which puzzled everyone. I was able to find a small room with a kitchenette for rent in an old hotel. The cost of living in Los Angeles was confining, leaving me few options, none of which fit into our budget.

The months that followed after Holly left and I couldn't see our kids took me to the lowest lows as I struggled with the stress from the trauma. Being alone at that time was difficult. I tried to distract myself with the small TV in the hotel room, only to realize that most of the TV shows centered around police or detectives going after the "bad guys," whom everyone seemed to hate. They were the scum of the earth, and now I was listed as one of them. The rest of the channels seemed to be centered on news portraying similar images of society and the bad guys. So I couldn't watch TV to take my mind off things. It was too traumatic in my state of post-trauma.

Every time a bus or police car drove by, my adrenalin would pump erratically. My blood pressure would rise along with my stress. I couldn't go anywhere without looking over my shoulder, wondering if someone was going to suddenly grab me to abduct me again and drag me away. Everywhere I went I had to carry my court paperwork in case I was stopped for anything. I had to call the court officer every week and mail paperwork monthly identifying my every move. I constantly questioned everything I did to make sure I wasn't violating any laws. I couldn't even cross the street if a police car was near. My room was on the third floor, where I felt trapped, thinking that at any moment someone would burst through the door and grab me. When I left for work in the morning, I would always wonder if I'd ever return to my room again, or if I would be taken during the day. Paranoia gripped me.

I could barely make it through my days. Most of the time I would feel the pressure so tight in my body that I thought I would drop from a stroke or my heart would burst. I sat on the aged furniture staring at the threadbare carpet in my room, waiting for the door to burst open and my life to end. In the evenings I would go through mounds of files from our business, trying to prepare for the trial. I felt I couldn't spend any money, since my family would need every dime we had left if something happened to me. I ate as cheaply as possible, or not at all sometimes.

I was able to talk with Holly on the phone, which helped tremendously. She became my connection to sanity at times. Nonetheless, I kept falling deeper and deeper into a depressed state, with seemingly no hope of ever escaping. I felt like an alien on a strange planet. Everyone seemed to be staring at me when I went outside. There was no semblance of "normal" in my life anymore. My family was in another country and everything seemed foreign and distant, with nothing to hold on to, and the black hole I was falling into kept getting deeper.

Hidden in a parking lot behind an aged hotel, a Chevy Impala sat low to the ground with smoke rising through a slit in the window. Four glassy-eyed occupants nodded to the hypnotic beat thumping against the windows, not even noticing the unconcealed dwellers accompanying them. Horrid creatures drifted between the upholstery, making faces and taunting the human occupants. On the hood of the car in the shadows cast by the setting sun, a large cloaked creature sat watching the hotel windows.

Two dark shadows skimmed the parking lot until they reached the cloaked creature. "Nothing yet, but the taunting is having an effect. Our guy is on the edge of a nervous breakdown."

From a silhouette hidden in the darkness of the hooded cloak, two eyes of fire lit up. "Excellent. I am not going to lose this guy again. Keep it up, and push him harder. Rattle the door knob occasionally when he is falling asleep. Now get back in there; it's still your turn for patrol."

"Sham, we can do the door knob and lob thoughts through the window, but there's no way we can get in there. The angelic cover is growing stronger by the minute. There must be a lot of humans praying"

"Yes, I know. I can feel it out here. Stop complaining and get back in there anyway."

Pointing through the car window, Sham yelled, "You two get over here."

Two of the horrid creatures floated through the glass. "What do you want, Sham?"

"I want you to find some police cars and drive them past the hotel. Make sure you have them hit their sirens a couple of times when they are near our victim's window." The two shadows skimmed through the trees and over the hill. A larger shadow flew over the trees before drifting to a stop on the hood of the Impala.

"Sham, I come to report on the deceiving humans you wanted to interact with your victim."

With red twisted horns starting to appear through the edges of the hood, the large creature focused on the large shadow, "And . . . ?"

"I had two humans who were perfect for this task. The plan was to befriend your victim and then lure him away and deceive him again. They could have driven him deeper into depression and darkness."

Sliding the hood back to reveal a large mouth of sharp teeth and burning red eyes, the cloaked creature simply uttered, "Could?"

"Yes, Sham . . . could. The power of his heavenly Father is too strong. The angelic beings wouldn't let my humans get close."

Physically bouncing the Impala in place, the cloaked creature pounded his fists on the hood. "They are praying again! Stop the praying. Stop it, stop it, and stop it!"

"Uh, Sham, the prayer cover is coming from all over the place. Our victim is calling to his heavenly Father, but there are many others praying on his behalf as well."

Sham reached through the window, clutching the human in the driver's seat, and began slamming the driver's head against the horn until blood ran down his face. With lights flashing a police cruiser raced into the parking lot with a dark shadow sitting on the hood. The cruiser raced toward the repeated horn blowing. The police cruiser screeched to a stop with sirens screaming just as Sham reached in and started the car. Glassy-eyed occupants sat oblivious to what was going on. Sham reached a hoofed leg through the door and punched the accelerator, sending the car across the parking lot into a tree.

Followed by a horde of horrid creature shadows, Sham adjusted his cloak and hood and then made his way down the street. A squad of police cruisers raced past the horde, screaming in pursuit of the drug dealers now trapped in the Impala, not even noticing the shadowy figures.

28

Higher Vision

---

*The most wonderful thing about this harsh life is the
One who brings peace through it all.*

God whispers to us in our pleasures, speaks in
our conscience, but shouts in our pains; it is His
megaphone to rouse a deaf world.
—C. S. Lewis, The Problem of Pain

Even to your old age and gray hairs I am he, I am
he who will sustain you. I have made you and I will
carry you; I will sustain you and I will rescue you.
—Isaiah 46:4 (NIV)

I felt like I walked through this time in my life in some sort of a
dream—or nightmare—most of the time. I don't know how things
were getting taken care of, but they were. There seemed to be
enough money to pay the bills each month, although on paper the
budget didn't add up. The projects I had at work were doing very
well, although I could barely concentrate on most days. I somehow
became surrounded with people who were highly motivated and
very skilled at what they did, and we worked well together. I had
to return to Denver several times for court appearances, but every
time I had to be in Denver, a business trip came up that put me in
Denver at the same time, for one strange reason after another.

I plummeted so low that I felt I had one foot in the grave, and
at times I wished that I had both. I asked my heavenly Father again
to save me, but I somehow felt it wasn't even possible anymore.

My brother gave me the name of a guy he had known years before. He said I should look him up. I didn't have anything to lose and desperately needed someone to reach out to, so I did. His name was Jared. I found out that he was the pastor of a church near the old hotel I lived in. The church was called Higher Vision. God pointed, and I ran for help. His church had a men's group that met at a coffee shop. I remember showing up early the first night, and then walking the parking lot to try and reduce the unending stress and pressure that throbbed through my body. The guys I met were awesome. They didn't judge me or treat me like some convict or terrible person. They listened and prayed. Together we reached out to our heavenly Father.

In the midst of my turmoil my Father continued to provide. Jared met with me at his office to pray. The people from the Higher Vision church, whom I'd never met before, came around me and my family and cared for us in more ways than they will ever know. The presence of my Father was strong at the Higher Vision church. On the days when I needed it the most, which was often, my heavenly Father surrounded me with his family. Teresa and Elgin invited me over often for walks and on holiday occasions. My good friend Austin was going through a very trying time of his own. We called each other daily to talk and listen to the pain we each were suffering through. When I could barely breathe from the strain, God would give me just enough to make it through one more minute, one more hour, and eventually one day at a time.

Although my job often required me to travel, I had to get approval from the court each time and have my paperwork updated before I was allowed to go. Hearing my kids tell me how much they missed me on the phone was heart-wrenching, and my Father knew it. I'll never forget the day when out of nowhere a sudden need for me to be in our Buffalo office came up. I leaped with joy when I got the call. Buffalo was just over the border from our home in Canada. Even though I couldn't cross the border, my heavenly Father gave me a week with my wife and kids in Buffalo. I had to work, but what a marvelous thing it was to be with them every evening.

The court appearances and trips to Denver went on for months and months. In early December I had been returning to the court for six months, and I didn't know what the next day would hold, as usual. There was no end in sight to the court appearances. The lease on my room at the old hotel had ended. Everything I owned in the United States was in my little pickup back in Los Angeles. The truck was tucked away in a parking garage where I had left it when I boarded the plane for Denver. I didn't know where I was going to sleep or where I was going to go when I returned to Los Angeles. I planned on spending a couple nights in my truck and prayed that God had a better plan. I had seen him weave his plan through the pattern of my life constantly over the past months, and he never left me or let go of me, so I had to trust him completely.

I can remember sitting in the courtroom with my sister that day. She had accompanied me many times so I wouldn't have to appear before the judge alone. We were looking at my calendar for the next appearance. I had a business trip that would allow me to lay over in Denver, but it was two months away on the sixteenth of the month. Other than the sixteenth, no other date would work and I would have to find a way to Denver on my own, so we prayed. Within minutes my attorney sat down with his calendar and said, "The only date that works for the district attorney is in two months on the sixteenth. Can you make that work?" We just smiled at each other as God reconfirmed once again that he was in charge. My Father reassured me continually. His affirmation was what kept me going daily, and the more I trusted in him, the better things got.

The thing that was weighing on me the most that day was being away from home on Christmas. Everyone kept telling me that leaving the country would be impossible; the court would never allow it. I had seen my heavenly Father do so many things that seemed impossible that I had to ask. My attorney said it would take a miracle, but he took the request to the judge anyway. I was in the middle of a felony case, out of jail without bail, after an international fugitive warrant was issued, and I was asking to leave the country?

My heavenly Father is beyond the understanding of man or the courts, and he is in the miracle business. He gave me the most wonderful Christmas gift that year. I got to go home, even though the hearings continued. As my attorney put it, "That's a miracle, because it never happens that way."

My Father let me make my own choices and ignore him a year earlier, knowing that it would cause pain. But he didn't leave me there. Like any good father, he lifted me back up and restored my faith in him. He made it clear that he was there every minute of every day providing for me, and he brought me home for Christmas.

They did say that Canada probably wouldn't allow me back across the border. Nonetheless, they gave me permission to leave the country, along with more travel paperwork. I wasn't free of the weight on my shoulders but I was grateful that my Father carried me as I struggled through the mess.

The next day I was en route back to Los Angeles, where I got my bags out of the little truck, and immediately boarded an international flight to Toronto. When I left the truck and all of my bags in the parking garage in Los Angeles, on my way to Denver, my Father knew where I was headed next. I just had to trust in him. When my lease ended, he already had a new place for me. He sent me home to be with my wife and kids. I never had to sleep in my truck, although I was only hours from the reality of it. I was on my way home with one border crossing between me and my family. The trip turned out to be more than I could have imagined once again. But then, my Father never ceased to be amazing.

In the early hours of a Colorado morning a large hooded creature paced the parking lot between the trees in front of the courthouse. Shadows darted between parked cars, making their way to the hooded creature. The creature stopped and sat on the bumper of an SUV as two shadows arrived and reported, "Sham, we can't find him."

Red flaming eyes appeared in the darkness of the hood. "He had an appointment today. What do you mean, you can't find him? He never misses his appointments. Something is wrong here."

"Uh, Sham, we looked on the court roster, and his appointment already happened. I couldn't find another appointment for him this month either."

Ripping his cloak off and throwing his hood to the ground, revealing twisted, charred horns and a vile red body, Sham screamed while kicking the side of the SUV repeatedly. "*What do you mean?!* Why didn't I know about this? Do any of you feebleminded fiends know where he is now?"

Meekly staring at the ground, a sinister shadow replied, "Well, we can't get close to him. He is surrounded by a host of angels. We can't get near his sister's house where he was staying either, so we can't watch his every move. There is a legion of angels guarding that house. The prayer cover must be coming from all over, it is very strong around him right now. If he left with his sister we could have missed him."

Scurrying across the parking lot, another shadow darted to the SUV. "Sham, he was spotted at the airport headed back to Los Angeles."

Calming down, Sham scratched his horns as he thought. "Do we have the drunk driver ready?"

"Yes, sir. The minute he gets on the 405 freeway with his little pickup in Los Angeles, we'll send the drunk driver after him. We have the driver sedated and possessed by one of ours."

Sham stopped to stare at the ground in deep thought, and his hateful eyes dimmed back to a light ember. "Okay, we have that covered."

Pointing to another dark shadow under the SUV, Sham continued his investigation. "Did you make sure the Harrigans are steaming angry like I ordered? Did you make sure they are still raging for revenge?"

Moving like a lost shadow flickering under a candle, a demonic creature replied in a spiteful tone, "I did my job. I have several creatures with them right now. I know where my victims are and what they're doing."

Growling at the shadow under the SUV, the first two shadows bit back. "Did you plant the greed thing in the Harrigans like you were supposed to?"

"Yes, but did you do your part?" the flickering creature spit out.

"We did our part at the bank. We know our human doesn't have any money and can't borrow any either, so no matter what the Harrigans demand, our human will be doomed as planned. They will throw him in prison for sure."

Watching the bickering, Sham took delight in the moment. The lost shadow stopped in its tracks before materializing into a lizard with a large scaled frill around its neck and a long single horn protruding from its head. "The Harrigans want a million dollars, but I also overheard the district attorney discussing a plea deal for the amount owed on the invoice that wasn't paid. The Harrigans will become as angry and hateful as we are if that deal goes through. Is there any way your human can come up with that money? If he does, it will ruin this glorious opportunity to destroy them both."

The bickering shadow hovered in circles while holding his ground in the argument. "That doesn't matter, because he doesn't have anything—like I already told you. He will be doomed either way."

"That's not entirely true," said the lizard-like creature. "I was informed by my many friends at the Internal Revenue Service that he has a large tax refund coming that he wasn't expecting. It could be close to enough for the plea deal."

Sham stepped into the middle of the quarrel. "All right, all right. There is no way they'll let him go back to Canada to be with his family for Christmas, and I know his family can't afford to come down here. We'll have a window of opportunity when he is all alone for Christmas. He may be protected, but he has been tremendously beaten up too. All we need is a short window of opportunity to attack."

Jumping into the conversation, a demon hovering behind Sham cheered. "Yeah, we have a job to do here."

Grabbing the cheering dark creature, Sham yelled in his face, "Shut up! And make sure you have your drunk driver ready on the 405 freeway. We're headed back to Los Angeles, and this time I'm not taking any chances."

29

Saturday before Dawn

When his people pray, he hears, and things happen.

Do not cast me from your presence or take your Holy Spirit from me. Restore to me the joy of your salvation and grant me a willing spirit, to sustain me. Then I will teach transgressors your ways, so that sinners will turn back to you.

—Psalm 51:11-13 (NIV)

What no eye has seen, what no ear has heard, and what no human mind has conceived—the things God has prepared for those who love him—

—1 Corinthians 2:9 (NIV)

Over six months had passed since I last touched Canadian soil. The place I once tried to leave, I now longed to stay. My heavenly Father wanted us in Canada. He made that obvious to me in so many ways. The home that wouldn't sell was waiting for me with my family in that great neighborhood when I returned. My office was minutes from our home, and I still had a job there. God made a great life for us there, and now I was finally returning. I was somewhat apprehensive about the border crossing originally, but if it hadn't been in my Father's plans, I wouldn't have been allowed to return anyway. My work visa needed to be renewed, but that was in his hands as well, even if it seemed more impossible than ever after everything that had taken place. The thing we didn't have in Canada and missed the most was extended family.

I can remember asking my heavenly Father for an extended family and friends if this was where he wanted us to make our home. I specifically asked him for a group of guys who knew him like I did. I asked for a group that I could pray with and share my life with. I asked for a place where my kids could connect with others who knew him, and a group of women that Holly could bond with.

When the plane touched down in Toronto, I felt safe for the first time since being taken and locked up. As I gathered my bags and made my way to the customs agent, excitement rose inside me. I absorbed the familiar surroundings with a hint of worry as I moved up in the customs line. When the moment arrived and I handed my passport to the customs agent, the lady smiled. She scanned my passport and looked at her screen for a moment; then she said, "Welcome home." My heart jumped with excitement as I held back a tear of joy. There were no angry, abusive officials, just a pleasant person in uniform who welcomed me back to the home God had prepared for me. When I stepped out the door, I had to touch the ground and give thanks to my heavenly Father. My first call was to Holly, followed by my immigration attorney, who said I wouldn't be allowed to return. When she said it wasn't possible, I originally told her it would take a miracle and I'd let her know when it happened, so I did.

All I could think of after that six months was *I'm home, I'm really home, I'm where my Father wants me to be.* The cab ride home filled my vision with a beautiful city and peaceful warmth. The trauma seemed to fade, and the fear of being taken subsided. My mind was flooded with the anticipation of seeing my wife and kids again. When the cab reached my driveway, it really sank in. As I walked up to my front door, I recalled when seeing my family at home was something I had dreamed of but didn't think I'd ever experience again.

When the door opened, I felt like Jimmy Stewart in *It's a Wonderful Life.* I was greeted at the door by Holly and my kids standing beneath a banner and balloons. The dogs tackled me, and we all hugged and cried together. I drank it all in and thanked my heavenly Father for being my dad and loving me so much that he brought me back to where I needed to be. He adopted me when I was just a kid who needed a father, and he never made me feel second best. He took me through the hard times and lessons learned and never let go of me.

The following day I ran into a friend who without prompting told me about a great men's group he had recently discovered. After he invited me, I knew I was meant to accept the invitation and go. God had once again heard me and answered my prayer from the day before.

The guys met very early Saturday mornings, and I'm not a morning person, but I had to be there. At 5:30 in the morning a group of praying men gathered every week before the 7:00 a.m. men's group. When I walked in the door of that little church, I could feel the presence of my heavenly Father. In an ever-present way, it was strong there. The road ahead of me was still unclear, and I had many impossible obstacles ahead, but the power in that room in the early hours of the morning was ecstatic when these guys prayed. I remember the first time I was there I said, "My situation is going to take a miracle," and the response was, "We know the One who does those." There were so many little things every day that my heavenly Father provided for. The miracles were more about his personal relationship with me than impressing others.

Although the Harrigans were uncooperative, my attorney and the district attorney started discussing a plea deal as opposed to a full trial. The clock was ticking on my work visa for my stay in Canada, and although I feared crossing the border into the United States, I had business trips I had to attend to. As much as I wanted to avoid the object of my anguish and fears, I had to return to the United States to fulfill the obligations I had to appear at the Colorado court as well. All I could do was walk blindly in faith with my dad.

We took our home off the market, and immediately people started making offers on it, but we knew it didn't sell for reason, so it wasn't for sale any longer. God had preserved that home for us to live in. My work visa had expired, and the paperwork had been filed for a renewal, although I didn't know if it would be accepted. I was living on what was called "implied status," so I could stay in

Canada and work. But if I left the country, I couldn't return without a renewed work permit. By leaving the country I would lose my status. My next court date in Colorado was also approaching, so I prayed along with the guys at the men's group and waited. In the same way my life had been shaped over the previous year, I had to trust my heavenly Father with whatever came next. I can't say that I didn't have elevated levels of anxiety many times, but my Father showed me on a daily basis how he was in charge. The connection to our new church at Burlington Alliance was growing stronger daily, and God continued to put things in place and take care of us. God connected me with a strong group of guys like I had prayed for, but he also connected my family with an amazing youth group for the kids and a women's group for Holly. He gave us the extended family that I had asked him for.

When I was three weeks away from my next court appearance in Colorado, I was told that the new work visa would take another six months. There was a backlog of immigrant applications in the system. I even went and tried to meet with my MP (member of Parliament) to see if there was anything that could be done to expedite things, but it being a campaign year, he was rarely in his office. I remember asking my heavenly Father for some encouragement in the situation. The next day my MP knocked on my front door on his campaign route. He couldn't do much to expedite things and agreed with the six-month backlog, but the fact that my heavenly Father had sent him to my front door was encouraging. The three weeks came and went. I was at home packing my suitcase to leave for my next appearance in Colorado with no idea when I'd be back, or if I would be able to return at all. As I prepared for my trip, my phone beeped with an e-mail message. I could see it was from my immigration attorney. I opened the e-mail to find that my renewed work visa had been approved and it had just arrived in their office. I could read the surprise in the words at how quickly it had been processed. My Father continued to show me that he was in control.

My court appearances in Colorado went on for about a year. I was finally offered the plea deal by the district attorney. If I pleaded guilty to a permanent minor charge, a 30 day temporary major charge and paid the missing invoice, plus fees and court costs, the ordeal would finally be over. I knew in my heart that I didn't do anything purposely wrong, and I did everything I could to make it right. The deal they offered sounded pretty good to remove the weight that I'd been carrying on my shoulders. However, the money they wanted from a guy who was living on faith seemed almost insurmountable, unless you knew my heavenly Father. By some odd circumstance I was overpaying taxes in two countries, since I worked only six months in each and lived in both. Before going to court for the final appearance, I had received the largest tax refunds that I'd ever seen (which never happened to me before), plus a work bonus that I wasn't expecting. It all came out to just enough. My attorney was paid, all of my travel was paid, we still had a home, and I still had a job. Somehow my heavenly Father provided just enough for what we needed, when we needed it, every step of the way.

On my way back from my final Colorado court hearing, my immigration attorney called me and told me I couldn't come back to Canada until after the 30 day major charge was removed and the proper court paperwork was officially filed, or I would be denied reentry. Staying in the United States for a month would have forced me to find a place to live, which I couldn't afford. Plus, I needed to get back to my job and family in Canada. I felt my Father had cleared the way for me to go home. After all, he was the one in charge. He was the one who continually opened the doors and pointed the way back home. I had a peace about going home, but I had no idea what would take place when I arrived at the border crossing, especially with the court case now posted on my record for all to see, even if it was only temporary.

A shadow of ominous proportions swallowed up everything in its path as it moved swiftly through the Southern California neighborhood. Passing the rusty farm equipment and broken fences in front of the once stately old home, the shadow stopped in front of the opening before drifting through the missing floorboards to the basement below. In the cavern of old basement walls, a thick sulfurous stench filled the air. The shadow materialized into a dark hideous winged being with sharp teeth showing through its torn skin just below its burning eyes. The sinister creature bowed on its sharp talons in the middle of the room and spoke. "Beelzebub, my liege, you called for me?"

As the darkness set in the room, many repulsive creatures could be seen darting back and forth in the moonlight. The ghostly room seemed to be alive with movement focused toward a shadowy corner on the far side of the basement. From the corner, slits of green eyes opened and glared in an icy stare at the hideous creature kneeling before him in the middle of the room.

"Do not appear so surprised, Chief Demon. Reports about some of your victims are not good. Our enemy has held a stronghold that you have been unable to extinguish."

"Yes, my liege. I can explain."

"Explain? You destroyed the leader of the family, but once the head was bitten off, the body of the family should have died. The family has spread out and grows stronger with our enemy. The mother, the sister, and the brothers all still call on their heavenly Father. And now, there is another generation who calls on him too. Why have you failed me with the family, and especially the boy, who should have been your easiest prey?"

"My liege, Sham—"

"Don't give me excuses, you poignant feeble excuse of a creature. I know about Sham and his failures, Drach and his inabilities, Mole, Reptile, and your other pathetic excuses for demons."

Moving slowly around the room, the dominant creature slowly circled Chief Demon as his voice echoed through the basement and into an unearthly realm.

"In your overconfidence, you misjudged the power of prayer that these worthless humans can tap into. Let me remind you that our enemy, their God, is the only thing that stands between us and them. Prayer is their power to call on their heavenly Father. This prayer ability was granted them a mere two thousand years ago, as you should remember. If they pray, we have no power over them. If we have no power over them, they will not be ours in hell and we will not feast on these piteous creatures for eternity."

"Yes, my liege."

"If we do not have these human creatures to feast upon in hell, would you rather that I feast upon you and your minions?"

"No, my liege."

"There is only one thing worse than losing one of these humans to their Father of Light, their so-called heavenly Father."

"What is that, my Liege?"

Turning in burning fury to bore his eyes of daggers through Chief Demon, he paused before continuing.

"Having them affect one another! Letting them undo the deception we have worked so hard for centuries to beguile them with! You are failing the ambition of darkness in this world, the eradication of humans from this earth, the gathering of them in hell to feast upon, and most of all plundering them from their Father of Light. Why he created these feeble beings in his own image I'll never understand."

"Yes, my liege."

Stopping to ponder what he had just said, the dominant creature smiled, stretching the green eyes into slits before turning to Chief Demon once again.

"Nonetheless, these humans were given a freewill choice, which has become our greatest asset. Much like us, they are not forced to follow their heavenly Father. However, if they don't want to be with him in his heavenly world, they have nowhere else to go. Once they leave this physical world, they become no match for us, and we'll be happy to take them."

The walls shook from the rumbling laughter the creature billowed through the night. Then he stopped, refocused his attention on Chief Demon once again, and concluded his discourse.

"Your job is to deceive them. Turn them from the welcome mat their heavenly Father laid out for them on that cross. If they accept him, we lose them to the heaven he has created for them—the heaven we are not allowed to enter. They don't have to hate the

Father of Light like we do. They just have to be lulled to sleep until they are dead. Don't let them call on their heavenly Father. Never let them pray for one another, and keep them away from those who do. Do you understand me, Chief Demon?"

"Yes, my liege."

"All they have to do is accept him, and we lose. If these humans ever figure out what we are up to, or worst yet, that the Creator of the universe actually cares for these egotistical, infinitesimal humans, they'll flee so fast that you'll never taste the flesh of humans again!"

"Yes, my liege."

"Now get out there and do the job I commanded you to do."

The overpowering creature backed into the shadows of the corner before Chief Demon spread his wings and discreetly vanished into the night.

Hours later in the dead of night a burning red creature with twisted horns stood next to a little pickup deep in a parking garage in Los Angeles. The host of beastly dark creatures accompanying Sham darted between cars and concrete pillars in anticipation. Without notice an enormous shadow of darkness filled the parking space like pitch black ink oozing into every crevice. The beastly creatures ejected in every direction, leaving Sham standing alone in the shadows. "What are you waiting for, Sham?"

Startled and overpowered, Sham stuttered. "Uh . . . my . . . um . . . human victim of course. What are you doing here, Chief?"

"You don't know where he is, do you?"

"Now wait a minute, Chief. We've been a little behind with this human, but the prayer cover is pretty thick right now, so give me a break. He should be here any minute, and I have a couple of plans lined up to finish him off. So bear with me just a little longer and you'll be pleased."

"Sham . . . he's in Toronto. He crossed the border some time ago."

Stomping a hoof on the ground, Sham threw his head back in disgust. "I quit! This is your human. I have my own victims to lull away from the Light with fancy cars, homes, planes, and the wealth of this world. And my other victims don't have this blasted prayer cover to deal with."

Chief Demon latched onto Sham's horns and swung him up through the wall into the street, where a teenager swerved to miss the unidentifiable object rolling through his car. The teenager slammed on the brakes as he saw the creature stand up in the rearview mirror. Then, thinking twice about the large red horned object in the mirror, he slammed down the accelerator and sped away.

Before anyone else could see him, Sham threw a fist into the air in anger; then faded into the darkness, leaving car alarms and dogs barking into the Los Angeles night.

30

Home Is Where My Father Is

---

*No matter where you go or who you become in this life,
there is no peace until you find your heavenly Father.*

Then I heard the voice of the Lord saying, "Whom
shall I send? And who will go for us?"
And I said, "Here am I. Send me!"

—Isaiah 6:8 (NIV)

I waited patiently for the LORD; he turned to me
and heard my cry. He lifted me out of the slimy pit,
out of the mud and mire; he set my feet on a rock
and gave me a firm place to stand. He put a new
song in my mouth, a hymn of praise to our God.
Many will see and fear the LORD and put their trust
in him.

—Psalms 40:1-3 (NIV)

At the Toronto international airport I walked down the long corridors
leading away from the plane. The memories of everything that had
happened over the past few years hung fresh in my mind. People
hurried by me on their way to greet a relative or catch their next
flight. The smiles of officers directing traffic at each corner projected
a happy sense of contentment that greeted the travelers to this friendly
country. The fears and paranoia instilled in me from the traumatic
year I recently had traveled through seemed to subside as I walked
down the gateway to my new home. My heavenly Father performed
so many miracles every single day that I could never write them all

down. I wouldn't have survived the ordeal I went through without him. The time in prayer with the praying men at Burlington Alliance Church meant more to me than I could ever express. My heavenly Father gave me my family back, reunited me with my loving wife, my kids and surrounded me with an extended family and great friends. And now I walked this passage facing the unknown but knowing who was in control. How would I respond with what my heavenly Father had given me? How would I cherish the gifts and the grace? How could my suffering be used for my heavenly Father's good to help and encourage others, and do his will?

Approaching the line to meet with a customs agent, I saw several scurrying individuals frantically trying to find the proper paperwork and necessary forms. In an earthly sense I should have been fearful knowing that my immigration attorney had warned me not to return. In a worldly realm he was correct, but I'd seen a glimpse of a realm that existed beyond this world. I'd seen miracle after miracle where the world said I couldn't or it wouldn't happen, and my heavenly Father had trumped all and things did happen. I saw my heavenly dad embrace me unconditionally, like no earthly dad could. I had found my Father, and he was more than anything I could ever have dreamed of. He continually carried me through the challenges and triumphs of this life. He never left me. When I walked away from his path, he patiently waited, and then he carried me back to the road from the pit I got myself stuck in. I love my Father, but what puzzles me the most is that he loves me.

At the customs counter a friendly lady smiled and asked about my trip while checking things on her computer. She handed my passport back and directed me to a second checkpoint, where I would need to meet with another agent. As I made my way to the second checkpoint, I reflected on my time in the Twin Towers Correctional Facility and the harsh treatment, the terrifying inmates, and the monstrous political machine that seemed to grind up and swallow everyone who entered. The desire for a toothbrush, a pillow, or even a pencil refocused my view of the meager existence on this planet. Things that seemed so important before I was aggressively cuffed and paraded through the Los Angeles airport became so insignificant afterward. The six months away from my family with the weight of the world on my shoulders took me to the darkest hours of my life. But my journey wasn't about the pain and hardship. It was about my Father and his love for me. My heavenly Father provided daily for me and brought people into my life who helped me through this journey. Many times he sent people who would call or just show up and encourage me when I couldn't go on. There were so many people who knew my Father and prayed for me, and I saw those prayers answered. So many contributed to the intertwining of the tapestry, and they might never know the ultimate impact they had on my life until we meet in heaven.

The second customs agent was pleasant and easy to talk with. He checked my renewal paperwork and updated my work visa while we discussed the possibility of my making Canada my permanent residence. I still consider the United States my country of origin, but after what I had just gone through, I didn't feel any hurry to return. The past months living in Canada had allowed a healing from the traumatic experiences I had endured to begin. I don't know my Father's plans for me next, but wherever he leads, I have to go. No matter what I do, I can never take my focus off him again. I couldn't imagine living this life or enjoying anything of this world without him.

The customs agent stamped my paperwork and finished up with those words that I've grown to enjoy so much when crossing the border to Canada, and one day will hear from my heavenly Father: "Welcome home."

The shadow of a passing commercial airliner momentarily darkened the doorway of the Canadian customs office as a man dressed in business attire stepped into the beautiful August daylight. Pausing for a moment, the man knelt next to his travel bag and looked toward the sky, and then he looked down and touched the sidewalk. A beautiful blond woman stepped into his shadow and touched his shoulder. Within moments the two embraced with great enthusiasm.

Standing near the curb, two angelic beings radiated with joy. The larger of the two put a hand on the other's shoulder.

"It's been a rough road. I think our Father has something special planned for these two."

The man picked up his travel bag, and the two locked arms and strolled toward the parking garage. The man turned to the woman. "So where do you think our heavenly Father is leading us next?"

With a big smile the woman nodded her head. "Right here, Kevin. Right here. We're home, and I think that has been made very clear to us."

Nodding his head playfully, the man replied, "I'm perfectly fine with that. I am just so grateful to be here with you and the kids and to be doing whatever he asks. I can hardly believe it's over. I never thought I would see this day. I want to be close to my Father and go wherever he wants us to go, no matter where that is, and I never want to lose my focus again."

The angelic beings sat on top of an older economy car watching intently. The man opened the trunk and loaded his travel bag before walking around and opening the woman's car door.

Standing next to the open passenger door, the man pondered deeply while contemplating out loud. "Holly, our heavenly Father has been so good to us. He has changed me and blessed me beyond anything I deserve. I feel him calling me do something more and to share my experience in a way that will help others find him. I want to share what he has done for me because I know there are so many others in this world who need to find their Father, but I'm not sure what I can do."

While the man walked around the small car, the angelic beings observed the human conversation intently. The smaller being started to fade through the roof into the backseat while addressing his companion. "I think he is getting the big picture here."

Opening the driver's door and squeezing into the small car, the man adjusted the seat as the woman answered, "Why don't you start writing down your story and see where God leads, maybe a book?"

Squished in the backseat of the small car, an angelic being spread a large smile and patted the man on the back. Pausing for a moment, the man contemplated the statement while starting the engine.

"That's an interesting idea; I've never done that before. It would take a miracle, but then, I do know the one who does those."

The small economy car rattled to life and made its way down through the parking garage and out of sight.

The End

Next to a concrete pillar at the Toronto Pearson International Airport parking garage, a defeated, dark, hideous creature angrily tapped a talon on the ground while observing the couple through burning red eyes as they drove away.

Tap, tap, tap . . .

About the Author

Kevin was born and raised in the United States. His journey has taken him around the globe often in the face of world events. As a writer, engineer, entrepreneur, and story teller he views the world from a technical yet creative perspective with a spiritual viewpoint. As an author he has published in news and trade publications. His greatest joy comes from being a husband and father. His greatest passion is the pursuit of his heavenly Father. Today he resides with his wife Holly of over 17 years, and two children near Toronto, Canada.

As a speaker he shares with audiences about his most valuable lessons learned and true fulfillment in this life, which is far more than the things that can be acquired. The storms of life, although devastating, are part of the journey. It is through the hard times this world has thrown at him that he has found the true meaning of life.

www.findingmyfather.org

Resources

We invite you to continue your journey, it isn't always easy, but the reward is beyond measure. Your heavenly Father promised that he would never leave you or abandon you. Share your story and find support in others, who are on their journey from the father who caused the scars to the one who heals them. Join us at our web site.

www.FindingMyFather.org

If the message of this book has impacted you we welcome you to share this message with others. Give a copy to friends, even strangers, as a gift. They not only get a thrilling supernatural novel, they also get a glimpse of the true Father who wants to love them beyond anything they could imagine.

If you have a website or blog, consider sharing your experience of how this story has touched your life. Share your journey with those who need to find their Father, and those who need him to heal their scars.

CPSIA information can be obtained at www.ICGtesting.com
Printed in the USA
BVOW071237161212

308290BV00001B/2/P